Sol T. Plaatje
MHUDI

Sol T. Plaatje
MHUDI

*An Epic of South African Native Life a
Hundred Years Ago*

This edition first published by Jacana Media (Pty) Ltd in 2021

10 Orange Street
Sunnyside
Auckland Park 2092
South Africa
+2711 628 3200
www.jacana.co.za

Mhudi by Sol Plaatje was first published by the Lovedale Press in 1930.

Introduction © Sabata-mpho Mokae, 2021
Editorial note © Brian Willan, 2021

The financial assistance of the National Institute for the Humanities and Social Sciences (NIHSS) towards this publication is hereby acknowledged. Opinions expressed and those arrived at are those of the author and are not necessarily to be attributed to the NIHSS.

ISBN 978-1-4314-3067-3

Also available as an ebook.

Cover design by publicide
Proofreading by Russell Martin
Set in Ehrhardt MT Std 10.5/13.5pt
Printed by Creda Communications
Job no. 003802

See a complete list of Jacana titles at www.jacana.co.za

To the Memory of
OUR BELOVED OLIVE
One of the many youthful Victims of
A SETTLED SYSTEM
and in Pleasant Recollection
of her life work, accomplished, at the age of 13, during the
INFLUENZA EPIDEMIC
This Book is Affectionately Dedicated

'Death wounds to cure we fall, we rise, we reign,
  Spring from our fetters, fasten in the skies,
  Where blooming Eden withers in our sight:
  Death gives us more than was in Eden lost:
  The King of Terrors is the Prince of Peace.'

Contents

Principal characters in the story

Mhudi (a harvester), heroine of the tale (pron. *Moody*)
Ra-Thaga (the bird man), her husband
Mzilikazi (the female mourner), King of the Matabele and
    Emperor of Central South Africa
Umnandi (the sweet one), his favourite spouse
Nomenti, another spouse, bitterly jealous of Umnandi
Langa (sun), Crown Prince of the Matabele
Gubuza, Commander-in-Chief of the Matabele impis

Qanda
Tabata
Sitonga   }   Other warriors, and uncles of Langa
Dambuza
Dingiswayo

Tauana (lion's whelp), Chief of the Barolong
Moroka (rainmaker), Chief of another Barolong clan
Taaibos, a Koranna Chief

Ton-Qon (his headman), a villain

Potgieter
Sarel Cilliers
} Boer Voortrekker leaders

De Villiers, a noble Boer

Viljoen
Van Zijl
} his friends

Annetje, De Villiers's fiancée and sister to Van Zijl

Preface

SOUTH AFRICAN LITERATURE has hitherto been almost exclusively European, so that a foreword seems necessary to give reasons for a Native venture.

In all the tales of battle I have ever read, or heard of, the cause of the war is invariably ascribed to the other side. Similarly, we have been taught almost from childhood, to fear the Matabele – a fierce nation – so unreasoning in its ferocity that it will attack any individual or tribe, at sight, without the slightest provocation. Their destruction of our people, we were told, had no justification in fact or in reason; they were actuated by sheer lust for human blood.

By the merest accident, while collecting stray scraps of tribal history, later in life, the writer incidentally heard of 'the day Mzilikazi's tax collectors were killed'. Tracing this bit of information further back, he elicited from old people that the slaying of Bhoya and his companion, about the year 1830, constituted the *casus belli* which unleashed the war dogs and precipitated the Barolong nation headlong into the horrors described in these pages.

This book should have been published over ten years ago, but circumstances beyond the control of the writer delayed its

13

appearance. If, however, the objects can be attained, it will have come not a moment too soon.

This book has been written with two objects in view, viz., (a) to interpret to the reading public, one phase of 'the back of the Native mind'; and (b), with the readers' money, to collect and print (for Bantu schools) Sechuana folk-tales, which, with the spread of European ideas, are fast being forgotten. It is thus hoped to arrest this process by cultivating a love for art and literature in the vernacular. The latter object interests not missionaries alone, but also eminent scholars like Dr C.T. Loram, Dr C.M. Doke and other professors of the University of the Witwatersrand, not to mention commercial men of the stamp of Mr J.W. Mushet, chairman of the Cape Town Chamber of Commerce.

The last time I wrote a booklet, it was to pay my way through the United States. It was a disquisition on a delicate social problem known to Europeans in South Africa as the *Black Peril* and to the Bantu as the *White Peril*. I called it *The Mote and the Beam*. It more than fulfilled its purpose, for, by the time I left the States, over 18,000 copies had been sold and helped to pay my research journeys through several farms and cities of nineteen different States; and it is the author's sincere hope that the objects of this book will likewise be fulfilled.

In conclusion, I have to thank Rev. R.H. Shepherd, Chaplain of Lovedale, and Mr M.R. van Reenen, principal of the Coloured public school, Beaconsfield, for helping to correct the proofs.

SOL T. PLAATJE

32 Angel Street
Kimberley
August 1930

Introduction

WRITTEN IN 1920 AND published for the first time in 1930, Sol Plaatje's *Mhudi* is as relevant to our concerns now as it was back then. A century after Plaatje sat down in the cold concrete jungle of London, to write this novel, readers all over the world are still finding their thoughts and feelings in his text, with its language so powerful yet so beautiful.

Mhudi is set in the 1830s when Matabele under Mzilikazi attacked Barolong in Kunana (the present-day Setlagole in the North West province of South Africa). Following the attack, a young Morolong woman named Mhudi, the heroine in the novel, was under the impression that she was the only survivor until she met Ra-Thaga, a young man who also survived the massacre. They fell in love, got married, made a home for themselves in the forest and named it Re-Nosi, meaning "we are alone".

Later in the story Mhudi and Ra-Thaga met other Barolong who also survived the calamities in Kunana and later the Boers who were trekking into the interior from the Cape. The Barolong entered into a pact with the Boers to fight the Matabele, whom they eventually defeated and succeeded in chasing off their land.

Ra-Thaga had left Mhudi alone with the children to go and take part in this battle. After having a dream about Ra-Thaga being injured in the battle, Mhudi left her children with her cousin Baile and embarked on a journey to go and find her husband. On her way to the battlefield she met and made friends with Annetjie, a young Boer woman and Umnandi, the wife of Mzilikazi. Umnandi had fled her home because of the apparent scheming against her of Mzilikazi's other wives. Mhudi eventually found Ra-Thaga, who was indeed injured just as she saw him in the dream. She nursed him back to health.

After the battle Mhudi and Ra-Thaga bade their new friends goodbye, got on the oxwagon gifted by Annetje and her husband, De Villiers, and returned to join their people in Thaba Nchu.

Plaatje wrote *Mhudi* after he had arrived in England as part of the second deputation of the South African Native National Congress in 1919. Due to challenges relating to publishing, *Mhudi* was only published ten years later, in 1930. "This book should have been published over ten years ago, but circumstances beyond the control of the writer delayed its appearance," wrote Plaatje in the foreword of the 1930 Lovedale edition.

Mhudi was the first full-length English novel to be written by a black South African. Through it Plaatje carved out a path which, years later, other African writers would follow. These include Peter Abrahams who wrote *Mine Boy* in 1946, Amos Tutuola's *The Palm-Wine Drinkard* in 1952, Mongo Beti's *The Poor Christ of Bomba* in 1956 and Chinua Achebe's *Things Fall Apart* in 1958.

Plaatje added that at the time when he wrote *Mhudi*, South African literature was "almost exclusively European". *Mhudi* was an example of what Chinua Achebe meant when he later wrote in *The Empire Fights Back* about "new ways to write about Africa", which he argued were also efforts of "reinvesting the continent and its people with humanity, free at last of those stock situations and stock characters, 'never completely human', that had dominated European writing about Africa for hundreds of years".

By acknowledging that South African literature was "almost exclusively European", Plaatje took it upon himself to be the *righter* of that which he deemed wrong with the "almost exclusively European" South African literature, what Achebe described as "the colonisation of one people's story by another". This was the task at hand for Plaatje and other African writers of his generation and those who came after them.

To portray the extent of the destruction that came with Western civilisation, writers like Plaatje would use their imagination to paint the picture of a world in which a white man had not set foot, as he did in the opening paragraphs of *Mhudi*:

Two centuries ago the Bechuana tribes inhabited the extensive areas between Central Transvaal and the Kalahari Desert. Their entire world lay in the geography covered by the story in these pages.

In this domain they led their patriarchal life under their several chiefs who owed no allegiance to any king or emperor. They raised their native corn which satisfied their simple wants and, when not engaged in hunting or in pastoral duties, the peasants whiled away their days in tanning skins or sewing magnificent fur rugs. They also smelted iron and manufactured useful implements which today would be pronounced very crude by their semi-westernised descendants.

Interestingly it was not Plaatje alone who looked to an unadulterated Africa to show what the continent could have been had European colonists not set foot on it. Chinua Achebe does this even later in his nonfiction; in *My Home under Imperial Fire*, he takes the reader to the world of the precolonial Igbo:

> The Igbo nation in precolonial times was not quite like any nation most people are familiar with. It did not have the apparatus of centralized government but a conglomeration of hundreds of independent towns and villages each of which shared the running of its affairs among its menfolk according to title, age, occupation, etc.; and its womenfolk who had domestic responsibilities, as well as the management of the scores of four-day and eight-day markets that bound the entire region and its neighbours in a network of daily exchange of goods and news, from far and near.

What Plaatje, as well as other writers including Chinua Achebe, Amos Tutuola, Mongo Beti, Peter Abrahams and Thomas Mofolo, did was to reimagine the African into a story into which he was thrust in a way he would not like to see himself, nor believe the portrayal was real or affirming. These African writers took it upon themselves to re-story Africa and the African.

One of the questions that have been keeping mainly African language and literature scholars awake at night, especially in regard to *Mhudi*, is: why did Plaatje, who had already made his name as *modibelapuo*, the one who had put up a defence for literary expression in mother tongue and had invested time in its development, choose to write his first novel in English and not Setswana?

In the reasons Plaatje outlined for writing *Mhudi*, in the

foreword, the answer to the above question has been answered: "This book has been written with two objects in view, viz. (a) to interpret to the reading public one phase of the 'back of the Native mind'; and (b) with the readers' money, to collect and print (for Bantu Schools) Sechuana folk-tales which, with the spread of European ideas, are fast being forgotten. It is thus hoped to arrest this process by cultivating a love for art and literature in the Vernacular."

Some scholars have expressed regret that *Mhudi* was written in English. They have argued that had it been written in the author's mother tongue, it would have given Setswana a great first full-length novel. In fact, some have even gone to the lengths to argue that *Mhudi* was the first Setswana novel! In their essay entitled "*Maropeng: On Repatriating Mhudi as a Setswana Novel*", in the volume *Sol Plaatje's Mhudi: History, Criticism, Celebration* (2020), Shole J. Shole and Eileen Pooe go beyond expressing this regret; they make a plausible argument for the repatriative translation of *Mhudi*.

"*Mhudi*, like all African literary works linguistically exiled in the languages of European colonialists, needs to be reclaimed and reimagined in the native language of its author and his people through a special form of translation, a 'repatriative transcreation', for which a Setswana neologism, *phetsolelo*, has been coined. *Phetsolelo* (derived from *phetsola*) means 'revert, flip, turn inside out or upside down; make a turnaround' (as in *phetsophetso*)."

Shole and Pooe also argue that *Mhudi* is the work of a patriotic Motswana which has as its subject the Batswana people and the Setswana universe. "It is inspired by, and owes its being to, the Setswana setting, history and socio-cultural world." By being written in English, they argue, *Mhudi* has been linguistically exiled from its language base and needs to be reclaimed.

Shole and Pooe's argument finds harmony in Kenyan scholar Ngugi wa Thiong'o, who argues in *Decolonising the Mind: The Politics of Language in African Literature* that the future of the African novel is dependent on being translated into an African language or between African languages:

> The future of the African novel is then dependent on a willing writer (ready to invest time and talent in African languages); a willing translator (ready to invest time and talent in the art of translating from one African language into another); a willing publisher (ready to invest time and money) or a progressive state which would overhaul the current neo-colonial linguistic policies.

In *Politics and Politicians of Language in African Literature*, Achebe explicates the position in which Plaatje found himself with regard to the language in which he chose to write *Mhudi*: "No serious writer can possibly be indifferent to the fate of any language, let alone his own mother tongue. For most writers in the world, there is never any conflict – the mother tongue and the writing language are one and the same. But from time to time, and as a result of grave historical reasons, a writer may be trapped unhappily and invidiously between two imperatives", a situation which Plaatje's people would describe as being "mo gare ga 'naka tsa kukama".

Plaatje has also been lauded by many for his portrayal of women in the person of the heroine of the novel, Mhudi, as visionary and being way ahead of his time. D. S. Matjila and Karen Haire in *Bringing Plaatje Home - Ga e Phetsolele Nageng: 'Re-storying' the African and Batswana Sensibilities in His Oeuvre*, argue that Mhudi in the novel "exhibits an independence that challenges the stereotypical, traditional conception of a woman as a minor and dependant". By so doing, they add, "Plaatje implicitly critiques African society for its exclusion of women from public decision-making and, by extension, African society's general disregard for their potential in public life.

"He [Plaatje] frequently shows the superior judgement of women, as when Mhudi instinctively distrusts the headman who invites her husband, Ra-Thaga, on a hunting trip. Ra-Thaga, who misses the finer subtleties of character, accepts the offer, putting both his wife and himself in considerable danger.

"Indeed, Ra-Thaga decides to accept the invitation to the hunt, despite Mhudi's premonitions and warnings. Male chauvinism brings Mhudi into direct conflict with her husband."

Plaatje's elevation of women, through Mhudi in the novel, may have its genesis in his childhood and the women who lived in Pniel. Brian Willan details this in the biography, *Sol Plaatje: A Life of Solomon Tshekisho Plaatje 1876–1932.*

"Plaatje's mother was one of several women in Pniel who told him of family and tribal traditions, and from whom he learned Setswana, his first language. 'The best Sechuana speakers known to me', he observed later in life, 'owe their knowledge to the teachings of a grandmother, or a mother, just as I myself … am indebted to the teachings of my mother and two aunts.' Among these 'teachings' was a fund of fables and proverbs, highly valued as repositories of the inherited wisdom of their people and passed on from generation to generation," writes Willan.

Another woman who left a deep impression on the young Plaatje was his paternal grandmother 'Au Magritte' from whom he learned in detail about his ancestry. Willan adds that it was also during Plaatje's childhood that he was told about his paternal great-grandmother's bravery.

"She was gathering wood one day with some other girls in

the bush near Kunana hills (so Plaatje related many years later) when they suddenly came upon a lion feasting on the carcass of a freshly killed eland. She rushed at the lion, waving her sheepskin in his face, causing him to turn tail and run off. When the girls returned home in triumph with the meat, the men would not believe their story. Only after returning to the scene were they convinced by the evidence of the spoors which revealed where the lion stood over the carcass, and how it ran away," Willan wrote.

Mhudi can also be seen, to some extent, as a tribute to many other women who fell and rose up with Plaatje in difficult times, especially while he was writing *Native Life in South Africa* and *Mhudi*. On both occasions he was left alone when his comrades departed, and dedicated his time to writing the two books alongside doing the important political work.

A short biography of Sol Plaatje

Solomon Tshekisho Plaatje was born on the farm Doornfontein in the district of Boshof in the Orange Free State on October 9, 1876 to Kushumane and Martha Lokgosi. The Plaatjes were a family of Christian converts following contact with the Berlin Missionary Society, which in southern Africa today is known as the Evangelical Lutheran Church. Shortly after Plaatje's birth, his family moved to Pniel, a mission station about twenty kilometres from Kimberley towards Barkly West, soon to become part of the Cape Colony.

In Pniel, a small yet multilingual community, Plaatje attended school and was taught by the resident minister Ernst Westphal and his wife Marie. From an early age it was evident that Plaatje was bright and gifted. He asked Marie Westphal if she could teach him English, German and Dutch, which she and her husband gladly did. Unfortunately the highest level of education the mission school offered was Standard Three, which Plaatje attained. He was also appointed a pupil-teacher at the school.

In 1894 Plaatje left the mission station for the bright lights of the fast-growing town of Kimberley where fortune seekers, from other parts of southern Africa and Europe, had descended following the discovery of diamonds and the frantic digging on a hillock that later became the famous Big Hole. Upon arrival in Kimberley, Plaatje took up a position as messenger at the post office. Kimberley was a multiracial and multicultural community. It was during this time that he met other young black men who had come to work in the city, including an interpreter called Isaiah Bud-M'Belle, whose sister, Elizabeth, Plaatje later married. It was also in Kimberley that Plaatje for the first time saw the play *Hamlet*, by William Shakespeare, at the Kimberley Theatre. Seeing that play ignited his interest in Shakespeare's work. Just over two decades later, he translated some of Shakespeare's plays into Setswana; *Julius Caesar* to *Dintšhontšho tsa bo-Juliuse Kesara* and *Comedy of Errors* to *Diphoshophosho*. The Shakespearean translation was the first on the African continent.

For somebody with such a huge body of work, Plaatje did not live long. According to his protégé Modiri Molema in a Setswana biography *Sol Plaatje: Morata Wabo*, later translated into English by Karen Haire and Daniel Sekepe Matjila as *Lover of his People: A Biography of Sol Plaatje*, Plaatje lived just fifty-five years, eight months and ten days. He died on June 19, 1932 in Johannesburg.

"His departure felt like the disappearance of the shadow of a great rock in a dry and thirsty land," Molema wrote.

Molema also argued further that Plaatje died with his boots on: "He pursued knowledge and shared it selflessly with all. In the end, Plaatje, it must be said, had loved and lived for his people, sacrificing his own health for their advancement."

Plaatje's works, especially *Mhudi* and *Native Life in South Africa*, continue to draw the international attention of scholars and inspire works of art over a century after they were written. The timelessness of Plaatje's work is evidenced by volumes of essays in this day and age, analysing and grappling with the issues he wrote about then. His work gives us the means to examine life, question the centuries-old injustices and confront the assumptions that characterise life as it is at the moment long after he ceased breathing.

Brain Willan writes that *Mhudi* was "the literary creation of a man of complex sensibilities, who found in writing not just an escape from the day-to-day struggles that preoccupied him at the time he wrote it in 1920, but also the opportunity to give imaginative expression to many of his underlying values and beliefs."

Mhudi, Willan writes, sheds light upon what sustained Plaatje in a lifetime of endeavour:

"In this sense *Mhudi*'s value is that it brings all this together, and at a level of detachment from reality which provides a glimpse into a sensibility so obscured by the many different guises Plaatje had to adopt in circumstances over which, as he often complained, he could exercise little control.

"In *Mhudi* it is different. He is in control of both his characters and their circumstances, released from the constraints imposed upon his own activities and ambitions. Here there is scope for free expression of his imagination, his fascination with the traditions of his people, his exploration of the literary and cultural possibilities of mixing Tswana and English traditions, his admiration for the qualities he believed women to possess, his vision of the consequences of continued injustice in South Africa," adds Willan.

The truth in *Mhudi* lies in its timelessness, in its stubborn relevance. The history it presents us with refuses to be history, it lives with us daily and torments us. Mhudi, despite her wisdom and bravery, is yet to know how it feels to be equal to a man in this world. Sol Plaatje's truth in *Mhudi* is as real as concrete.

Sabata-mpho Mokae
Sol Plaatje University
Kimberley
February 2021

Editorial note

A NUMBER OF EDITIONS of *Mhudi* have been published since the 1970s. Several of these have returned to the typescript used by the Lovedale Press to typeset the first edition of the book in 1930, and they have preferred to incorporate elements of the typescript which Plaatje subsequently changed or corrected. This edition, by contrast, takes as its basis the published Lovedale text, since this reflected not only the final version of Plaatje's typescript but also incorporated subsequent corrections which he made to the proofs of the book during the course of its production. It thus aims to reflect Plaatje's last thoughts on the text.

At the same time, we have corrected obvious typographical errors and inconsistencies and have modernised spelling of commonly used names. We have made some amendments to reflect the fact that this edition of *Mhudi* is published for a South African audience, whereas the original edition of *Mhudi* incorporated some features that addressed the needs of the overseas audience Plaatje initially envisaged. So we have deleted some superfluous explanatory notes, and incorporated others into the text. For similar reasons we have returned to the original names of Cilliers, De Villiers and Viljoen in place of the phonetic representations that Plaatje devised for his anticipated overseas readers.

Brian Willan
Sol Plaatje University
Kimberley
February 2021

Chapter One

A Tragedy and Its Vendetta

TWO CENTURIES AGO the Bechuana tribes inhabited the extensive areas between central Transvaal and the Kalahari desert. Their entire world lay in the geography covered by the story in these pages.

In this domain they led their patriarchal life under their several chiefs who owed no allegiance to any king or emperor. They raised their native corn which satisfied their simple wants, and, when not engaged in hunting or in pastoral duties, the peasants whiled away their days in tanning skins or sewing magnificent fur rugs. They also smelted iron and manufactured useful implements which today would be pronounced very crude by their semi-westernised descendants.

Cattle breeding was the rich man's calling, and hunting a national enterprise. Their cattle, which carried enormous horns, ran almost wild and multiplied as prolifically as the wild animals of the day. Work was of a perfunctory nature, for mother earth yielded her bounties and the maiden soil provided ample sustenance for man and beast.

But woman's work was never out of season. In the summer she cleared the cornfields of weeds and subsequently helped to winnow and garner the crops. In the winter she cut the grass and helped to renovate her dwelling. In addition to the inevitable cooking, basket-making, and weaving, all the artpainting for mural decorations was done by women. Childless marriages were as rare as freaks, so, early and late in summer and winter, during years of drought and of plenty, every mother had to nourish her growing brood, besides fattening and beautifying her daughters for the competition of eligible swains.

Fulfilling these multifarious duties of the household was not regarded as a drudgery by any means; on the contrary, the women looked upon marriage as an art. The daughter of a well-to-do peasant, surrounded by all the luxuries of her mother's home, would be the object of commiseration if she were a long time finding a man. And the simple women of the tribes accepted wifehood and transacted their onerous duties with the same satisfaction and pride as an English artist would the job of conducting an orchestra.

Kunana, near the present boundary between Cape Colony and western Transvaal, was the capital city of the Barolong, the original stock of the several tribes, who also followed the humdrum yet interesting life of the other Bechuana Natives. They planted their stations in different directions over scores of miles; and it was often easier to kill wild animals nearer home than go to the cattle-post for meat. Very often the big game ran *thalala-motse* (when wild animals continued their frolics straight through a Native village) when there would be systematic slaughter of antelopes and orgies of wild-beef eating.

Barolong cattlemen at times attempted to create a new species of animal by cross-breeding between an eland and an ox. One cattle-owner, named Motonosi, not very far from

Kunana, raised two dozen calves all sired by a buffalo. The result proved so disastrous that Barolong tradition still holds up his achievement as a masterpiece of folly, and attempts at cross-breeding thereafter became taboo.

These peasants were content to live their monotonous lives, and thought naught of their overseas kinsmen who were making history on the plantations and harbours of Virginia and Mississippi at that time; nor did they know or care about the relations of the Hottentots and the Boers at Cape Town nearer home. The topography of the Cape peninsula would have had no interest for them; and had anyone mentioned the beauty spots of the Cape and the glory of the silver trees on their own subcontinent they would have felt disappointed on hearing that they bore no edible fruit.

To them the limit of the world was Monomotapa (Portuguese East Africa) – a white man's country – which they had no ambition to see. Of monetary wealth they had none except their flocks and herds. A little bartering was done with neighbouring tribes in exchange for other commodities, and none could be so mean as to make a charge for supplying a fellow-tribesman with the necessaries of life. When the rainy season was good everyone had too much corn, and in years of drought the majority went short of porridge.

Strange to relate, these simple folk were perfectly happy without money and without silver watches. Abject poverty was practically unknown; they had no orphanages because there were no nameless babies. When a man had a couple of karosses to make he invited the neighbours to spend the day with him cutting, fitting in and sewing together the sixty grey jackal pelts into two rugs, and there would be intervals of feasting throughout the day. On such an occasion, someone would announce a field day at another place where there was a dwelling to thatch; here too the guests might receive an invitation from a peasant who had a stockade to erect at a third homestead on a subsequent day; and great would be the expectation of the fat bullock to be slaughtered by the good man, to say nothing of the good things to be prepared by the kind hostess. Thus a month's job would be accomplished in a day.

But the anomaly of this community life was that, while the many seams in a rich man's kaross carried all kinds of knittings – good, bad and indifferent – the wife of a poor man, who could not afford such a feast, was often gowned in flawless furs. It being the skilled handiwork of her own husband, the nicety of its seams seldom failed to evoke the admiration of experts.

Upon these peaceful regions over one hundred years ago there descended one Mzilikazi, king of a ferocious tribe called the Matabele, a powerful usurper of determined character who by his sword proclaimed himself ruler over all the land.

Mzilikazi's tribe originally was a branch of the Zulu nation which Shaka once ruled with an iron rod. Irritated by the stern rule of that monarch, Mzilikazi led out his own people who thereupon broke away from Shaka's rule and turned their faces westward.

Sweeping through the northern areas of Port Natal, they advanced along both banks of the Vaal River, driving terror into man and beast with whom they came in contact. They continued their march very much like a swarm of locusts; scattering the Swazis, terrifying the Basuto and the Bapedi on their outposts, they drove them back to the mountains at the point of the assegai; and, trekking through the heart of the Transvaal, they eventually invaded Bechuanaland where they reduced the Natives to submission.

At length the Matabele established as their capital the city of Inzwinyani in Bahurutshe territory, the Bechuana inhabitants being permitted to remain on condition that their chiefs should pay tribute to Mzilikazi. Gradually enlarging their dominion, the Matabele enforced taxation first upon one and then another of the surrounding Bechuana clans, including the Barolong at Kunana, whose chief at the time was Tauana.

Perhaps the new administration might have worked well enough; but, unfortunately, the conquerors not only imported a fresh discipline but they also introduced manners that were extremely offensive even for these primitive people. For instance, the victorious soldiers were in the habit of walking about in their birthday garb, thereby forcing the modest Bechuana women and children to retire on each appearance of Matabele men. This hide-and-seek life, which proved more inconvenient than accommodating, was ill calculated to inspire respect for the new authority. Needless to say this outrage, so shocking to local susceptibilities, was resented by the original population and became a perpetual source of discontent. Still, the new discipline was not stern; and as long as each chief paid taxes each springtime in acknowledgement of his fealty to Mzilikazi, the Bechuana were left in undisturbed possession of their old homes and haunts.

One of Tauana's righthand men was a wealthy chieftain, Notto by name. Besides his home in the capital he owned three cattle-stations and many cornfields in the country. His son, Ra-Thaga, minded one of the herds at a place called Mhuhucho.

One day, Notto set out to spend some time in the country with his son in order to fulfil his pastoral duties, such as earmarking the lambs and calves and braying skins and riems. One morning, while Notto was engaged in these occupations at the cattle-post, two men came from Kunana who walked like bearers of very important news. After greeting him they related this startling information: 'Two Matabele indunas, Bhoya and Bangela, had come to Kunana to gather the annual tribute. They duly announced the object of their visit and asked that six young men should be supplied to carry the Barolong tribute for them and lay it "at the feet of Mzilikazi, ruler of earth and skies".

'Chief Tauana', the messengers went on, 'received the visitors with indifference and, without informing his counsellors in any way, he commanded some young men to take the two to the ravine and "lose them", which is equivalent to a death sentence. The tax collectors were dragged away without notice and almost before they realised their doom they were stabbed to death.

'I am told', said the narrator, 'that, before his death, Bhoya, with his hands manacled, gesticulated and cried: "You dogs of a Western breed, you are going to suffer for this. You shall pay with your own blood and the blood of your children for laying your base hands on the courier of King Mzilikazi. A Matabele's blood never mingled with the earth without portending death and destruction. Kill me with your accursed hands, you menial descendants of mercenary hammersmiths [Barolong], and you have sown the seed of your own doom. Do you hear me?"

'He was still speaking when Rauwe stabbed him in the breast. He fell forward, gave a gasp and a groan, rolled up the whites of his large dull eyes, and after uttering a dread imprecation, sank back lifeless.'

'You can well understand', said the emissary, 'that Mzilikazi is not going to take such treatment lying down; consequently the chief counsellors decided to take immediate steps to make amends. But as the chief would probably refuse to apologise, it was decided to summon home from the cattle-posts all men of influence, to attend a tribal picho and arrange a settlement before it is too late.'

Accordingly, Notto issued word that all men of importance should leave their fields at once and accompany him to the city. Two days later, a contingent of men, some walking, others mounted on oxen (young Ra-Thaga among them), might have been seen making their way in the direction of Kunana.

So, towards evening, about six miles from the city, the party was met by a large number of fleeing women. The fugitives told them that Kunana was being attacked, and the would-be interceders had to abandon peace and forthwith arm for the fight.

To speak the truth, Ra-Thaga and the other young bloods were glad. Old men liked to recount their wondrous deeds of valour in the wars they had fought, and young men were always pining for an opportunity to test their own strength in a really good fight.

The young people had been complaining that these Zulus from the east were having things too much their own way and should be checked. Hence their delight on hearing that the two nations were at grips. But it must be confessed that Notto held views of quite another character; yet how little did they dream when the fight began that evening in the twilight, that they were about to make their last stand together; or that Ra-Thaga would never again set his eyes upon the man who gave him life.

They all stood waiting for Notto's orders when a melancholy shout rent the evening air in the bush hard by. Not having reached the town, they were till then not aware that they were in the thick of the fight already; but women began to scream in the bush around and they could hear the Matabele swords at work. Notto gave the order to fall to, and they hurled themselves into the bush from which emanated the sickening wail. It was clear, from that moment, that the sun of the peacemaker had set, never to rise again, for, by the faint light of the new moon, they noticed with horror that the Matabele were not fighting men only; they were actually spearing fleeing women and children. Ra-Thaga saw one of them killing a woman and, as she fell back, the man grasped her little baby and dashed its skull against the trunk of a tree. The sight almost took his breath away. The next moment a woman fell beside a tree, her fall hastened by a stab from behind. She carried her baby in a springbok skin, strapped to her back. The skin loosened as she fell and a Matabele, withdrawing the assegai from the mother's side, pierced her child with it, and held the baby transfixed in the air.

Maddened by these awful scenes, the Barolong hurled themselves against the enemy and fought like fiends possessed.

The bush, by this time, was a howling pandemonium, and what was seen and heard made the survivors almost delirious with grief. Looking away they saw the flames shooting up from hundreds of blazing huts at Kunana, and licking the air in a reddish glow that almost turned the night into day. Then Ra-Thaga recognised his father in the turmoil, holding a number of assegais. He had evidently done much already for he was panting heavily.

'Charge and kill these beasts of prey!' the headman cried.

Just at that moment a woman ran past him and a Matabele from behind a tree, close by, speared her also. Ra-Thaga drove his assegai into his armpit; he could not pull it out again so he left him with it, saying as he did so, 'Feel what these mothers have felt, you vampire, and may the spirits scorch your soul hereafter.'

'I couldn't tell', he used to relate, 'how long our struggle lasted, but eventually I found myself alone amongst a number of corpses, groaning men and expiring women.

'At length I rose and searched through the field of carnage,' he said, 'then came upon my father's body which lay lifeless between pools of blood. He was dead. "My father, Oh my father," I cried. "I wonder where and how mother is."

'Not far from there lay a woman between two dead children. She was suffering frightful agonies, having fallen with her head

bent down beneath her body and being too weak to straighten
herself. I straightened her out which eased her pain a bit,
and she lived just long enough to tell me what had happened;
and that was the only story I ever heard of the origin of the
massacre, and the conflagration in the city. It was clear that she
was not far from the door of death; so, thinking of my mother
and sisters, I decided to return to the burning city to learn
something about them.

'On the way I heard two men coming from the opposite
direction, speaking in undertones, in our tongue, and so I knew
they were not enemies. I spoke and they replied that they too
were hurrying away to discover the fate of their women folk.
"Kunana is in ruins," they said, "the Barolong are wiped out
and their home shall know them no more." Nevertheless, I
decided to risk a journey into the burning town. At the chief's
court, hordes of Matabele soldiers were dancing round a
bonfire; evidently celebrating the avenging of Bhoya's death.
The crossings and passages between the huts were full of dead
bodies of friends and enemies, and many of our women and
children. In our quarters, I saw none of our folk. The corn in
the mud bin was still smouldering, so, removing the parched
grain from the top, I took out from underneath some good
sound corn, carried this in a knapsack, and left the hideous
place as quickly and as quietly as I had entered it.'

Ra-Thaga then made for the cattle-post which he and his
father had left the day before. Arriving there next morning, he
could hardly recognise the old place. The huts, the cattlefold,
like the whole terrain from Kunana to Mhuhucho, bore
gruesome traces of the ravages of the Matabele in the shape of
dead bodies, burnt huts and destroyed crops. Up to that time he
had seen no sign of a living being, only abundant evidences of
death.

After pondering for a while among the ruins, he made for

some adjacent kopje and surveyed the country from the crest of the highest hillock.

He saw parties of the victors reconnoitring on the plains, under the direction of others who were signalling from the hilltops. Now and again he observed a number of Barolong in full flight, and hordes of Matabele at their heels. It was not difficult to divine the result of such a chase.

Ra-Thaga travelled nearly two months without meeting a single soul. The loneliness was frightful. During his flight, and when he thought of the devastation of the country, he often wondered what had become of the chief. He fully believed that he, too, was killed with his wives and children and all his people.

Chapter Two

Dark Days

RA-THAGA, IN ORDER not to be attacked by wild animals, was wont to sleep in the top branches of some large tree, where he would weave a hammock of ramblers and ropes of inner barks, tying it up with twigs. In this manner he spent many nights alone in different woods. This was a wise precaution, for occasionally his sleep and the stillness of the night were disturbed by the awful roar of the king of beasts, making thunder in the forest. One morning, at the end of another restless night, when the wood pigeons began to address one another in their language, after the dawn of day had caused the whining of the hyenas to cease, the sun rose slowly, and Ra-Thaga, descending from his late solitary nest, commenced the misery of another day. Each of his mornings was but the resumption of his fruitless search for the company of human beings, which it seemed he was never to find in this world. As he dragged his feet through the dewy grass he seemed to have no particular destination in view. He wondered how much longer this solitude would last. With a drooping spirit he mused over the gloom of existence and asked himself if he still could speak his own language or if, supposing he met anyone and was addressed, he could still understand it.

These thoughts tormented him for the sixtieth time, when he suddenly saw a slender figure running swiftly towards him. It was clear that the maiden was frightened by something terrible, for she ran unseeingly towards him, and as he arrested her progress, the girl stood panting like a hunted fox. It was only after some moments that with a supreme effort she could utter the short disyllable, *tau* (that is a lion).

'Where?' asked Ra-Thaga.

'Oh stranger!' gasped the girl, recovering her voice, 'how good of you to appear just when my succession of misfortunes had reached a climax. I almost stumbled over a huge lion just beyond that ridge, not far from here – I am afraid he will hear us if we speak above a whisper. I did not notice the brute at first because his hair looked just like the tops of the autumn grass. He must have been eating something, for straight in front of me I heard a sound like the breaking of a tree. I think he was crushing the leg of a cow – oh, how silly of me to forget that there are no cows in this wilderness. Anyway,' continued the girl between her gasps, 'I noticed that in front of me there was not a tuft of grass, but a living animal feeding on something. So I stepped quietly backward, without turning round, until I was at some distance, and then I turned and ran.

Ra-Thaga, successfully concealing his own fears, asked, 'You were not, then, observed by the animal, were you?'

'No,' she replied, 'I believe that he is still devouring his prey.'

Ra-Thaga did not know what to do, for if there were two things he was against meeting, they were a Matabele and a lion. 'But here is an awkward position,' he thought, 'a young woman fleeing to me for protection. What is best to be done?'

His native gallantry urged him to go after the beast; the young woman persisted in following close behind him. Vainly he tried to persuade her to remain where she was, but she was obdurate. 'Nay,' she replied, in a loud whisper, 'I dare not remain alone.'

Ra-Thaga thought he knew what was passing through her mind before she spoke. She added: 'I have wandered through this lonely wilderness for days and nights, since my people were scattered at Kunana; I have lived on roots and bulbs and wild berries, yearning to meet some human being, and now that I have met you, you cannot leave me again so quickly. In fact, I am not quite certain that you are a man, and even if you are a dream I will stay with you and dream on while the vision lasts; whether you are man or ghost I have enjoyed the pleasure of a few words with you. I am prepared to see ten other lions with you rather than stay alone of my own free will. Walk on to the lion, I will follow you.'

Ra-Thaga heard this with a shiver. He believed that women were timid creatures, but here was one actually volunteering to guide him to where the lion was, instead of commanding him to take her far away from the man-eater. How he wished that he might find it gone! However, he summoned up courage and proceeded, his companion following. At times he felt pleased that she had not obeyed him, for her presence stimulated his bravery. As they proceeded, however, he certainly began to doubt the wisdom of his adventure. 'In our country,' he said to himself, 'lions were usually hunted by large companies of men armed with spears and clubs, with the aid of fierce mastiffs, and not by one badly armed man guided by a strange girl.'

Suddenly, their extreme peril struck him, and before he had time to ponder over it, the maiden touched his shoulder and pointed to what looked like a tuft of moving grass, some fifty yards ahead – it was a black-maned lion.

The king of beasts was leisurely gorging himself with

chunks of meat torn from the carcases of an eland which he had recently killed. Ra-Thaga, realising that not only his own safety depended upon his prowess, but also that of the young woman who had appeared as if from the clouds, and commended herself to his care, his fears vanished. Yelling at the top of his voice and waving his cloak of skin in the air, he rushed at the feasting lion, the girl doing the same. This violent interruption of his meal caused the lion to jerk his head, whereupon he took fright and darted off as hard as he could go with his tail between his legs. The lion ran through the trees across the grassy plain and never stopped till he was out of view, thus leaving Ra-Thaga complete master of the situation. With the lion out of sight Ra-Thaga was able to rejoice; though his pride was not greater than the joy of the girl who realised that her trust in him had not been misplaced. At last his eyes fell on the damsel who in her turn cast furtive glances at her unknown hero. 'My man, my man,' she seemed to say, 'my stranger man, whom the spirits have sent to save me from loneliness, starvation, and the lion's jaw, I would willingly pass through another Matabele raid and suffer hairbreadth escapes if but to meet one like you! And to herself she said, 'I wonder what his name is?'

Ra-Thaga was also wondering who she was and whence she came; and guessing what questions were crossing her mind, he came nearer and offered her his hand.

'*Dumela* (Good-day), my sister,' he said, 'I am Ra-Thaga, the son of Notto. I belonged to the Sehuba clan of the Barolong at Kunana, the burnt city. Pray who art thou?'

'My name is Mhudi,' replied the girl, 'my people belonged to the Kgoro tribe. I, too, came from the doomed city – curse that Matabele king! My father and mother are slain, also my two sisters and little brothers – tiny little children. I have never heard of any lions killing children, but Matabele seem to be fiercer than beasts of prey. Tell me, father, are these Zulus really human beings?'

'Well, Mhudi,' replied Ra-Thaga, 'I too would like an answer to that poser. We are both very tired and hungry. The gods of our ancestors have watched over us these many lonely days and nights since the destruction of our homes, and now we have met. See, here is the carcass of a fully developed young eland bull, of which the lion has eaten but little, there is the *mothanthanyane* shrub, I will spin a stick against its limb and start a spark while you keep watch. We will then roast some meat and appease our hunger, after which there ought to be plenty of time to relate our experiences to each other; although it seems, I think, that our stories will not be dissimilar.'

Ra-Thaga was nearly half an hour labouring to ignite the sticks, while Mhudi stooped beside him holding a bunch of grass in both hands, ready to encourage the first spark into a flame. The continued friction between the two sticks finally generated a spark which, shooting into the tuft of grass, started a comfortable blaze. Mhudi entered quickly upon the duties of providing a meal and, not long after, the roast was sizzling on the coals.

While the girl nimbly did her part, Ra-Thaga made a careful study of the unexpected being who had so dramatically altered the trend of his life, and he determined never to let her pass out of it again. Her curly hair was as carefully trimmed as though she had come from her mother's house that morning, but her general appearance showed that, even for a bucolic girl, she was frightfully travel-stained. For all that, Mhudi had a magnificent figure. Her forehead completed the lovely contour of a slightly emaciated face, the colour of her skin being a deep brown that set off to advantage her brilliant black eyes. A pretty pair of dimples danced around her cheeks when she smiled; and the smile revealed an even set of ivories as pure as that of any child. Her bewitching mouth and beautiful lips created a sense of charm, and when she blew the fire she seemed to blow something into Ra-Thaga that almost maddened him with ecstasy and he wondered if her breath was charmed. In front she wore an apron of thin twisted strips, suspended evenly from a belt round her waist, reaching just above the knees, while a springbok skin drooping from her hips downward formed the kirtle that matched her beautiful form. Round her shoulders hung a furry rug of speckled lambskins very carefully tanned. This she had put aside while preparing the meal. Her agile movements as she carefully piled up more and more wood on the now blazing fire, or turned the eland ribs on the glowing embers, so fascinated Ra-Thaga that he never tired of looking at her. He thought she had above her beaded anklets the most beautiful limbs he had ever seen. He recalled the halcyon days at Kunana, when pretty girls bedecked with ornaments pranced about the courtyards, but could not remember one so perfectly proportioned and elegant in every movement.

Chapter Three

Mhudi's Alarming Experiences

A ROYAL PAIR NEVER sat down to a meal with greater relish than the rescued Mhudi and her chivalrous comrade, as together they partook of the wild beef from a flat stone, which served as an improvised dish and table in one. Musing the while over their unexpected meeting, 'And after all,' thought Ra-Thaga, 'the gods are indeed propitious to allow someone to comfort me after the massacre of our people.' Each of them thought it rather fortunate that the other was of the opposite sex.

'Now tell me,' said Ra-Thaga at the end of their meal, 'where did you come from, my friend, and how did you get here?'

'No,' replied Mhudi, 'though I have lost my people, I have not lost my manners. Men first; you have the right of way. You tell me, brother, how you came here in time to save me from the lion, and I will give you my story afterwards.'

They exchanged a few more pleasantries, then Ra-Thaga,

having recounted his part in the memorable cataclysm, added: 'Future generations will never know war, for the Barolong are an exterminated people. The famous race of warriors and descendants of Tau – the Lion of the North – who in their wars never tarnished their spears with children's blood, are no more. The Barolong, noted for their agility and dexterity with the sword – a clean sword that never stained itself with the blood of a woman – are wiped out. Their fire is extinguished, their city flattened and their name blotted off the face of the earth. In our wars men killed other warriors, and captured the unarmed and non-resisting. They took the women and children home. But the Matabele, oh, the Matabele! Could it be real or was it only a dream? In fact, I am not even certain whether the bloody operations I have described took place in two or more nights, or only one. Until I met you, I did not believe that another of our tribe existed, and I had never expected to hear our language spoken again. On seeing you I did not believe that you were a Morolong. But it turns out that two of us, at any rate, are left alive to tell the story, but – to whom? Ah, yes, to whom …?

'Now, do tell me how you left Kunana that used to be our home. Kunana, where we enjoyed a peace and prosperity that were unequalled anywhere; where our cattle waxed fat along the green valleys and bred like so many wild animals; where our flocks with the jocund lambs around their dams would frolic, while the she-goats fed from two to three kids each, till we were forced to increase and extend our outposts to give them more and still more space to roam about; Kunana, where maidens sang and danced in the moonlight and made life merry with their mirth; Kunana, our former home, but now one of the Matabele outposts. Do tell me, my sister, how you escaped and how you ever reached here.'

'How can I explain?' commenced Mhudi. 'Where shall I begin, for who could have foretold in my childhood days that the sweet life at Kunana would end like this?

'On that terrible day after the sun had risen and cleared the horizon, we girls took our water-pails as usual and fetched the sweet water from the spring near the valley. The flocks had left the fold and we separated the kids from their mothers in order to milk the goats on their return from the bush next afternoon. The summer sun shone overhead and the shades of the camelthorn trees were cool; so we took our wooden pestles, sat merrily in a circle under the shady branches busily pounding the corn to prepare porridge for the evening meal.

'On that last afternoon I had taken a pestle to hurry along with my cookery duties, when, suddenly, the watchmen's horns sounded in different parts of the town. Being preoccupied with my work I paid but passing attention to such masculine affairs, until I observed my mother hurrying indoors – I know not whence – and was terrified to see her weeping. At the same moment I noticed a commotion among the crowd of men all around, everybody hurrying towards the chief's court. Rushing forward to find out the cause of my mother's grief, and how I could help her, I learned from the dear soul the meaning of the alarm.

'My mother had told us one evening that two Matabele had been killed. In our girlish simplicity we hardly enquired for the reason. We took it that these Khonkhobes [foreigners] had no business in our country, and that it was just and proper that they should be sent off or put to death. We had often heard how they carry off women and children, and we felt that we were safer with Bhoya's dead bones in the ravine than with Bhoya himself prowling about the country and levying taxes; but, ah! that's where we were mistaken. The news of the death of the two Matabele indunas had hardly got about when the alarm was sounded. We were ordered to prepare to leave with the children at nightfall, and while we were tying up some provisions, a hideous cry rent the air to the north end of the town as the enemy attacked, and we had to flee before sunset. Mother had the baby, and I carried my little brother and a few articles. The bushes on the southern outskirts of the town were swarming with a moving mass of women and children; while the tramp, tramp of the march of many pairs of feet was drowned by the wild screams of thousands of people at the far end of the town, as they received the thrusts of the Matabele spears.

'A young mother and friend of mine who joined me later in the course of our flight, gave me some harrowing details of the attack. She herself had one of her breasts ripped open by one of those human vultures and the running and bleeding exhausted her soon after she joined me. She begged me to leave her and fly with the little ones. She told me that the Matabele took her baby from her and dashed its little head upon a rock till its brains bespattered those around. Other women, she told me, met their death heroically. My cousin Baile, she said, was near her when she received a stab from a Matabele who spoke our tongue fluently; and Baile said to him: "Kill me, you coward, go back and brag that you have killed a woman in kirtles. If that be your Zulu prowess, I admire the Bechuana trait of measuring strength with bearded men, and never defiling their spears with women's blood." She was still speaking when another stabbed her from behind; and, as she dropped, this Matabele speared his comrade for allowing the dog of a Chuana woman time to curse his king's armies; many similar incidents she told me before she entreated me to leave her and flee.

'We had not gone far out of Kunana when we found that the place was completely surrounded, and there was little hope of escape. Some women were already turning back, but we, who came last, had seen enough to satisfy us that it was better to meet our death endeavouring to get away. I shall never forget the happenings of that night. The screams of women and children as the Matabele hordes met us reminded me of the shambles of which my mother used to tell us; for, up till then, the women were unaware how carefully they were waylaid. There were five or six Matabele behind every little bush greeting a woman with a stab as she tried to pass a tree. And if one woman managed to pass while these gallant soldiers were engaged in slaying another woman and her children, there would be another soldier behind the next tree ready to prod her, and so things went on until my turn came. As I passed a shrub, behind which it was impossible to suspect that a man could be hiding, a big naked soldier waved his assegai in the air, and brought it down upon my little brother who was still strapped to my back. The point of the assegai just grazed the skin of my nape. The force felled me and the Matabele withdrew his spear and left me and the child on the ground. It was then, while in this position, that I saw more butchery than I had ever heard of. Here a defenceless woman, there an innocent child would be ambushed and stabbed to death; the ferocious brutes were evidently pleased with the evening's work.

'My little brother on my back only moaned a little and died shortly after. I noticed that the blood around me was the poor child's and not my own, and that I had escaped with a slight scratch. Placing the child beneath the tree, near other victims, I fled from the hideous place. With my relatives wiped out, I wondered why I still cared to live, but I ran from the field of carnage to where I do not know. I had lost my bearings and knew not which was east, west or home; but I knew that so long as I kept my back towards the lurid sky, reddened by the flames of the burning city, I was running away from danger.'

Chapter Four

Rays of Sunshine

MHUDI CONTINUES HER STORY. 'At daybreak I found myself at the bottom of a deep ravine, in which I crouched for the greater part of the day – afraid of the crawling, venomous snakes, if I lay there long – and in fear of the tigers, if I wandered out of it; but hunger and thirst forced me to get out eventually and find something just to moisten my parched throat. So dry was my tongue that it seemed to have stuck to the roof of my mouth. When I raised myself, my limbs ached so painfully that I imagined I was a mass of sores. I was stiff as a result of the night's running and perpetual anxiety.

'Raising myself, I stumbled along the ravine afraid lest I should meet Matabele or fierce wild beasts. The loneliness was nerve-racking. I saw rows and rows of trees covered with ripe berries, but hungry as I was, I felt too thirsty to eat the fruit. At length I saw a couple of hartebeest in the distance, which shied at me. As they bolted, four smaller buck also darted away from the same place. This satisfied me that there must be some drinking water and no Matabele about; as the animals would not then come near the place. The spot from which the antelopes ran was but two hundred yards distant; yet, being so stiff and footsore, I was all the afternoon trying to get there. I reached the place eventually and found a beautiful pool of water.

'Shaded as it was by trees and the scarp above the ravine, it was nice and cool. I must have drunk too much of it, for though my thirst was gone, my pains had become worse. Passing slowly along the gully I picked and ate some woodberries; and before I had gone very far the sun had set. There was an uncanny stillness all around me in the gathering darkness and the hideous silence accentuated my loneliness. Finding a convenient cove, sheltered by a cluster of trees, I lay down upon it and afterwards fell asleep. In my sleep during the night, I suffered from awful hallucinations. I saw all over again the butcheries at Kunana and the terrible faces of the ferocious *majahas* (soldiers). More than once I would dream of a stark naked Matabele rushing at me open-mouthed and ready to fling his spear at me. The terror would force me to scream aloud and, screaming, I would wake up with a start to find it was only a dream. After each such awakening, my heart would beat loudly, for I feared that the scream had penetrated the darkness that shielded me from the view of dangerous nocturnal prowlers. The howling of wolves and jackals, some of them uncomfortably near to my hiding place, did not allay my fears. Then I would lie awake, my heart beating rapidly, before I could fall asleep again.

'When my fears had become unbearable, it was with some relief that I heard the first notes of the singing of the early birds and knew that they were harbingers of the dawn which would soon dispel the night and its unseen terrors.

'I continued my stay at this spot for several days. Beginning to feel less fearful, I used to saunter out by day, refresh myself with a drink of water at the pool, then wander along the gully to gather some roots and woodberries about the slope; then I would get back to my recess and remain in hiding in an attitude that enabled me to see without being seen.

'In this position I would watch the different kinds of game that came to the pool or wandered away from there, in groups or in files, after browsing about the undergrowth around the water. I couldn't tell what I was expecting from my continued stay at that place. My one desire was not to be seen at all.

'One day, I decided to walk along the stony slope to the summit of a kopje at the far end of the ridge. My limbs being much better in spite of the abiding stiffness, I could pick my way much more easily over the rocks. I couldn't tell what part of the world that was, but when I reached the summit, a wide stretch of country was exposed to view and the sight of the outer world fascinated me immensely. Emerging from my limited outlook of many days in the ravine, where only the music of the birds could reach my ears, the sight of the extensive landscape was like being born afresh. The succession of woods and clearings, depressions and rising ground, with now and then the gambols of a frisky troop of gnu among the distant trees, where the woods were less dense, refreshed me, for I had never seen the world to such perfection.

'A gentle breeze was blowing with a rustle over the grasstops; the leaves of the mimosa and wag-'n-bietjie bushes and the silvery leaves of the yellowwood tree waved like fans in the path of the wind; it was bracing to find so much life in the air in spite of the awe of death by which I had been surrounded.

'As I inhaled the fragrance of the leafy trees, the wind, which had a stimulating effect, acted like medicine upon my system. Now and again I would hear some rustle behind the trees nearest to me as a duiker or two, having suddenly descried me, took fright and scampered down the hillside.

'I enjoyed the refreshing view for a time, although haunted by fear and loneliness; then I retraced my steps and wandered back towards the ravine where there was food and water. Moving along the vaal-bush overlooking the gully on which my cover was nestled, I noticed two men walking in the hollow gully bottom near the foot of the kopje where I happened to be. A chilly thrill of terror passed through me as I noticed that they were following my footmarks. They walked round and round the little tree from which I had picked some berries. They followed my spoors to the side of the kopje, where on the stony slope my footmarks became invisible; then my alarm increased when they returned to the pool, apparently to waylay me there; and before they went back I had seen enough to convince me that they were not Bechuana but Matabele on the warpath.

'The water of that pool, fresh as it was, had no further attraction for me; the berries of the neighbouring slopes had lost their taste; and I decided to leave the place.

'Descending the kopje on the further side, I ran as fast as I did on my first night out of Kunana. The poignant memories of the massacre helped me to accelerate my paces, but I had once more lost my bearings. I knew that my safest course was to run with my right hand towards the sunset, but after dark it became difficult to follow my direction. When I stopped in the woods to take a breath and get some bearings, my heart beat so loudly that I feared the Matabele would hear it.

'The darkness covered the woods like a heavy skin rug. Some jackals started to bark, and the wild hounds commenced to howl, while some near and distant cries of wolves caused a chill of fright to run all down my spine. The big star, Kopadilalelo (Venus), shone brightly, supported by myriads of smaller planets, but it did not help me to find my bearings.

'Suddenly a red glow appeared towards what I took to be the Western horizon. The skies grew red and brilliant to the

West, and reminded me of a tale that I had heard long ago. It was to this effect: Two men, it was said, decided to determine the course of the sun from west to east, or how he managed, after setting in the west, to return and resume his journey from the east every morning. Someone told them that those desirous of watching the sun's homecoming could do so by staying up all night with their eyes fixed to the west. Their curiosity would be satisfied, so the story went, but they could never live to tell the tale; for none but children of death ever beheld the sun going east.

'These men, the story proceeds, having taken a strong dose of medicine to prevent death, made up their minds to stay up and chance the consequences.

'One of them got afraid and entered his hut, leaving his companion to wait and watch alone. As he prepared to go to sleep he heard his friend shouting outside the hut: "Come! come and see, there he is! there he is . . . a big round ball as red as blood! Come quickly, he is tearing the skies like a meteor! . . . Come and see, he is now returning east!" The man in the hut trembled with fear and would not come out; but when he got up in the morning, he who had seen the big red ball going east, was no more. He had died before the dawn.

'I meditated over this story as I stood and watched the sky in the west becoming redder. I believed that I was about to witness the appearance of "the blood-red ball", see the return of the sun, and die before dawn. I wondered why, after what I had gone through, I should still be afraid of death, which should put an end to all my sufferings, yet, there I was, afraid to die.

'My heart beat quicker and louder while I could not keep my eyes from the West. At length a wide red rim rose from behind the hills – it emerged slowly – a huge red round ball. It cleared the horizon, grew appreciably smaller, and became whiter the higher it ascended the heavens; then it changed into a silvery white disc, the size of a melon, and I realised that what I had seen was nothing more dangerous than the rising of the moon. Her appearance in the west simply meant that I had not yet found my bearings and it coincided with the appearance of the big star in the east. So, remembering the two Matabele of the previous afternoon, I decided once more to journey on. Every night, thereafter, had its dangers and it seemed that life could not last much longer. Two nights after, I was awakened by a tremendous roar and I started to run. I kept on running, I know not whither nor for how long, till an uncanny premonition checked my flight in time to hear a disturbing rustle in the bush to the right of me. Then I felt that I had fled from one danger straight into the horns of another. I had the presence of mind to stand absolutely motionless, when a huge dark object emerged from the woods alongside and waddled along slowly yet uncomfortably near to where I stood. What the animal was, I knew not, but truly it petrified me with fear, for each moment I expected it to turn round and rush at me. Now and then it would stop as though scenting my presence, then move on slowly again.

'Cold drops of perspiration rolled down my face and the fright caused shivers to run all over me. It was all I could do to stifle my trembling, maintain a deathlike silence and so avert detection. The tension was unbearable for the beast was in no hurry to get away. Each of its slow movements was like an age and intensified my agony. To my relief, the brute at length vanished into the dark woods; but my joy was of short duration for, soon afterwards, I heard the approach of another coming in the same direction almost straight up to me. As it came nearer, my endurance entirely gave out for it seemed that I stood right in the creature's way. I held my breath and assumed a standing posture as the animal, halting in front of me, chewed with a champing noise, and swallowed a mouthful of herbs. Whether it was unconscious of my presence, or mistook me for a tree trunk, I know not. By the curved horn over its nose I concluded that it must be a rhinoceros, and mate to the one that first frightened me. Passing so close to me, it seemed that my shaking alone should betray me and provoke an attack. Happily I was left trembling where I stood and my enemy disappeared in the wake of his fellow.

'After both creatures had gone I started to run. In my haste to get away I found no time to avoid the thorny trees, and the briars played havoc with my limbs.

'In the course of my flight I thought that someone had struck me a nasty blow across both knees. The earth seemed to give way beneath my feet and I dropped vertically downwards. My chin hit the ground almost at the same time as my elbow, nearly dislocating my right shoulder. I found myself standing straight up, and being partly underground I was unable to move. Then at last I was no longer afraid to die. I had done everything to avoid danger and death, and further endurance seemed impossible. All things in this world have an ending, thought I, and my pursuers had now overtaken me; and so surrendering myself to the impending tragedy, I calmly awaited my doom . . . I waited but nothing happened. Then, pulling myself together, I found that I had stumbled into a porcupine's hole or it may have been that of an anteater, from which I extricated myself after a long struggle.

'Happily the moon and stars were there to guide my course, for, on emerging from the hole, I had lost all sense of direction. So I ran and ran; and then I ran again, until I dropped down from sheer exhaustion.

'It was late in the morning when I woke to dig for roots and continue my aimless wanderings, ever haunted by the melancholy feeling that I would never see my people again.

'Proceeding after sunset, along a sparsely wooded field, I came upon an inviting little nook between two trees. Here I crouched down for the night, and slept like a log. In my sleep, I dreamt that I was travelling alone in search of human company. Pursuing my quest in the heat of a broiling sun, I reached a gigantic tree standing on the bank of a running rivulet, its branches overhanging the flooded spruit. The roaring torrent of the stream dispelled all my hopes of ever venturing across. Being fatigued and footsore, I rested my weary limbs in the shade of the weeping branches of this giant of the woods. Bees had evidently built their hives in the dim cavities around its mighty trunk, for they flew up and down and gathered honey from the blossoms that ornamented its drooping branches. In a familiar buzzing language, they hummed an invitation to me to take shelter in the shade of their stronghold, to eat of their fruit and honey and be happy. Notwithstanding this hospitality, I dreamt that I was oppressed by the absence of any sign of human life. Then I was frightened by a rhinoceros approaching me from the river bank. At sight of the beast, I shook in every limb, and I wept as the monster made for me. At that moment a handsome man descended from the tree top, raised me into a hammock which he carefully fastened to two branches high up beyond the reach of the curved horn of the rhinoceros. He was a well-spoken man with a beautiful voice, and he treated me to the joy of hearing our language spoken once again.

'Awakened from this vision by the cooing of the friendly doves, and the *coo-coor-r-ro* of the bush pigeons, at daybreak I found myself in a strange country and a different landscape from the land I travelled through at sunset the day before. The koorhaan, at the bottom of nearly every grass knoll, made the morning lively with their friendly cackling, while the butcher-birds and other warblers also sang or whistled in a variety of dialects.

'Continuing my ramble I spent the morning in silent thought over the happy import of that dream. Since this morning, I have been wishing to dream again. My only living friends were the turtle doves whose language I thought I could almost understand. I think that if this solitude had been prolonged for another month, I should have been able to sing their songs and learn to converse with them; yet I longed for the company of a man, like the one who appeared in my dream. After my dream, something I couldn't say what, but inwardly I had a feeling that something was about to happen and effect a change in my solitary existence. With my mind thus occupied, I walked over a grassy ridge, where the trees were rather sparse. Proceeding more like a girl wandering through her mother's cornfield than one lost in the wilderness, I finally reached the point where I thought I saw the moving tuft of grass, but really a lion, which frightened me and caused me to run straight into your arms.'

Chapter Five

Revels after Victory

THE TOWN OF THE Barolong having been mercilessly sacked, their cattle-posts and homesteads flattened to the ground and the surviving occupants scattered in all directions, all their belongings having fallen into the hands of Mzilikazi's victorious army, the king, on learning of their success, ordered the warriors to remain on the Malmani River with their booty until he had prepared a feast for their reception. The Feast of Welcome and an elaborate programme having been decided upon, the king sent messengers to the Ngwaketsi, Bakwena, Bakgatla and other Bechuana tribes, inviting their chiefs to attend a Matabele festival or send representatives to Inzwinyani, if they could not attend in person.

This army of destruction was led by Langa, second living son of Mzilikazi – an impetuous youth, very jealous of the dignity pertaining to his station. Despite his extreme youth, he had several times vowed to wage war against his people if, on the death of his father, they attempted to pass him over in favour of his elder half-brother of another house. This lightning raid on Kunana was his first military exploit. His army was composed mainly of young men supplemented by a few of the senior divisions.

By daybreak, on the day of the feast, there was a significant stir among the Matabele people. The call had sounded the previous afternoon from hill-top to hill-top, so cowmen left their herds in charge of small boys, villagers left the women behind and, travelling all night, hastened towards the capital, where they were that day expecting to count the booty and divide the trophies of victory. By the first streak of dawn, thousands of men began to assemble at the great rallying place, the circular stockade in the centre of the city, surrounded by the king's headquarters. It was already crowded with a curious and expectant multitude from every quarter of the king's dominion. There were tall men and short men, old men and young men, stout brawny fellows and lanky or wiry ones – a motley mass of black manhood. Some wore furry jackal-skin caps, others wore feathers on their caps. Some had woolly heads, others had their heads cropped while, here and there, a few appeared with black circlets on their heads – the insignia of their rank – others wore nothing at all; but every one of them carried his spears and his shield.

When Mzilikazi emerged from his dwelling, surrounded by his bodyguard and accompanied by his chiefs, arrayed in their brilliant tiger-skins, the effect of the recent victory was manifest by the satisfaction on every face. The appearance of the royal party was hailed with tumultuous shouts. The rattle of the assegais on the shields rivalled even the rattle of a heavy hailstorm. The court jesters sang and leaped, bedecked in all manner of fantastic headdresses, till the cat tails round their loins literally whirled in the air.

The king, with more than usual dignity, acknowledged the royal salute of 'Bayete' from thousands of leather-lunged

Matabele. Having seated himself upon his wooden throne, which was decorated for the occasion with lion and leopard skins, King Mzilikazi surveyed the excited mass of humanity before him. With so many thousands in attendance, it was no uncommon thing for a joyous festival of the kind to end with a death sentence on any who might upset the uncertain temper of Mzilikazi the Terrible; therefore men grasped their shields and gripped their spears and stood erect, lest a faulty pose should irritate the eye and rouse the ire of the Great One. The crowd stood breathless and at high tension, while court jesters and mbongis were lauding the greatness of Mzilikazi and reciting the prowess and deeds of valour associated with his ancestry.

Whistles blew, drums began to sound and hundreds of men chanted a song of victory, while thousands of warriors stamped a rhythmical mark-time in harmony with the tom-toms. The excitement grew, while the soldiers broke into their familiar war dance.

The infection was not limited to the men. Long files of Matabele women were descending the hills along the tortuous footpaths leading into the capital from every direction. They carried on their heads earthen pots full of beer for the entertainment of the conquering heroes, singing at the same time praises of the victors. Nearly every one of the files of singing women was headed by a group of syncopating cymbalists, ringing or beating time with their iron cymbals in rhythm with their steps, as they wound their way down towards the level valley bottom, across which the city lay. The women of the city were busy in between their huts, outside the frenzied crowd of warriors. Their business was to cook and to prepare the eatables for the festival which was to follow the great indaba in the assembly; yet they also caught the infection. Beside the numerous fireplaces in the courtyards, groups of shimmying girls sang the praises of Langa – a high-born son of the Great

One – and warbled national ditties to the glory of Matabele arms. Some women carrying their babies astride their hips minded the boiling meat pots and joined the chorus of singers, while others tinkled little rattles in harmony with the shimmy.

They had heard that such an enormous booty of horned cattle had never before been captured in the history of human warfare. No one, much less a woman, cared to know the cause of the raid, for the end had amply justified the means. They knew, and for them the knowledge was enough, that Prince Langa had raided the Barolong cattle-posts, killed the owners and captured every beast. Hence their joy was too great to consider the relatives of their own young fighters who fell at the point of the spears of the Barolong defenders. The members of a constantly warring nation like the Matabele had been drilled from childhood to face the most devastating situation without the tremor of an eyelid. Today, especially, the booty more than counterbalanced the loss of the good Matabele blood spilled in the enterprise. With this magnificent addition to the national wealth and the national food supply, it should be impossible in future, for the sister, wife, or mother of a spearman, to run short of beef; so the women of the city were in high glee.

They danced and sang:

Come, let us sing!
  Mzilikazi has a son.
Come, let us sing!
  Langa is the name of his son.
Come, let us sing!
  Langa has a spear.
Come, let us prance!
  His sword is a sharp-pointed spear.
Go forth and summon the girls of Soduza
  To the dance;
Go call the maidens to the Puza,

And the dance;
For Mzilikazi has a son!
Langa, the Fighter, is his son!

The whole of the city was in a swirl, for the music of the merrymakers was keeping the dancers in motion.

Suddenly, King Mzilikazi gave a signal, and the dancing and the singing in the inner circle ceased; far away in the distant outskirts of the city was to be heard a swelling chant mingled with the rumble of tom-toms; ever louder and louder droned the barbaric music – the victorious army of Langa was returning; the victorious army from Kunana laden with the spoils of victory. As they entered the great enclosure, the home regiments squeezed aside and prepared a way for Langa and his young warriors to approach the king. The newcomers had their own mbongis who loudly proclaimed the latest success that the youthful army had scored for the Matabele arms.

At another signal from the king the drums within the enclosure began again to beat in unison with those of the victorious army now also within the enclosure. The young warriors were elated at receiving from their elders that shout of welcome hitherto given only to veterans, and they knew that their king was more than satisfied with their martial deed. Sitonga, a tall induna, with a big sonorous voice, stood forth from among the King's bodyguard and harangued the crowd.

'My lord, and chiefs!' he said. 'Who is Sitonga, that King Mzilikazi the Great, the terrible ruler of land and clouds, should select him to congratulate his heroes after so great a feat of arms. Yet I am as proud of the honour conferred on me as I am of the achievement of these youths. We are here to celebrate the success of an expedition led by Langa, a worthy son of a royal father and a noble mother.' To this there were loud shouts of 'Bayete!' The speaker proceeded, 'To greet the success of an expedition against Tauana the rebellious Rolong chief, and what a success! Langa has blotted his name off the face of the earth. Tauana will die nameless and unhonoured.

'You know, my chiefs, that there are certain croakers in our midst, their ears are deaf and their eyes are blind to Matabele virtues. They have only one philosophy and that is the decadence of the Matabele nation; they say the milk of the mothers of today is not conducive to the growth of bravery in our children's livers. All that the milk of the present-day mothers can nourish, they say, is faintheartedness. Where are those croakers now? Let them stand forth and eat their words, for Langa has shattered their contention. The fact is, there is not a drop of bastard blood in Langa's body – there runs through his veins the reddest of Matabele blood regulated by the throbbing of a royal heart that knows no fear. (*Bayete!*)

'We heard with dismay the wrongful murder of Bhoya by a Barolong brigand. This brigand enjoyed the King's magnanimity, and was allowed to share the sunshine and the blessing of rain with us. His wives, like our women, we permitted to garner the produce of the land. But as soon as he was drunk with the brew of his wives, he dared to lay his wretched hands on the person of the envoy of his king. While some of us were stunned by this villainy, Langa wasted no time, he quickly taught the brigand the lesson of his life. Thanks to Langa, son of the Terrible One, all Barolongs, if any are still alive, shall henceforth know how to run when a Matabele appears in view. Oh Langa, you are a prince! Your royal father is pleased with your achievement and so are all the people here assembled.'

This oration was punctuated by vociferous cries of 'Bayete'. Sitonga proceeded: 'The Great One has sent invitations to all the Bechuana chiefs: Makabe is here and Sechele too. The Bahurutshe are strongly represented and the Bafokeng have also sent delegates. These visitors join our festival with their chieftainship undiminished. Each of these chiefs shall drive home a share of the booty, and show his people that as long as the Bechuana are loyal to us, Mzilikazi is their shield; but let an enemy provoke us and he shall taste the full force of Matabele temper. Tauana was foolhardy enough to brave the anger of Mzilikazi, the most high; and the anger of Mzilikazi fell upon him. I have seen the ashes of his city and the corpses of his wives and children. I have also seen the dead bodies of his chicken-hearted blacksmiths, who knew as little about fighting as they did about the dignity due to royalty. Tauana shall offend us no more. The vultures are feeding on the corpses of his people, and those of them who were fleet-footed enough to outrun Langa's spearmen are eating dirt today. The jwala you will drink this afternoon is brewed with the grain from Tauana's corn-bins, and this evening we will be dividing his cattle.

'Oh Langa, descendant of the Great Matshobana, we are proud of you! No race with such valiant princes should be ashamed of its royal house.'

Vigorous speeches, just as loudly cheered, were delivered by other orators doing homage to Prince Langa. 'As long as you are alive', they said, 'we will sleep and rest secure in the belief that you are guarding us from every danger.'

Following these speakers came Gubuza, commander-in-chief of all Mzilikazi's armies; a man with a striking personality. He had an arresting glance that always commanded respect. He carried a round head with little ears, over a shapely pair of broad shoulders. Although the Matabele usually walked unshod, Gubuza was distinguished by using sandals like those worn by the Barolong. For some reason, the soles of his sandals were invariably made from the dewlap of an eland, instead of the ordinary cowhide. As he discarded his leopard kaross on rising, his smooth black skin shone over his ample frame, the blackness of it throwing into relief his bare thighs and arms.

The splendid proportions of his immense symmetrical frame struck the attention of men and women and gained their admiration even before he spoke. Hence, he received an ovation that befitted not only his personality but his position as leader of the terrible armies of Mzilikazi; but as his speech developed, the cheers gradually diminished until at length there was a manifest feeling of disappointment on the faces of the excited populace.

He said, 'No, my chiefs, I am not so hopeful as the previous speakers. Gubuza has sat at the feet of many a wise man; I have been to Zululand, to Swaziland, to Tongaland and to Basutoland. I know the northern forests, I know the western deserts and I know the eastern and southern seas. Wiseacres of different nationalities are agreed that cheap successes are always followed by grievous aftermaths. Old people likewise declare that individuals, especially nations, should beware of the impetuosity of youth. Are we sure that Bhoya was guiltless?' He asked, 'Was there provocation? Supposing there was, are we satisfied that the Barolong could have maintained order in any manner short of killing Bhoya and his companion? Did Bhoya simply deliver his message or did he violate Barolong rights in any way? Did he not perhaps terrorise the children or molest Barolong women? My lord and my chiefs, I am a king's servant and know what I am talking about. I ask these questions because men of my circle too often forget that they are emissaries of the king. They sometimes think that they are their own ambassadors; they are too apt to forget that without their ambassadorship they are but menials of low station. Royal appointments have on some of them the same effect as strong drink in the heads of other men.'

By this time the buzz of dissenting voices was making it

positively difficult to follow the speaker, who continued amid frequent interruptions. 'I have heard nothing from previous speakers to indicate that the prince had asked Tauana for any reasons; nothing to show that he would not in due course have appeared in Inzwinyani and explained his action.'

Several voices already interjected 'Tula', for the crowd had heard enough and were not disposed to submit to any further infliction of Gubuza's unpatriotic views.

In the ensuing din only his last remark could be distinguished amidst the uproar when the speaker concluded: 'My lord and my chiefs, I am afraid we have made a fresh enemy.' Several speakers jumped up all eager to reply. Dambuza, one of them, refusing to give way, raised his powerful voice and thundered: 'Gubuza, I am ashamed of you.' Cries of 'Bravo, Dambuza.'

Thus encouraged, Dambuza continued: 'We all know you as a warrior and nothing can rob you of your military distinction. There is no need that you should be jealous over the success of the Prince who received from your training all the prowess and valour he displayed against the rebellious Barolong. Surrounded, as we are, by unknown people in a not too friendly world, how could we command respect if not only Matabele but even ambassadors of our king may be killed by anyone who might be disposed to do it?

'My lord, I am a pure-blooded Ndebele – (*loud applause*) – and I breathe the pure air in the belief that should a man or a beast shed a drop of my blood, the king's majahas would settle him before he had time to relent; but if I may be killed with impunity by anyone, whatever his grievance, then life is not worth living. It matters not whether it be a beast with four paws or only two, anyone or anything spilling Matabele blood should suffer a violent death. I, for one, feel certain that Tauana got much less than he deserved. He should not have been allowed to escape. I will never again salute Gubuza, if he would tolerate the life of anyone who killed a Matabele person. I would rather be a bushman and eat scorpions than that Matabele could be hunted and killed as freely as rock-rabbits.'

The speech was received with uproarious cheers, with which the king seemed delighted. With a laugh, Mzilikazi vacated his seat as a sign that the speeches were over. Dancing proceeded with boisterous fury, after which there was great feasting and revelry.

Up on the plateau above the city, herdsmen were ascending and descending the escarpment above which large herds of horned cattle were gathered. After much singing and dancing, beef eating and beer drinking, the male portion of the revellers surged up the hillside to the top of the plateau where they inspected the captured Barolong herds. The animals were not chewing the cud after the manner of kine. They, too, seemed to feel a disturbance in the atmosphere. On the surrounding hills, bushbuck and rhebuck peeped through the tree-stems from the distance and marvelled at the commotion. They had never seen so vast an assembly of man and beast, and they wondered what was in course that today these proverbial hunters should pay no heed to them.

It would seem that the surprise of the cattle was not a bit less than that of the game. Oxen bellowed and cows lowed for they all failed to recognise the cowmen. Wherever they looked the Barolong oxen saw only strange men with strange faces and stranger methods. The calves had been separated from their mothers early that day and the latter were now being milked and the milk (straight from the teats of looted cows) was distributed among Matabele piccaninnies with distended bellies to incite their courage thus early in life.

Hundreds of calves remonstrated loudly against this wholesale theft of their mother's milk. They seemed to ask what their elders had their big horns for, if hornless people could with impunity practise such systematic robbery at their expense. Hundreds of cows seemed to low some explanation in reply. What it was, they alone knew, but the bulls and bullocks on the other hand held down their heads, switched their tails and waved their dewlaps as if lamenting their impotence. They seemed to take the situation mechanically as the ways of men and wars.

The chiefs were now admiring the booty and dividing the spoils of war. This kept them busy till after sunset. The rejoicings were continued after the disposal of the large booty, for the whole nation had gone pleasure-mad.

The moon rose above the hills, and appeared like a huge ruddy orb of fire above the treetops. As she cleaved her way upward and mounted higher and higher up the skies, she laid aside her orange glow and assumed a silvery hue. She lit the night with her everlasting radiance as though doing her best to serve the revellers as brilliantly as did her sister orb throughout the day.

Mzilikazi withdrew from the crowded circus and summoned his privy council to a night meeting. Retracing his steps in the moonlight, he left his bodyguard at the gate of the stockade beside his quarters, and entered the spacious dwelling of his youngest and dearest wife. She regaled the councillors with some beer of her own brewing, and, as they drank, her lord rejoiced in their adoration of the excellence of her brewing.

Ntongolwane the magician was there, and so was Gubuza, the leader of the armies, Matambo and Dingiswayo being among the indunas present as well as Tabata and Dambuza. Everybody was in a merry mood, for the king was pleased with himself.

'Well, Tabata,' asked Mzilikazi, 'how did you like the boys and their revels?'

'O, most noble king,' replied Tabata, 'it was the grandest sight I ever saw. Thy servant rejoiced at every turn. It was a feast for the ears and a feast for the eyes as well as for the mouth.'

'Quite true, Tabata,' said Dambuza, 'quite true. The feast was grand – I liked the martial bearing of the serried ranks of the several divisions. What a tremendous impression they must have made on our Bechuana visitors! I liked the dances, I liked the drums, I liked the lot of cattle; in fact I liked everything, not excluding the shimmy of the girls. There was only one thing to mar the splendour, which, I am sorry to say, irritated and offended my ears. Gubuza, my chief, your speech was the only fly in the milk. Your unworthy words stung like needles in my ears. You would do better in future to confine your activities to fighting, of which you know everything, and leave speeches to men who can talk. A woman would have made a better speech, for you have not spoken like a warrior, you spoke like a coward. You would do more good if you went and told the dancers on the hill that you are sorry for what you said this morning.'

Gubuza made a reluctant reply. He said, 'I am sorry if my words wounded the feelings of the chiefs. When I spoke this morning, I had seen some of the cattle but was not then aware that the booty was so large. When I reached the plateau and saw the swarms of Barolong cattle I felt a quiver on my breast as though it had been touched by a spear; for I am convinced that the owners of so many cattle will never rest until they recover them. It should not be forgotten that all these cattle belonged to men and not to children. It is clear that they increased and multiplied under the wands of clever magicians or they would never have bred in such abundance. We know not the manner in which the Barolong prepare their spells, and I shudder when I think of the day when the revengeful owners of those herds will come back for them. The carousals of those who are now enjoying themselves outside will not save us from their wrath.'

Now the Great One joined the discussion, which meant that everybody else had to listen and applaud. 'To me,' said Mzilikazi, 'everything went off successfully. If Gubuza had not spoken I should have been very sorry. You see, a man has two legs so as to enable him to walk properly. He cannot go far if he hops on one leg. In like manner a man has two hands; to hold his spear in the one and his shield in the other. With a spear in his right hand, without the shield in his left, be he ever so agile, he is entirely at the mercy of his opponent. For the same reason he has two eyes in order to see better. A man has two ears so as to hear both sides of a dispute. A man who joins in a discussion with the acts of one side only, will often find himself in the wrong.

'In every grade of life there are two sides to every matter. There are riches and poverty; beauty and ugliness; health and sickness; wisdom and folly; right and wrong; day and night; summer and winter; fire and water. One cannot exist without the other. Without you, I could be no king, and without me you could be no nation; and it was wise of Gubuza to remind us that side by side with our infectious joy, there is such a thing as sorrow. Langa paid a price for his victory, and in the midst of our rejoicings some mothers' eyes were wet with tears. But taking everything into consideration, notwithstanding Gubuza's warning in my ears, I feel that the balance is entirely in our favour.

'Gubuza will remember the last time we returned from a buffalo hunt. Our pack-oxen were laden with beef and eland hides and everybody was satisfied; yet some men had been gored to death by infuriated wounded buffaloes. I commanded Gubuza to start vigorously and train the young men for a bigger chase on the track of human buffaloes. I told him that, when the training of the army was complete, all the neighbouring nations must be subjugated and broken down until our law should govern from the desert to the sea. He promised me he would train and never stop until rebellious tribes are subdued and distant nations, from Sekuku's mountains to the Tembu and Pondo seas are conquered, and Shaka himself acknowledged our supremacy. That sounded like a child's dream, but today's events have proved that before we are very much older the dream will become a reality, and the Matabele sword shall become the terror of the nations of the world.'

The speech was interrupted by grunts of approbation and the king asked: 'Did you see our Bechuana visitors? What did they say of the fate of their rebellious compatriots?'

'Oh, we saw them,' said three of the listeners. 'They were lost in admiration. When they heard that this great and successful enterprise was the achievement mainly of beardless youths, they expressed their conviction that no king has ever commanded an army as invincible as the spearmen of Moroa Matshobana.'

To this there was a chorus of laughter in which the king joined heartily, and after sundry helpings to more beer, Mzilikazi said: 'I think, Gubuza, we should reward the boy for his daring. We could promote him to the command of the Sibongo regiments and make him chief of the Amasizi. And if he likes, he may settle them on the territories from which he has cleared the Barolong pest. The further training of these young fellows should be carefully watched so as to make them fit for the next great conquest in the expansion of our authority. Let this success be known among the nations so that foreign armies may tremble each time they hear the mention of the name, Amandebele.'

This terminated the midnight council – a termination which registered another landmark in the history of the Matabele.

Out in the moonlight, the drums were still busy and the revellers were dancing and the hills resounded to the shrill voices and handclapping of the women until dawn, by which time, the voices of some of the revellers were hoarse with over-exertion.

Chapter Six

The Forest Home

THAT EXACTLY IS HOW our hero and heroine met and became man and wife. There were no home ceremonials, such as the seeking and obtaining of parental consent, because there were no parents; no conferences by uncles and grand-uncles, or exhortations by grandmothers and aunts; no male relatives to arrange the marriage knot, nor female relations to herald the family union, and no uncles of the bride to divide the *bogadi* (dowry) cattle, as, of course, there were no cattle. It was a simple matter: taking each other for good or ill with the blessing of the 'God of Rain.' The forest was their home, the rustling trees their relations, the sky their guardian, and the birds, who sealed the marriage contract with their songs, the only guests. Here they established their home and named it Re-Nosi (We are alone).

They were certain now that, once beyond the reach of the bloodthirsty Matabele, each would be sufficient for the other's company until they should have children of their own.

Ra-Thaga being a trained hunter, they had plenty of

venison. He caught bucks with primitive snares which he set nearby in the evening; also jackals, whose furs would be needed for their bed during the coming winter. In the adjacent valley near the fountain they secured potclay, and Mhudi became quite a clever potter. Her husband likewise carved numerous spoons and dishes and other vessels from the trunks of trees. One or two of these vessels were filled with the eland lard which always served to flavour their venison. What a change from the coarse and scanty fare of their previous solitary wanderings! Ra-Thaga was already beginning to regard himself as a king reigning in his own kingdom, and the animals of the valley as his wealth. To say that Mhudi was happy would really not be saying too much, for here was a woman who possessed her husband's undivided attentions. There was no room for suspicion of faithlessness, no danger of desertion, no long absences from home, no nights out! Always there when he was wanted. She thankfully realised that the gods were 'wiping away her tears', and requiting her for all the suffering she had undergone since the destruction of Kunana. What a boon to be able to speak to her husband alone all the time, his attention not being claimed by social or tribal matters, to say nothing of running distant errands for chiefs – as was the case with her brothers at Kunana – or of game drives and political missions to neighbouring tribes.

'My mother had to share my father's affections with two other wives,' she said to herself. 'Why should I be thus singled out for exceptional favour? Jealousy! My word! With such a monopoly in a man, and a noble man at that! Did they not say that man is by nature polygamous and could never be trusted to be true to only one wife? But here is one as manly as you could wish, and I have never, never seen a husband of any number of wives as happy as mine is with me alone!'

Such were Mhudi's thoughts by day whenever she was left

alone; and it naturally followed that when she was alone, he too was alone; and when she had company, he too had company. There being no third person, she spoke only to him and he to her. When she was thus meditating, he would perhaps be 'abroad' (which was seldom further than a mile, and hardly ever as far as three miles away), also cogitating on his one ambition which was to make his young and pretty wife very happy. He felt that she – his queen – should be free as the birds of the air were free, nay, even more so; she should be a queen ruling over her own dominion, and he her protector guarding her safety and happiness. Then Ra-Thaga would return or leave the shady tree under which he had been braying a buck-skin, and stealthily approaching his wife, he would hear her speaking to herself: 'My little father, my other self, my guide, my protector, my all, while I remain his little mother, his sister, his other self, his helpmate, his life, his everything. How can I help him to be more manly!'

One morning Ra-Thaga climbed the lofty tree beside the hut, as he was wont to do, to survey the land in every direction and see what was going on; at least between his home and the horizon. He observed a certain movement some distance off among the trees. Hastily he called out, 'Mhudi, have you any food? I think some visitors are approaching. These will be the first since our marriage, and I should like them to see what a good hostess my wife will make.'

'Just assure me that they are not Matabele,' cried Mhudi, beneath the shade of the awning, 'and you will not be disappointed; for I can entertain as many wayfarers as choose to come.'

'They have left their burdens in the grass,' continued Ra-Thaga, still regarding the unusual spectacle from the treetop, 'and are quenching their thirst in a pool near the pan. I can see, passing through the high grass in single file, six faggoters with loads of wood on their heads coming almost directly towards us.'

'Now I see that you are joking, dear, for nobody would go to an uninhabited country for wood,' said Mhudi.

'You are right, Mhudi, that did not occur to me – Great Tau's Barolong! Those are not faggots, they are lions' manes. Lions, six lions, I see!'

From his elevated post Ra-Thaga finally noticed that the lions were changing their course and making for the ridge where he had chased the one notorious lion on the morning he first met his wife. A shudder went through him as he saw them sauntering about the place, examining the ground and smelling at the few eland bones left about. He felt that with half a dozen lions prowling in the neighbourhood, he could not claim the sole proprietorship of Re-Nosi – the name he had given to the valley. It would be a case of the survival of the fittest, and it seemed certain that he could not measure strength with the claws and jaws of six black-maned lions. What was to be done? For the first time since the forest home was planned, Ra-Thaga felt helpless and afraid.

But his wife, far from entertaining any fears, considered herself quite safe under the protection of her husband.

'Are they gone?' she asked, more out of curiosity than alarm.

'Apparently,' replied Ra-Thaga, 'for I cannot see what has become of them.' Mhudi added: 'Don't worry. Our old friend may have been among them for all we know, and explained to the others something of his past experience and his narrow escape from you. It is possible that animals converse in their own way. By the by, I see by the smoke that the wind is blowing towards the spot where you spotted them. They have probably scented our presence and gone for good. Come down and have a drink of berry-beer; they are far away by now.'

Ra-Thaga, who had been wondering whether the sudden appearance and disappearance and no further reappearance of the lions were a reality or but a phantom of his mind, now thought that there was a possible solution of the puzzle in Mhudi's process of reasoning; so he asked her, 'Are you not afraid, Mhudi?'

'Why should I fear?' she said. 'Who would be afraid in your company, while fear is afraid of you? I feel ready to meet any number of lions as long as you are about.'

He said little after this, but thought much.

For a long time Ra-Thaga considered it unsafe to set any more traps except for jackals; antelopes he feared would attract lions and make his place untenable, so he fell back on what dried venison they had, and they were seldom able to eat freshly killed game. The juicy *lerisho* (a sort of wild turnip) and similar roots which formerly served as their vegetable food became scarce, as his wife would not hear of his going out alone, for whenever he did she would count the moments and work herself up into a frenzy until his return. He could not bear to see her in an unhappy mood, so the better to maintain her cheerfulness, he seldom wandered far from the enclosure.

Some weeks passed in this manner, till, no doubt owing to the hard and dry fare on which they were obliged to subsist, Mhudi suffered an attack of malarial fever and could not leave her bed. After several wakeful nights, she one afternoon fell into a heavy sleep, and Ra-Thaga sat watching her. Thinking over their unfortunate condition, his mind naturally turned to the old easy life of Kunana among his people, now dead and gone. He remembered how, when people were ill, they consulted a herbalist and how the *longana* bush (the Bechuana wormwood) served as a tonic and cure for every ailment. He therefore resolved to go out in search of this herb and risk his wife discovering his absence. He left her asleep and hoped to return before she awoke.

He examined every root and plant as he went, and although

not able to find at once what he wanted, he presently came upon something not less welcome. The ears of a young duiker buck appeared above the grass-tops where the animal was crouching. Fortune favoured Ra-Thaga for, as he raised his heavy knobkerrie, the buck took fright, and, darting off, tried to clear a little bush with one spring; at the same moment the kerrie, propelled by the force of a powerful arm and healthy broad shoulders, broke both its hind legs, and our hunter pounced upon it and killed it. Knowing that the fresh tender venison would be as good for his patient as the medicine, he threw it over his shoulder and proceeded cheerfully on his search.

Very late that afternoon Ra-Thaga found the *longana* herb and hastened homeward with his bundle, impelled by anxiety to reach his sick and lonely wife. He wondered whether she were better or worse. How had she felt on waking and finding him gone? Would the sight of the medicine and fresh meat appease her into forgiving him? His heart palpitated as he was nearing his home, propelled, as it were, by some mysterious force. Indeed he could not account for his nervousness which was increased rather than allayed by the sight of the enclosure round his hut. He paused at once beside a tree. But what was that moving stealthily, and menacingly, outside the enclosure to the hut? Could it be that Mhudi was still there, or had a lion devoured her in her sleep? As the beast came opposite him, it stood still, with its tail towards him. There was no mistaking the fact that he scented life and was preparing to leap the fence. Ra-Thaga's presence of mind did not desert him. Carefully putting down his load, he slipped off his sandals, thinking as he did so of an old acquaintance who, while travelling in the wilds many years before, fell asleep in the shade of a big yellowwood tree. He was suddenly awakened by the roar of a lion rushing at his dog. Knowing that the animal would make for him after it had destroyed the dog, the traveller seized it by the tail while it was mauling his pet. He held it tight and never slackened his hold for two days and nights, until a party of trekkers who chanced to come that way speared the lion for him.

'Oh!' thought Ra-Thaga, 'if only I could get at the lion's tail! I would not care how many days and nights I had to hold it so long as I could keep the beast from reaching Mhudi.' But how could he accomplish such a feat?

With these thoughts crossing and re-crossing his mind, Ra-Thaga, with his senses keyed up, was breathlessly and without noise making an effort to reach the lion. Circumstances favoured him. First of all, the wind was in his favour; secondly, the beast was so engrossed with its intent to enter the enclosure that it was indifferent to aught else.

He never could describe how he managed to reach that lion unobserved and to grip it by the tail. The frightened animal leaped into the air, lifting him up so high that he was nearly thrown on to its back; but he held on tenaciously by the tail till the lion, abandoning its prey, was only struggling to get away; but Ra-Thaga would not let it go.

Inside the hut, his wife had slept nearly all the afternoon, waking up just in time to hear the scuffle outside. She rose to her feet, and, hearing his frantic calls for her to come out with his assegai, she was quickly on the scene.

Most Bechuana women in such circumstances would have uttered loud screams for help. Mhudi yielded to the humour of the picture of her husband having a tug of war with the lion; feeling highly amused, she gripped the situation, stepped forward in obedience to Ra-Thaga, and summoning all her strength, she aimed a stab at the lion's heart. The infuriated animal fell over with a growl that almost caused the earth to vibrate.

Leaving the dead lion, Ra-Thaga fetched his herbs and his

buck, secured the openings to his enclosure with fresh wag-'n-bietjie bush, and followed Mhudi into the hut where he skinned his buck while sunning himself in the adoration of his devoted wife. Her trust in him, which had never waned, was this evening greater than ever. She forgot that she herself was the only female native of Kunana who had thrice faced the king of beasts, and had finally killed one with her own hand. Needless to say, Ra-Thaga was a proud husband that night.

Chapter Seven

Mhudi and I

AT TIMES MHUDI and Ra-Thaga found fruitful subjects for animated discussion. On one topic there was a sharp difference of opinion between man and wife. Ra-Thaga at times felt inclined to believe that the land on which they lived belonged to Mzilikazi, and that Mzilikazi was justified in sending his marauding expedition against Kunana. This roused the feminine ire of Mhudi. She could not be persuaded that the crime of one chief who murdered two indunas was sufficient justification for the massacre of a whole nation.

'But,' protested Ra-Thaga, 'all the tribes who quietly paid their dues in kind were left unmolested. Mzilikazi did not even insist that larger tribes should increase the value of their tax in proportion to their numbers. So long as each tribe sent something each spring in acknowledgement of its fealty, he was satisfied.'

Mhudi, growing very irritated, cried: 'I begin to think that you are sorry that you met and married me, holding such extraordinary views. You would surely have been happier with a

Matabele wife. Fancy my husband justifying our exploitation by wild Khonkhobes, who fled from the poverty in their own land and came down to fatten on us!'

'On this subject you can never be logical, Mhudi; you forget that Mzilikazi does not care for riches and wealth, he has enough in his vast regions where every living animal, wild or tame, belongs to him.'

'Nonsense,' pouted Mhudi in disgust.

'Yes,' retorted her husband, 'even the lion that we chased the other day – the lion that killed the eland for us – is his property.'

'Oh Ra-Thaga, you are incorrigible! After this I will not be surprised to hear you say that the rain which causes the growth of the grass is bestowed by Mzilikazi and his hordes of murderers. The fact is, they are interlopers and intruders. We will chase them from here as surely as you chased the lion the other day, and kill their fighters as you killed the other lion. They had no right to slaughter women and children as they did.'

'Oh, my little dear, you are too optimistic. Bear in mind that might is right. If Mzilikazi had no right to occupy this country, it follows that we had no right to chase the lion, the lion had no right to kill the eland, and by the same process of reasoning we had no right to eat the lovely eland beef that we enjoyed on our wedding day.'

'And by the same process of reasoning,' Mhudi set forth, 'we will overthrow their perverted might, which takes women and children unawares, by a force that is more powerful than treachery.'

'Where will you get it, I wonder,' retorted the husband.

'I used to have a high respect for the sense of men, especially your sense, Ra-Thaga; but I am beginning to change my good opinion about it. On the first day we met, you said the Barolong were exterminated and their name shall be known no more. I refused to believe it. You know, I don't know where, but somewhere in this vast country, at a place called Motlhan'oapitse, Sehunelo's tribe – the Seleka branch of the Barolong – is still intact. They include the brave Sehubas, your fellow clansmen, who boldly snatched the Barolong chieftainship from Modiboa, and led the hammersmiths from victory to victory, through the Central African lakes and forests, and on the banks of the Zambesi right over Mosi-oa-Thunya (the Victoria Falls) down to Bechuanaland. These include my own clansmen, as merry and valiant, as they were found swimming in streams of the milk of their own cows; they include the descendants of Makgetla who never quailed before a foe; and the Ra-Pulanas whose furnaces have smelted the iron that supplied other nations with hoes, knives, hammers and scimitars; they are famous as the only travellers who fearlessly traversed the jungle of Mafika-kgochoana, by day and night, a region on the Molopo which is shunned by travellers because of the lairs of lions and tigers, as well as ferocious buffaloes roaming or crouching there. The Ra-Tlou clan is still intact; and surely nothing has happened to the Beef-eaters and the Lion-trackers and the other clansmen who venerate the elephant, or the koodoo, or the rhinoceros; nor to the other members of the Sehunelo's council with the hippopotamus as their tribal totem.

'I am sure that at this moment their foundries are busy and it is not difficult to divine the result, as they can handle an iron spear or battle-axe as well as make one. Someday, somewhere, and somehow, they will turn up and teach Mzilikazi that the crime of one man killing two potential women-slayers is no excuse for massacring whole generations of innocent men, women and children.'

'Let's change the subject,' said Ra-Thaga in despair.

'Yes,' agreed Mhudi abruptly, 'let's speak of something

different, or else I won't talk any more.'

'Tell me, Mhudi,' queried Ra-Thaga, 'were you ever in love before you met me?'

To this she ingenuously said, 'You know the day I met you was not the first occasion on which I had a narrow escape from a roaring lion.'

Ra-Thaga was not very pleased with this evasive remark, but he listened as she went on.

'Your life was spent mainly at the cattle-posts or in the hunting field, so probably you never heard the story. I have had some exciting times in my young life, but my first encounter with a lion is known far and wide; and I was told that it had even reached the wicked ears of Mzilikazi.'

Ra-Thaga, at first impatient, now became intensely interested. His wife continued:

'It happened in this way. A couple of years ago a group of us set out from our cattle-stations on the banks of the Setlagole River to gather berries in the direction of Motlhokaditse valley. There were two score and three girls beside myself. They were the jolliest lot of maidens you have ever met – most daring too, or I would not be here to cook this hare for you. There was some competition as to who should first fill her bag with berries, and her knapsack with the mola fruit from the creeping plant on the sands. We picked and gathered and sacked and bagged the fruit, proceeding as we did so from vine to vine, and from tree to tree. Presently, some of us became so engrossed in our work that we left the majority of the girls far behind a sand dune with wood-berries so numerous and ripe that they literally hid the green leaves and gave a maroon colour to the trees. I made straight for that bush, and saw my knapsack filling in imagination before my companions arrived. Coming up to the tree I started picking its fruit. Suddenly, there was a frightful growl and the terror drove the blood from all my veins. I was face to face with a monster of a dog which, in my awe, seemed several times magnified. As it opened its terrible mouth it gave a startling roar that shook the earth beneath my feet, and bathed my face in its steaming saliva which drenched me all over; the tree appeared to vibrate and spin round, and only the growling monster appeared stationary. I must have been unconscious with fright, and could barely see the animal in front of me. Subsequently I heard the shouts of girls' voices around me, and after what seemed an eternity, the animal turned and disappeared behind the tree.'

'So then,' said the astonished Ra-Thaga now lost in admiration, 'you were the heroine of Motlhokaditse, whose bravery was the pride of the countryside! Why, the thrilling tale of your adventure will live as long as there breathes a member of our tribe. I know the story. No man would believe the girls at first, until the next day when their footprints were tracked to the spot, and the men found the footmarks of a girl, face to face with a lion's paw only two paces apart. I remember hearing that it was a Kgoro girl whose bravery crowned the whole of her clan with glory. Who would have thought that I should live to marry the heroine of Motlhokaditse! How did these good girls manage to scare that lion away from you?'

'Just as you did on the morning I met you,' she said, 'by shouting and waving their peltries in the air. Of course, young women are timid and not as bold as men. They ran at first, but seeing my peril they returned – to die with me, as they thought, but in reality to rescue me.'

'Wonderful!' gasped Ra-Thaga in admiration. 'I feel certain that each of half a dozen boys of the same age would have shown their heels and left their comrade to his fate.'

'No, no,' said his wife, 'as true as my father was a Kgoro, the boys would have done just as well.'

'Now tell me,' insisted Ra-Thaga after a long pause of silent admiration, 'were you ever in love before you met me?'

Luckily recalling a way out of her dilemma, Mhudi said: 'Not exactly, but I remember when the girls of my agedivision passed their initiation into womanhood, our school broke up on a brilliant moonlight night. The dance of our thojane feast took place under a starry and cloudless sky with a silvery moon rendered more brilliant by the bonfires that marked the centres where stood the several thojane girls who had just qualified for young womanhood. This dance was held four nights after the full moon, yet before the same moon waned, and before I had discarded the ochre and the rest of the bojale garb, I was told there were no fewer than seventeen aspirants for my youthful hand, from which I was to choose one.

'My naughty aunt used to come and help me to sort out the names and examine the genealogy of each candidate. I rejected the first one because some generations back, so my aunt said, his forebears used to herd my mother's grand-uncle's cows. I preferred a man whose ancestors herded their own cows, you see. The next one I rejected because it was said that, once upon a time, there was famine in the land, and his grandparents appeased their hunger by eating dogs and scorpions – this was enough for me, that settled him, for as relations they were hopelessly repulsive.

'The next one's ancestry was obscure, and the next one I rejected because his father went out hunting one day and fled before a wounded wildebeest. A good-looking aspirant had two wives already, and wanted me as his third; whereas my ambition was to become wife No. 1 or remain unwedded. Auntie did not seem to know much about the remaining twelve so I gaily rejected the whole bunch because I thought they were too many. My naughty aunt has since dubbed me "The blind eye", because she said I could not see one suitor among so many. I never heard how all these wooers received their fate; I never troubled to find out what became of them for I knew them not, and cared much less.'

'And then?' enquired Ra-Thaga further. 'And then, of course,' said Mhudi, 'there was the massacre after which I was alone until I met you.'

After this they would descant upon their happiness in the wilderness, where their days were ideal and their nights long and pleasant. They had neither cares nor worries of any kind. They had almost forgotten the horrors of their bereavement and the fact that they were apparently the only survivors of a once-great race. The solitude of the wilderness had become dear to them and they craved for no other company. In afterlife, when things were not particularly to his liking, the demands of society often made Ra-Thaga long for the loneliness of Re-Nosi. Then he would plaintively exclaim:

> I long for the solitude of the woods,
> Far away from the quarrels of men,
> Their intrigues and vicissitudes;
> Away, where the air was clean
> And the morning dew
> Made all things new;
> Where nobody was by
> Save Mhudi and I.
> To me speak not of the comforts of home;
> Tell me but where the antelopes roam;
> Give me my hunting sticks and snares,
> In the gloaming of the wilderness;
> Give me the palmy days of our early felicity
> Away from the hurly-burly of your city
> And we'll be young again – aye:
> Sweet Mhudi and I.

Chapter Eight

Strangers

CONTINUING THEIR STAY at Re–Nosi, Ra-Thaga and his wife saw new moons wax and wane, and waning wax again, until one evening when he chanced to be walking out and thought that he heard human voices. This caused him to climb the look-out tree in the enclosure from which elevated position he saw the light of a fire some six hundred yards off. He told his wife and she agreed that he should go and examine at close quarters; for, if the strangers were Matabele, she said, the two of them would have to leave their home and forthwith make good their escape.

Ra-Thaga returned and told his wife that they were not Matabele but a party of Koranna hunters who were camping in the neighbourhood. His appearance, in what was known as an untenanted wilderness, caused a great surprise among the hunters who thought at first that their visitor was a ghost. Two of the Koranna men could speak a few Sechuana words. The meeting was very friendly as the hunters brought him and his wife the first news of the world since their marriage. Mhudi had on that day made quantities of berry-beer of which

93

the hunters partook with gusto. 'Bechuana women', said Ton-Qon the Koranna leader, 'are noted for the excellence of their kaffircorn beer. But I have never heard that they could brew such fine beer without any corn. How do you manage it?' he asked . . . 'I was on my way to Kunana last year to marry a Rolong woman when news of the massacre of their women and annihilation of their men reached us. They are clever, those Bldi women, although I am surprised to hear that they cannot milk their cows; only their men folk can milk, for they learnt it while working for our people. Still the plan would have worked well, as I was going to have a Kora wife to milk my cows and a Rolong wife to hoe the fields for corn seeds and brew beer.'

The idea of the daughter of a hammersmith marrying a man whose language was as full of clicks as that of the wild Masarwa, was too hard for Mhudi's conception. The destruction of her people and burning of their homes seemed to have had no effect on her tribal pride. She knew very little about the Koranna; in all her life she had never seen more than one; so that a group of them, nearly all sounding the Koranna clicks in turn, was a spectacle so grotesque that she felt it difficult to believe that they understood one another. 'What a life,' she thought, 'to be married to a man whose language a girl could not understand! What would have been my fate had I missed my husband and fallen in with these people? Why, a woman could not master their language in a lifetime. Barolong have crossed the desert at times and gone to Hereroland. When they returned after eight or twelve moons they could speak the Kalahari and Herero languages fluently; but I have never *met* anyone who could master the clicks and gibberish of the Masarwa.'

After nearly a whole night's talk, Ra-Thaga was persuaded to join the hunters who were now returning home to Maamuse. This was entirely against Mhudi's wish. She disliked the squint-eyed Koranna headman whose reckless conversation and crude manners did not appeal to her. Her husband, however, had made up his mind to give up Re-Nosi, which for over eight moons had been their home. He preferred to be near other people and so collect information concerning the fate of the remainder of his fellow tribesmen; so next day, Ra-Thaga and his wife joined Ton-Qon's party and proceeded to the land of the Korannas.

Ra-Thaga became great among the Koranna people. For hours men would sit at the chief's court and listen to the account of his experiences. 'He must be a witch,' said someone, 'to have magnetised unto himself such a pretty girl just when he needed company.' 'No,' replied others, 'she must be the witch to have influenced the arrival of such a brave man, just when she needed him most.'

Thus Mhudi also became the talk of the people and many were the yarns spun concerning the two supernatural Bldis, as the Korannas call the Bechuana. Anecdotes in the history of the strangers were related and exaggerated with each repetition. Gossipers wagged their tongues and twisted the story about. Some reported that Ton-Qon's party had returned with ten hides of lions killed single-handed by Mhudi, while the hunters could not bring back the pile of skins of other lions and tigers killed by Ra-Thaga. One chatterer had had ocular testimony of what he said, for he 'saw lions' skins in a hut at the chief's court'.

Another story was to the effect that Ra-Thaga alone had vanquished the armies of Mzilikazi after all the Barolong were slain, and rescued his beautiful wife, who was a captive among the Matabele. Again, that she herself slew two Matabele soldiers who were attempting to follow her and thus inspired the remainder with fear. Such were the wild stories that circulated in the Koranna huts, which the strangers unacquainted with the Koranna tongue were unable to correct.

Ra-Thaga during his stay at Re-Nosi had benefited much from the sober judgement of his clever wife. None of his countrymen ever adored his wife as intensely as he did Mhudi. He could not withhold his veneration from – as far as he could see – the only living Morolong besides himself, lest the change should reverse his fortunes. With regard to manly occupations, however, he recalled a Sechuana proverb which his comrades used to quote, viz., 'Never be led by a female lest thou fall over a precipice.' And so when Mhudi warned him against this powerful headman he put it down to some idiosyncrasy, peculiar to women, which would no doubt wear off in time. On his part he felt grateful to the man who brought them from the lonely wilderness to a place where, among other people, they could drink milk, eat meat and have company. When she was inclined to be fidgety he would remind her of her exclamation after their first morning at Maamuse when she said, 'What a treat to hear once again the hens cackle by day, the cocks crow at night, the raucous bark of the sheep dog, to say nothing of the jabbering of the children even if one knows not their language. It makes my heart swell with joy.' Therefore, in spite of her warning, he planned to go out hunting with a party of which Ton-Qon was the leader.

This headman was one of the few men in the village, besides the chief, who owned a musket – an old elephant flintlock muzzle-loader, the best rifle of those days. They left on foot, Ton-Qon and two others remaining behind to follow the party next day on horseback.

The evening after the departure of the men, Ra-Thaga among them, the Koranna leader called at Mhudi's hut and engaged her in some highly objectionable conversation. She thought of his popularity among his people and feared that she could never succeed in showing him up, as he could easily turn the tables against her. It was a situation as perilous as she had ever been in. She found herself in the power of a man who feared no lions, and who, besides other worldly signs of power, owned horses, a saddle and a gun; and above all commanded a following among a section of Koranna that would go through fire and water at his bidding. Never since she had met her husband in the woods of Re-Nosi, did she so need his presence as she did that evening, but his obstinacy had placed him out of her reach. Ra-Thaga was noble, but a man like the rest of them, or he would never have joined this wicked man's party against her advice; nevertheless, her cool judgement, which was the secret of the charmed life she bore, did not fail her. Ton-Qon did the talking in the light of the wood-fire on the hearth while she did the thinking.

'The fire is burning low,' she said at length, 'and we need more wood. Let me go for some!' leaving Ton-Qon to cogitate by the fire. Mhudi resolved not to return to her hut that night. She hastened to the chief's harem where by means of signs to aid her imperfect knowledge of the language, she informed the ladies that her husband being out hunting, she was afraid to spend the night alone in her hut. She at once found refuge with one of the chief's wives. During the night Mhudi decided to follow up her husband and call him back from the hunting field. She must get him home at any cost and leave the villain to hunt with the other Korannas.

By daybreak she was off. She carried a wooden jar full of milk and some boiled corn in a small bag, which she believed would last her until she could find Ra-Thaga. The way was dreary and lonely.

All afternoon, as long as the daylight lasted, she traced their spoor through the plains and forests, now running, now walking, until evening, when in the twilight it became invisible and made it necessary for her to rest till dawn. After a year of home life, the prospect of a night alone in the woods was far from bright.

The stars hung over the purple sky. For a while there was tense silence and not a breeze to stir the leaves until first a hyena, then a jackal, began to howl and soon she renewed her acquaintance with the bay of wolves and the yelping of wild dogs, while other animals made the night still more hideous with their cries.

Amidst these discordant sounds she found peace at the foot of a large tree in the centre of a thicket of shrubbery. Here she levelled a pile of grass – a really comfortable outdoor bed – across which she stretched herself for the night. The undergrowth served as a screen against the sharp south wind that rose later, while the top branches of the tree served her excellently as an awning. Crouching down for the night she opened her eyes and looked away into the immense depth of the skies overhead, reading something there that she had never observed before. This immense dome, so lofty and yet so brilliant, suggested the power of its Maker, who apparently also made the trees and birds, and beasts and men – yes, brutal men!

'Where is the God, this Spirit, that made all these things? Does He not stroll round sometimes and examine His handiwork, and even me? I wonder how long it took Him to make this immense universe? Is He satisfied with it all and with me? Surely He cannot be pleased with the Matabele or with Ton-Qon; and if they too are the creatures of the God of Life, what did He make such people for? Did He also make the dreadful venomous reptiles that infest the land, I wonder? And if so, why?'

She marvelled at the stars and at their numbers; she did not seem to have noticed that there were so many before. While she admired the greater and lesser brilliancy of each planet, she was baffled to find that what looked like vacant spaces betwixt the constellations proved, on closer scrutiny, to be no spaces at all but further clusters of numerous smaller stars. It was a glorious if immobile audience, watching her with eyes too numerous to be counted. She wondered if they too were classed into tribes such as the people were on earth. Can it be that the stars also engage in fighting sometimes, and if so, did they kill one another's wives and children? Could it be that the thunder and lightning and hailstones that accompany the rain at times were the result of aerial battles?

Then her native superstitions got the better of her. 'It is said that we should never attempt to count the stars. Have I not perhaps been trying to count them?' Her flesh began to creep. 'If so what could happen to me? Had someone been trying to count the stars and so brought about the fate of Kunana?'

After hours of timid wakefulness, she fell into a deep slumber and woke up at dawn to find that the wolves were quiet and the jackals had ceased to yelp; and that their noises had given place to the chatter of a host of monkeys. The jabbering of these denizens of the woods enlivened the forests on the right, while the hillocks opposite resounded with the echoes of their voices. Truly a lively prattle, enhanced by the damp of the dewy morning before the appearance of the rising sun. Mhudi thought at first that the noise was that of the men shouting to one another in the distance; so, concluding that it might be men of the hunting party, she listened more intently, only to shudder as she realised the true character of the babble. Again her native superstitious beliefs overcame her as she recalled the traditional folktales, according to which monkeys were among 'the things that should never be seen'. She thought of her own little chequered life and remembered that throughout that period of her early wanderings she had never seen any monkeys, hence her consistent safety. 'But why', she protested, 'should these mischievous creatures come to blight my prospects with their evil forebodings on this grave morning? The misery portended by their presence, was it meant for me or for my beloved Ra-Thaga?' Tears rolled down her cheeks as she thought of him. She had shed tears, it is true, on the morning of her first meeting with her husband, but they were tears of joy at the sensational termination of their lonesome and solitary hazards. But the stream of tears this morning told her that all was not well with him.

As Mhudi resumed her journey along the spoor of the hunters, where she had left it the previous night, the ugliest thoughts tormented her. Wondering if the Korannas had strangled him, she walked with her head bowed down through fear of sighting any of the 'things that should never be seen!'

Chapter Nine

A Perilous Adventure

RA-THAGA, ON HIS second morning out, left the Korannas in camp and went out in search of game. He had not gone very far, when he saw in the bush a tiger eating leisurely at the carcass of a buck. So he ran back the two miles to camp and asked Ton-Qon to come along and shoot the beast. He had himself learnt to shoot with the Chief Massouw's gun but did not think himself as good a marksman as the much-practised headman. Now, all this time, Ton-Qon, who, with his mounted companions, had overtaken the party during the night, was planning to kill Ra-Thaga so as to make a widow of Mhudi and then to woo her. Thus, when he heard about the tiger, he thought he had at hand the means to rid himself of Ra-Thaga, and accomplish his evil purpose without soiling his hands with human blood. So he told the other Natives that, he being such a good shot, it was unnecessary for anyone to go with them. Only Ra-Thaga was wanted to point out the position of the beast.

Accordingly Ton-Qon shouldered his rifle and followed Ra-Thaga into the bush. He kept close behind him while his guide was trying to locate the tiger. As they cautiously approached the place, Ra-Thaga leading and Ton-Qon following, the former saw the animal at the side of a bush not more than ten yards distant. Looking round, he said in a whisper: 'There it is,' when to his dismay, he discovered that he was addressing space, the Koranna having disappeared and taken his weapon with him.

Needless to say, the animal sprang upon Ra-Thaga, knocked him down, bit him about the head and right arm, and left him bleeding and unconscious. This tragedy was enacted in a few moments.

Ra-Thaga remembered nothing more until he found himself by the side of a brook, with a familiar feminine hand bathing his temples and applying some soft fatty substance to his wounds. In his semi-delirium, he raised his head, and cried: 'What is the matter, Mhudi, what has happened? . . . Where are the Matabele? . . . Has the lion bitten me?'

'Hush,' said his wife. 'Drink a little sour milk and I will tell you all. There are no Matabele, but that squint-eyed friend of yours has tried and almost succeeded in taking your life.'

'Oh Mhudi! Who would want to kill me; and for what reason?'

'That monster, Ton-Qon; because he says he wants me.'

'You are dreaming, Mhudi! But tell me, where are we and what has happened? Oh, I remember; the tiger! *Mo-galamakapa* (Goodness gracious!). Has it destroyed my arm?'

'Fortunately not; they are all flesh wounds.' And Mhudi related all that had happened during the previous two days, and how she had reached the hunters' camp about four hours before to find 'that you and Ton-Qon had left to go and kill a tiger. I persuaded the men to bring me to the place, as I could not trust Ton-Qon alone with you, and just as we were about to leave the camp, Ton-Qon ran in and told us that you had been torn to pieces by a tiger.'

As to Ton-Qon, he told a beautiful story in the camp. 'I was walking behind the deceased,' he said, 'when a tiger jumped out of the grass, caught the poor man by the throat and killed him instantaneously.' This concoction fortunately did not mislead the Korannas, who, emboldened by the presence of the widow, demanded Ton-Qon's reason for not shooting the beast.

'I did,' he replied, 'and wounded it on top of the Bldi. It limped away while I was loading for the second shot, but not before it had finished him.' The men declared, however, that they had not heard that rifle shot, although the morning was unusually quiet; so they asked, 'Then why do you object to the wife going to view the remains of her husband, seeing that the tiger has run away?'

'Don't you know? Have you never heard,' stammered Ton-Qon, 'a wounded tiger is always enraged by the sight of a woman, especially a beautiful woman like this one.'

'Well, then,' said one, 'order someone to go and fetch the dead man to her – his widow. This seems a more sensible arrangement.'

'Oh,' said Ton-Qon, in a fidgety tone, 'what is the good of sacrificing more lives over a dead body? I am responsible to the chief for every man in this party.'

Now this talk was in the tongue of the Korannas which Mhudi did not understand. In her anxiety to know the truth about her 'dead' husband, she was on the point of departing alone, when one of the Korannas, following her, cried: 'Ha-ha, *Xhwekaowo!* (Come on, run along!),' and three of them tracked the footprints on the grass to where Ra-Thaga lay.

The party, no longer satisfied with their leader, decided to give up the hunt; returning home with the wounded man they reported the matter to the chief. Ton-Qon tendered bribes, and tried every kind of persuasion to hush up the matter, but the other Korannas would not yield to him.

Ra-Thaga remained an invalid for a month, but, thanks to the unremitting attention of his devoted wife, he became strong enough to attend the court and give evidence against Ton-Qon.

A crowd of Korannas gathered at Maamuse to witness the trial of an important leader of their tribe. The tribesmen descanted at the court on the mean treachery of which he had been guilty, and if the crime went unredressed, they argued, the life of the husband of a beautiful woman would 'not be worth the value of a mouse skin!'

After the tribesmen had aired their views, the Chief Massouw gave judgment.

He delivered a tedious review of certain past events, many of them irrelevant to the case at issue. At times he gave the impression to those present that he was going to discharge Ton-Qon; then finally coming abruptly to the point, he said, 'A case of this character occurred among the Bloms, some years back, lower down on the banks of the Vaal, and our countrymen over there decided to drown the villain. His head was enclosed in a skin beside a heavy stone, the ends of the skin being strapped around his neck with the stone inside. Powerful young men were ordered to carry him to the top of a steep and rocky bank by the side of the river, and roll him into the raging torrent below. When I heard the news I congratulated myself that none of my people were ever implicated in a case that calls for such terrible punishment. But what is this that you have brought me today?

'Now, men of the Koranna tribe – the Tigheboshes, the Hochstetters, the Machilles and representatives of all the clans – hear me. Open wide your ears, if you have any, and hearken to the law of Massouw, your chief. I should blot out Ton-Qon so that his name shall be remembered no more, but for the instructions of the white Missioner Moffat of Coolman. Moffat

advised me never to shed my people's blood. You will recall the
circumstances as I related them to you at the time; but I will
adopt other means of punishing Ton-Qon, for this dog is not fit
to live. *Kxamase* (verily), he will lead my people into ways that
are wrong. I will degrade him and install some other headman
in his place (*general nods of assent*). He schemed to take the life
of this innocent Bldi, to rob a woman of the company of her
husband, whom through her bravery she had saved from death
more than once. Anyone capable of such blackguardly actions
might come out at night and kill me during my sleep. So let it
be understood that every person in my dominion, whether a
Bldi, a Hottentot, a Griqua or anything else, is one of us. My
home is his home, my lands are his lands, my cattle are his
cattle, and my law is his shield. And you, the relatives of Ton-
Qon, I want you to hand over, before sundown, twenty of Ton-
Qon's best cattle, his horse, his saddle and bridle, and his rifle.
Ten of the cows I will award to Ra-Thaga, the Bldi whose life
Ton-Qon attempted to take; and the remainder of the fine will
be mine. That is my law which you must obey and don't let
me ever hear of so brutal a case again.' He concluded with an
indignant command for the dispersal of the crowd.

Mhudi told Ra-Thaga that she had no wish to own Ton-
Qon's cattle. And such was her determination on the point
that, for the peace of Ra-Thaga's home, the aged chief gave
him some cows from his own herd, adding those of Ton-Qon to
his own herd. Ra-Thaga's head healed up entirely after a time,
although traces of the tiger's claws remained on his forehead
till his dying day. In subsequent years he often referred with
pride to the scars on his face, adding proudly that none could
be found upon his back.

Chapter Ten

Arrival of the Voortrekkers

RA-THAGA, AFTER A long stay at Maamuse, received some news concerning the Barolong. According to it, the Seleka branch of the tribe had removed from Motlhan'oapitse under the guidance of their Chief Moroka-a-Sehunelo, to Thaba Nchu in the land of the Basuto. As for the Ra-Tshidi – Ra-Thaga's own people – he learned that hardly a family had in its entirety escaped the slaughter. Many fleeing mothers with their children on their backs, were overtaken and slain. Those of the fugitives that escaped the assegais joined their chief, Tauana, who sought and obtained an asylum among the Selekas; he had gathered together the remnants of his scattered tribe and followed his cousin, Moroka, to Thaba Nchu, where they had been slowly recovering from the frightful experiences and the shock occasioned by the sacking of their town. The reports enlarged upon the phenomenal recovery made by the refugees at Thaba Nchu and their wonderful progress in agriculture and husbandry. The chiefs held court, the women brewed beer, and the men ploughed and hunted very much as they did in the halcyon days at Kunana. The little children, so violently unsettled by the raid and subsequent flight, had long since recovered from their nasty experience, and adversity seemed to have quickened their growth; so Ra-Thaga and Mhudi made up their minds to leave Maamuse, proceed east and join their own people in the land of plenty.

The journey was not undertaken until seven months after Mhudi had presented him with their second boy. Then he bade good-bye to the hospitable Korannas and took his departure eastwards. Two young men were ordered to accompany Ra-Thaga and his wife and help to drive their stock along, and to return later with news about everything of interest for the information of Chief Massouw and the Koranna tribes at Maamuse.

After nearly a month of travel, which included resting, straying, and enquiring the way, our little party, their hearts beating high with expectation, reached the outskirts of the town of Thaba Nchu in the land of hope and promise. They had little difficulty in following the main road leading to the chief's headquarters in quest of information as to whether any of their relatives were alive.

Having passed several houses without being questioned, they noticed crossing the road in front of them a young woman balancing a pail of water on her head. This woman – who was none other than Baile, Mhudi's cousin – turned round to look at the travellers. The look became a stare as she recognised her cousin, Mhudi. So profound was her surprise at a meeting which was entirely unexpected that in the excitement the earthenware vessel on her head fell off, was smashed, and its contents spilt. Baile was wild with joy, for Mhudi (like her husband) had been given up by her people as among the victims of the great massacre.

Now, good health and a sound pair of lungs go hand in

hand, and a Chuana woman in moments of excitement can generally give full play to these organs. This Baile did, and in leaping to embrace her cousin she shouted 'Barolong! what have I seen? Have the graves of our fathers opened and yielded their contents? Maiyo! Has death become so tame that one who has been in his jaws can return to earth and live again? Surely this is the dead daughter of my uncle, returned to us in life. Maiyo! Maiyo!'

News of the sensational meeting of the cousins spread from hut to hut, and while the two women stood clasped in each other's arms shedding tears of gladness, a crowd was collecting round them. More and still more women, and children, were hurrying to the scene to see the apparition, and witness a real resurrection; and this is what they heard.

Baile: 'O, my cousin, is it indeed you – alive! – and without a scratch?'

Mhudi: 'My own cousin; and where are dear uncle and – ?'

Baile: 'Dead, everyone.'

Mhudi: 'And where is auntie, and – ?'

Baile: 'All killed.'

Both (weeping): 'Iyo – Iyo – Iyo!'

Mhudi: 'And these blotches – these scars on your – ?'

Baile: 'Traces of Matabele spears.'

Mhudi: 'After seven years?'

Both: 'Curse those Khonkhobes.'

Baile (between sobs): 'And you escaped wholly unscathed?'

Mhudi (also sobbing): 'Yes, thanks to my husband.'

Baile: 'Where did my unmaidenly cousin find a husband?'

Mhudi: 'He rescued me from alarming adventures in the wilderness.'

Baile: 'These little boys are your children?'

Mhudi: 'And his.'

Baile (sobbing again): 'My uncle's own daughter!'

Mhudi (ditto): 'My own auntie's child.'

Both (weeping): 'Woe – woe – woe – Iyo!'

Mhudi: 'A poor dying woman told me you were stabbed to death.'

Baile: 'I got picked up and was saved.'

Mhudi: 'So, I am not wholly orphaned?'

Baile: 'And I am not the only one left, after all.'

Thus for a second time their dramatic arrival provided a fruitful subject for fireside conversation in and around Thaba Nchu. For months after, the women never tired of discussing their romantic story at home, or at work in the cornfields. Men whiled away their evenings spinning yarns about them, or in the daytime when engaged in braying skins or sewing karosses in the shade. People came long distances to see them and they brought them many presents. Indeed it seemed that their 'resurrection' was going to be an abiding conversational topic to the exclusion of all other questions until it was eclipsed one fine day by the arrival at Thaba Nchu of a party of white men.

They were mounted and each carried a rifle. It was a travel-stained party, and the faces of the older men bore traces of anxiety. Apart from that they were well-fed on the whole, as the open air of a sunny country had impressed health, vigour, and energy on their well-clothed bodies, especially the younger men of the party. The spokesman of the riders was their leader, a Boer named Sarel Cilliers, who headed a large band of Dutch emigrants from Cape Colony. They were travelling with their families in hooded waggons, and driving with their caravan their wealth of livestock into the hinterland in search of some unoccupied territory to colonise and to worship God in peace.

'But,' asked Chief Moroka, 'could you not worship God on the south of the Orange River?'

'We could,' replied Cilliers, 'but oppression is not conducive to piety. We are after freedom. The English laws of the Cape are not fair to us.'

'We Barolong have always heard that, since David and Solomon, no king has ruled so justly as King George of England.'

'It may be so,' replied the Boer leader, 'but there are always two points of view. The point of view of the ruler is not always the viewpoint of the ruled. We Boers are tired of foreign kings and rulers. We only want one ruler and that is God, our Creator. No man or woman can rule another.'

'Yours must be a very strange people,' said several chiefs simultaneously. 'The Bible says when the children of Israel had only God as their ruler, they gave Him no rest until He anointed a king for them. We are just like them. There are two persons that we Barolongs can never do without; these are a wife to mind the home and a king to call us to order, settle our disputes and lead us in battle.'

'Perhaps you are right,' said Sarel, 'but the English may soon have a woman for a king and you must admit that a woman could not lead an army.'

Then changing the subject abruptly, he asked them about the condition of the country to the north. Answering his questions, the Barolongs informed the Boers that the country round about was wide and there was plenty of land for all. There were, they said, plenty of lions and tigers, and smaller species of carnivora, all yielding valuable skins. They might now and then kill a cow or two, but with so many guns in hand the Boers need not be troubled by their presence.

'And what a lot of guns!' exclaimed one chief. 'Why, with so many rifles you would hardly want to kill any of your sheep or oxen for food. There are too many eland and zebra and wildebeest, and such antelopes as hartebeest, gemsbuck, blesbuck, and if you went a little further afield, you would find giraffe, buffalo and elephant, while the plains and woods are alive with huge and tasty birds of every plume.'

'Yes,' said the Boer, 'we have seen herds and herds of game of every kind along our trek from the south. Could you tell me, how are the Basutos?'

'Not unlike ourselves,' replied Chief Moroka. 'Often inordinately fond of meat, but one can always get even with them for they have a fine old king.'

'Yes,' agreed Sarel Cilliers, 'far down in the Colony we have heard of Moshoeshoe's reputation. He is noted for his fair dealing and sound judgement.'

'Quite true,' proceeded the Chief, 'it is a pity that men are not like cattle or Moshoeshoe would be set apart to propagate noble rulers much the same as we do with good bulls. This country is all right,' he went on, 'it has only one serious nuisance and that is, it is infested by Mzilikazi and his ferocious impis. If you helped us to rid the country of this pest, we could make of it the happiest land under the sun. If that came about, I, too, would turn a Christian, wouldn't you, Tauana?'

'Most decidedly,' replied the latter; 'who so wicked as not to become a Christian in sheer gratitude if the Matabele were blotted out?'

'What kind of people are the Matabele?' asked Cilliers further.

'They are nearly all much blacker than ourselves. Their men go about stark naked even in the presence of their children. The women are well-dressed just like ours. But the men! Even in winter, they scarcely ever cloak themselves against the cold winds. Winter cloaks are the luxury of a few of their nobility. But in the summer months no Matabele ever puts on anything. They only carry spears and shields; for the rest they walk about just like children!'

'Oh,' said an elderly Boer, 'they are the *kaalkaffers*.'

'No, no', said the Chief, who didn't know Dutch, 'I mean

the Matabele, Mzilikazi's people. Travelling in the country you will easily distinguish their footmarks from ours: unless the ground be very damp most of our men wear sandals, but not the Matabele. They nearly always go barefooted. Again, if you examine individual footprints, you will find that the Matabele feet are much shorter, yet half as stout again as Barolong feet. When they kill cattle or game they leave only the dung. They will eat up every bit of the animal, including the offal. When they kill men, you will notice by the dead bodies that they are impartial in their killing. Old men, young women, boys, girls and babies – everybody is speared without discrimination.'

Addressing Cilliers again, Chief Moroka said: 'Tauana here has good reason to feel bitter against Mzilikazi. When his city, Kunana, was destroyed, the Matabele killed all the noble women of his tribe; and Montsioa, his son and heir, could not find a suitable maiden to marry as the future queen of his tribe. Chieftain Montsioa in consequence was obliged to marry his own father's daughter from another house.'

'Have patience,' said Cilliers, 'I will pay Mzilikazi back for all the Barolong women killed by his army.'

The Barolong regaled the Boers with meat and milk and cornmash. Sarel and the elder Boers being entertained by the Chiefs, they invited Mr Archbell, their minister, to confer with and pray for the strangers; and Cilliers and his men, when returning to their waggons, had a royal send-off, many of the young men running alongside their horses for a long distance until they were well out of Thaba Nchu.

Chapter Eleven

A Timid Man

'Mhudi,' exclaimed Ra-Thaga, when he came home with two companions, 'you must see the visitors who arrived at the chief's court today. A most interesting group.'

Mhudi: 'Where from, Basutoland?'

Ra-Thaga: 'No, No! They come out of the sea – away beyond where the clouds end.'

Mhudi: 'And what best did you like about them? Are they good people like Moner' Atsi-bele (the Archbells, Wesleyan missionaries at Thaba Nchu) and his family?'

Ra-Thaga: 'They are white, but they don't look like missionaries. They can't be from the same sea. What did I like best? Oh Mhudi, you should see them. I have never seen so many *kololos* (horses) in one herd, as those in possession of the strangers. Not since that morning when you and I saw that troop of zebras in the Kolong valley. And every one of them with a rider.'

1st Companion: 'I was tremendously impressed by their guns – a forest of them – a gun for every Boer. I said to myself,

"If ever we acquire half as many guns, and the Matabele come again, they shan't kill any more Barolong.'"

2nd Companion: 'I liked their stately beards best. I have never in all my life seen so much beard as I saw today, hanging on the chins of those Boers. Mhudi should see those beards. Did you ever see a beard flowing down to a man's belly? Did you see that short, stout Boer, who laughed the loudest, and how he emptied the gourd of sour milk?'

1st Companion: 'Didn't I! Why, I should like to face the Matabele standing beside him, with his stout gun in his hand.'

2nd Companion: 'After he swallowed the milk, much of it stuck in his beard: he caught hold of his growth like that (*demonstrating*) – folded it like a cloth, mopped his mouth twice, and his face was as clean as that of a man who never drank milk. By the great dead Barolong, and the dead mother who gave me life, I wish I had a beard like that.'

'And what would you do with it?' queried Mhudi.

1st Companion: 'With a beard like that, I could chase a blesbuck against the south wind, throughout a wintry day and never catch a cold; then swagger back home, with the buck on my back, flop it down in the courtyard; swell out my chest and stroke my woolly chin, for the whole world to admire the dignified face of the master hunter.'

2nd Companion: 'Exactly what the Boers were doing all day to excite admiration.'

Mhudi: 'Did they bring their wives with them?'

Both Companions: 'By the way, were there any wives?'

Ra-Thaga: 'I did not see the wives unless they too be bearded.'

Mhudi: 'What a queer surmise!'

Ra-Thaga: 'I have heard that wanderers from the sea, when crossing the Bechuana forests, always leave their wives – at sea!'

Mhudi: 'I should like to have been there, and seen the Boer

wives (if there were any) and found out what they wore.'

A number of girls went to draw water at the pools outside the village. After filling their pails, and before leaving the pools, they entertained one another with the latest scandal and the current gossip, and having exhausted every other topic, one of them began to extol the heroism of Mhudi and Ra-Thaga.

Suddenly, on the distant plain, they noticed the approach of a man running bareheaded in their direction. The fugitive, swift of foot, came, as one of the girls put it, 'as if pursued by a tiger'.

'A man, a man running,' shouted Kong-goane, one of the girls, 'let us be off.'

'Nay,' cried Tsetsanyana, 'shall we not stay and find out the cause of his haste?'

'Let us run,' repeated Kong-goane, 'you will be finding out and finding out till it is too late for us to escape. Do you not see that a man, and not a woman, flees? What more would you find out? Let us be off.'

'Wait!' retorted Tsetsanyana, successfully concealing her own nervousness. 'Everybody's name is not Ra-Thaga, you know. Some men are braver than others, but one cannot always tell the difference merely by looking at them; for outwardly men look almost alike, and bestride the land in similar gait, but their physical resemblance proceeds no further than their beards. Even as some women who resemble one another outwardly; the breasts that feed their babes are so much alike, yet the diaphragm that harbours the courage of each woman is made of different clay to that which moulded the diaphragms of all the rest; hence, some women, like some men, are less plucky than others. If yonder runner be a coward, then Kong-goane would rob us of the laughter we might enjoy at his expense; moreover, *we* should appear to share in his cowardice. Again, if he be pursued by Matabele or by tigers that are not yet in sight, let him but come and tell us so, and I will assure him in advance that he will run no faster than we can.'

'Tsetsanyana is right,' said Matsitselele, with a security she was very far from feeling. 'Kong-goane is as white-livered as that man who comes flying so swiftly from the invisible bogey. I think I notice some similarity between that runner and a man that accompanied my father to last winter's chase. He roused the camp one night (so the men related on their return) with a plausible story about a lion preparing to spring on my father's party in their sleep – and what do you think it was that he mistook for a roaring lion? A bush, a stationary little bush.'

'Very well,' said Kong-goane, 'you may stop there gossiping, chuckling and cackling like a dozen hens that have all laid eggs at the same time. I must away. If that man be pursued by lions or Matabele, I shall be safe in my mother's hut when he overtakes you. Goodbye to the lot of you, I am off.' Having said so, she balanced the water-pail on her head and left the spot in a hurry. Two or three other girls soon remembered that their mothers were waiting for them, although it must be said that their memories were refreshed rather by the sight of the running man than by consideration for their mothers. The others were anxious to see the fun to the end. 'Women, women,' the fugitive, now almost in their midst, shouted at the top of his voice, panting heavily like a racehorse, 'women, take to your legs and let them save you; never mind the water pots, save your lives. I have seen a milk-white house filled with a load of bloodred devils, some hairy in the face, some smooth, some big, some small – devils in a moving white house crawling in this direction with all the sheep and cattle and livestock from Hades. Some of the devils had four legs, long tails and two heads – one head hairy and almost like that of a man, and the other shaped like that of a cow, but with great ears instead of horns. Women, run I say! The monsters are almost here.'

But the girls, far from running away, stood and scrutinised the horizon in the direction whence the man came and demanded ocular proof of the existence of the alleged monsters. Now, it would have been impossible for a man to run away and leave the girls to face the danger alone without risking his own reputation, so the fugitive had perforce to control his terror and check his flight. Stopping to look back, he seemed puzzled when he found that nothing was pursuing him. How could he explain his behaviour to the satisfaction of the girls? The humour of the situation created by his attitude appealed to the girls so strongly that he could scarcely look them in the face. He was beginning to wonder if instead of devils in a crawling house he had not really seen 'apparitions in the air, devils in space and a boggart [goblin] in every tree'.

Maupenyana, one of the girls, solved the riddle for him, to the intense amusement of the others.

'This man', explained Maupenyana, 'never saw the Boers who, mounted on many horses, visited the chief yesterday.'

'Nor a new waggon either,' cried another girl.

He admitted he had heard of waggons, but had never seen one and added 'What are Boers?'

This question produced a fresh outburst of hilarity which confused the timid man, and the hallucination of 'the man who had fled from imaginary sprites' supplied an absorbing topic for conversations in the village for many evenings after. Anyone betraying faintheartedness was at once pronounced 'as timid and as swift as Tlholo', which was the timid man's name. Tlholo had himself decided never to mention the episode to anyone. Whenever he heard the subject alluded to, he remembered a pressing appointment elsewhere; and throughout his life he never regretted anything so much as his inability, on that afternoon, to seal the lips of those chatterboxes who saw him running.

Barolong travellers, from near and far, continued to bring news of waggonloads of Boers, the cause of Tlholo's alarm that afternoon, all moving in a northerly direction, at distances of from twenty to fifty miles west of Thaba Nchu. They spoke of the number of sheep, cattle and horses accompanying the waggons, and of the quaint animals never before seen by the Barolong. Some of these weird creatures seemed to be cared for by the women among the emigrants; they looked almost like guineafowl and wild ducks though not of the same colour; and, unlike the familiar wild fowl, they were as tame as goats. Huge web-footed birds followed behind some waggons like flocks of sheep. When these walking birds reached the foot of a hill they flew up the hillock over the waggons, and over the heads of the Boers and of their native drivers, and waited for the people and the waggons on top, then continued the journey downhill on their web-feet as before. These were the first geese ever seen in that country.

Again, a certain Morolong came home one day with a report of 'a horse with very long ears, the size and shape of a zebra, but without its stripes', which he had seen among the animals accompanying a party of Boers. It was quite natural that his tribesmen, who had never before heard of an ass, should think that he was drawing on his imagination. Naturally these stories lost nothing by repetition, as they were passed on from speaker to speaker, and from village to village, during the months that followed. And, as five different narrators would each give a separate and distinct description of the same party of Boers, it became increasingly difficult to correctly estimate the actual numbers of the trekkers.

Chapter Twelve

Queen Umnandi

HERE, WE MAY BE permitted to digress and describe the beauty and virtues of one of King Mzilikazi's wives – the lily of his harem, by name Umnandi, the sweet one. She was a daughter of Umzinyati, the offspring of a lineage of brave warriors with many deeds of valour to their credit. Such was the description of her given to the writer by a hoary octogenarian that it reminded him of a remarkable passage in the Song of Songs, namely:

I am black but comely O ye daughters of Solomon
As the tents of Kedar and the curtains of Solomon.
Look not upon me because I am black
For the Sun hath looked upon me.
My mother's children were angry with me;
They made me the keeper of the vineyards;
But my own vineyard have I not kept.

And when he changed 'vineyards' into 'cornfields', he thought he could visualise her appearance in his mind's eye with accuracy.

She had been the favourite wife of the great monarch whose ambition at one time was to make of her the principal queen of the Matabele; for not only was she fair of countenance, but the stately way in which she received court guests filled the king with pride, and these visitors to the royal palace, on return to their several homes far and wide, spread news of her personal charms, the excellence of her cooking and the tastiness of her beer. Her reputation so gladdened her regal husband that he often asked with what she seasoned her food – and his other wives hated her.

In moments of indiscretion his majesty outraged the feelings of his other wives by sending their food to Umnandi to be cooked all over again. Such flagrant acts of favouritism only served to accentuate the hatred of which she was the victim.

Her worst luck was the misfortune of being childless. This in time tended almost to cool her husband's ardent affections towards her. Her sorrows were not diminished by the attitude of her co-wives who, intolerably jealous of the favours bestowed upon her by the king, constantly sneered and mocked at her. Let but the king confer upon her a token of recognition, and they gossiped about it: 'He thinks that this will give her a child,' they would sneer, 'let's wait and see if it will.' Every meritorious act of hers was just as laconically referred to by the ladies of the harem: 'She thinks that this will give her a child, let's wait and see if it will.' These reproaches she bore with fortitude, but the king's waning interest, in addition to their jeers, was more than she could stand. Umnandi would willingly have given up her beauty and stately mien and forgotten her skill in cookery, in return for the birth of a baby boy as a present to her husband and his people. She would gladly have gone through fire and water if the end of it was to nurse a royal child of her own. She took counsel with famous herbalists from Basutoland, Swaziland, Bechuanaland, and Bapediland; she went through painful and even distressing ordeals on their advice, just for the hope of becoming a mother but these wizards accomplished nothing, beyond filling her heart with a succession of hopes, each of which in turn proved worthless.

It so happened that after completing her domestic duties one evening, Umnandi sat down by the fire in her hut to rest. But though her limbs were at rest, her mind was active, and she could get no ease, thinking over her sad lot. She thought of a noted medicine man who had reached the city two days before from Zululand – a magician of the first eminence. Stories of the wisdom of the newcomer had filled the city and spread to the outlying villages; and as Umnandi sat cogitating at the fireside and pining for the blessing of the child that would never be hers, she thought of her previous false hopes and wondered if it were worthwhile consulting the newly arrived wizard. But Umnandi little dreamed that in one of the huts of the royal enclosure a plot was at that moment being hatched against her with that same wizard as its agent. Nomenti, one of the ladies of the harem, was bribing the Zulu doctor, promising him ornaments, livestock and other gifts, if he would consent to visit Umnandi's hut and lay at her door a charm that would end her life.

'No,' said the magician with emotion, 'a dog of a witchdoctor in my station is not great enough to take the life of a royal wife. Seek some wizard with bluer blood than mine to snatch a wife from the bosom of my lord, the king, and defy the consequences. I am not equal to so great a task as that of putting her to eternal sleep.'

'But you are not pursuing your pleasure, Oh wise man,' said Nomenti. 'It is the will of the rightful wife of Mzilikazi, who sends you to rid our harem of this troublesome upstart. In proof of this I will call another and yet another of the principal wives of the king, each of whom would gladly double and treble your fee if you will but consent to withdraw this "thorn-in-her-foot".'

'Oh mother,' said the magician, 'waste not your breath in wheedling supplications. All the fees in Inzwinyani will not persuade me to slay a royal wife.'

'Now, listen, Oh wise one, who knows all that stands before your eyes, and all that is happening behind your back. Listen! Perhaps you are not disposed to remove this mote from my eye; but you could do me a lesser favour for the self-same fee. Go to the hut of this lick-spittle; offer her your sympathies; pretend to be the sharer of her sorrow, but, in the guise of friendship, give her some poisoned cordial that will sterilise her so that her breasts may never feed a child. Let her suffer every conceivable pain, but never the pain of parturition; let every joy be hers except the supreme joy of child-bearing.

'You know, Oh wise man from the land of the rising sun, the fame of your wizardry is great, but not as great as Mzilikazi's power. Your charmed decoctions can extinguish by the hundred the lives of men like spears on the battlefield; but they are not strong enough to assuage my husband's wrath. Bear in mind that at this moment I hold your life in the hollow of my hands. Offend me, then I will say the word, and you will not leave this city alive.

'Now listen a second time. It is but a trifling matter I ask of you; deny me that, and all the charms and spells in your medicine-bag will not save your head from the terrible wrath of this harem. Will you make her barren? Yes, or no?'

'Your orders are confusing, Oh daughter-in-law of the Great Matshobana. They are uttered in two voices as from the cleft tongue of an alligator. One tongue says to me: "Rob the King of the brightest jewel in his harem." The other warns me of the fate in store for anyone who attempts to wrong his majesty – as much as to say, "don't do it." Did such conflicting orders ever issue from the same mouth in such rapid succession? Indeed, I wish I could kill her, and appease your wrath, but for the reason given in a part of your request. I will, however, injure her as you desire, but cannot persuade myself to take the life of Umnandi. Were she but a concubine, and not a Queen, in this harem, I would not dare to kill her.'

'Now you will insult me by calling her a queen in my presence and hearing – now lest the worst comes to the worst, I will order you to her at once.'

Nomenti led the doctor out into the dark and cloudy night and, pointing to the farther end of the enclosure, she said, 'Do you see that light? That is the opening to her hut. Speed forth and offer her your sympathy.'

She stood and watched the figure of the doctor receding in the darkness, until he approached and was admitted into Umnandi's hut. Thereupon Nomenti returned to her own, called a principal attendant named Umpitimpiti, and poured into his ears some wicked and untrue statements reflecting on the faithfulness of Umnandi who, she said, was at that moment busy making love to a strange wizard against the latter's wish, and charged the attendant forthwith to apprise the king.

Now Umnandi was a great favourite in the city. She was a mother to all the attendants at court, for whenever there was not enough meat to go round she would always provide for others at her own expense. If one evening an old woman ran short of water or firewood, she never appealed to her in vain. If the daughters of a light-footed mother were heavy-heeled one day, and pounded not enough corn for the cooking-pot, and she wanted a little to adjust the deficiency, Umnandi always had some to spare. These beneficiaries of her bounty literally worshipped her; hence the bitter jealousy of her co-wives, who, constantly scheming to bring about her fall, vied with one another in attempting to encompass her ruin. The menials in the harem resented this persecution to which she was perpetually subjected, and Nomenti exploited her rival's popularity among the maids and servants to get rid of her. Having despatched the attendant to the king, Nomenti called a maid to whom she said:

'Nomsindo, my daughter, I have great news for you; the most important since our tribe was forced to flee from Shaka's tyranny.'

'Oh Mother,' said the maid, 'do not repeat it for I know already. The doctors are unanimous that the days of our city are numbered.'

'Nonsense,' said Nomenti in disgust, 'don't speak to me of witches' yarns. I take my orders from the lips of the king.'

'Oh yes, mother, the king knows it too. He said that the army that went to Kunana years ago exceeded his orders. Instead of avenging Bhoya's death they left the guilty murderers alone and slew the innocent tribesmen and the women, consequently the fate prophesied for us is not unlike that of the Barolong. The magicians have divined that the spirits of the dead Barolong are coming back, some bleached, some reddened in the face through anger – thirsting for Matabele blood. Oh mother, what will become of me should I be called upon to die the violent death of a Morolong woman? It is too terrible. I'd rather be speared by a soldier than by angry spirits.'

'Nomsindo, you are mad, raving mad! But remember that you have not come here of your own accord. I called you here to listen to me, after which you may jabber about witches and Barolong until your tongue be stiff. Listen, I have just this minute seen the king. Since I became the queen of the Matabele,' she lied further, 'I have never seen my lord so furious?

'You don't say so, mother,' replied Nomsindo, 'and the cause?'

'I will tell you. The king was on his way to Umnandi's hut, and hearing whispers and clandestine words from within – one voice being distinctly masculine, however much disguised – he approached with caution and found, what do you think? That childless harlot, whom you would serve as a queen while she is not worthy to look you in the face, leaning on the bosom of a strange man, words of affection flowing from her guilty lips into his equally guilty ears, though the poor man did his best to shun her advances. She lavished upon the stranger such caresses and embraces as I would never extend to my twin brother who sucked the same breast as myself, my caresses now being the prerogative of my lord, the king.'

'Oh horror of horrors, mother! Who was the beastly witch?'

'The stranger who reached this city three days back. Can you conceive of anyone so low in breeding, so wanting in all sense of fitness, as to be willing to raise a grimy, snuffy mixer of medicines to the pedestal of Mzilikazi, ruler of earth and skies?

'Very soon the young men will be with the king; already they are sharpening their spears at his command to rid society of that misnamed idol of yours, and no victim of Mzilikazi's wrath will better deserve her fate.'

Nomsindo did not wait to hear the end of the story; she darted off immediately to warn Umnandi. Filled with terror, she thought of nothing but to render some last service to so noble a benefactress in the few hours remaining before her looming execution. As she approached, she observed in the darkness the new doctor leaving Umnandi's hut and walking in the opposite direction. In fear and trembling she entered the hut with a rush that almost took the owner's breath away; but the cruel climax was to follow the query:

'*Yinindaba* (What's the matter?), Nomsindo; what is chasing you in here?'

'Terror, mother, terror; and oh, why did you do it?'

'Do what?' asked Umnandi in surprise.

'The man – the very man I saw departing hence as I came.'

'What about him?' queried Umnandi again in astonishment.

The girl was struck dumb. Gazing at the beautiful form of Umnandi, she regarded her beaming countenance illumined in the glow of the wood fire on the hearth, and found it inconceivable that the idol of the court should be capable of any kind of infamy. She had seen the doctor depart and, knowing the tremendous jealousy of the other wives, she feared the worst. Horrible visions of what torture would mean to Umnandi distracted her mind and she dropped fainting at the queen's feet.

Suddenly waking to the full meaning of her perilous situation, Umnandi exclaimed, 'But child, I have done nothing, except for the best.'

Nobody, however, heard these words because the girl had swooned.

Chapter Thirteen

Soothsayers and Battles

THE BANGWAKETSE AT Kgwakge – eighty miles to the west of Inzwinyani – were near relatives of the Barolong. And it was natural that their hearts were still aflame with memories of the massacre of Tauana's people and sacking of their city. These remembrances were constantly sharpened by hints and rumours that floated across now and again from Mzilikazi's headquarters. The Matabele were evidently meditating a raid of a similar nature upon the Bangwaketse.

Alarmed at this prospect, Chief Makabe, wise in his generation, moved with the whole of his tribe into the Kalahari desert. His timely tactics saved the situation for, shortly afterwards, Mzilikazi's army swooped down upon the evacuated city like so many vultures thirsting for Ngwaketse blood.

Finding the place empty, and disappointed of their prey, the Matabele lost no time in tracking the fugitive tribe. Over the vales and woods of Selokolela and Sefereleleng they traced them; they followed them deep into the unknown forests of Sekoma and Khakea – through sunburnt desert dales that are as waterless as they are sandy. The soldiers were maddened by fatigue and the heat of the thirstland, for marching and skipping through the forests, and looking for water or for stones, they saw nothing but trees, trees and sand, sand, sand all the time. And, after long and maniacally forced marches through the desert they came upon the rearguard of Makabe's people who, moving in their own hinterland and familiar hunting ground, had local means of averting the thirst.

Hunger, fatigue and the broiling sun had in the meanwhile devitalised the Matabele hordes and rendered them harmless; so that when at length they came in contact with the Bangwaketse they were too exhausted to fight; and, instead of attacking, they asked their enemy for water. Far from granting their request the Bangwaketse fell upon their enfeebled pursuers with deadly effect. After killing many of their ranks, they put the remainder to flight, and celebrated a grand victory. Hundreds of Matabele bodies lay round the battlefield as evidence that Makabe had avenged the blood of his cousins the Barolong.

It was a bad day for the *majahas* who had hitherto known no reverses. Many of the survivors never left the forest as they escaped the Bangwaketse spears only to succumb to hunger and thirst on their way back; and when the news reached Inzwinyani it created a painful sensation. The tidings were brought by a swift runner despatched by Muti, the induna in charge of the western outposts. King Mzilikazi was furious. He called his magicians together and ordered them to divine the cause of this unusual calamity.

The bonethrowers having gone through their incantations, their spokesman said: 'The shadow of the massacre of Kunana had never really left our nation. Many of the fleeing Barolongs had picked the sand from the footprints of our soldiers who destroyed their city years ago; they are constantly

mixing medicines with this sand and the evil influence upon
the Matabele would last as long as they can remember that
massacre. The power of the Barolong spell is spending itself in
Inzwinyani, and the only remedy suggested by the bones is that
the King should move the nation to a far and unknown region
beyond the influence of the Barolong charms. Unless this
advice be followed, declare the bones, all the Matabele must die
and their sheep and cattle with them.'

On hearing this prediction Mzilikazi called thirty more
of the most noted witch-doctors from among his nation and
ordered them to invent a more powerful charm and subdue
the fatal spell. The witch-doctors implored the King to move
the nation north, in terms of the opinion of the bone-throwers,
for there their efforts would be more efficacious. Mzilikazi,
becoming very angry, replied that that would be equal to flight.
A Zulu, he said, had never turned his back upon trouble,
and he was not going to establish the degrading precedent;
therefore, unless the effects of the evil spell were subdued, the
witch-doctors would be put to death. He gave them three days
to find an antidote.

Turning to Muti's messenger, he who had been the bearer
of the evil tidings, the king said: 'Tell Muti that at the end of
three days he must deliver before me every survivor of the army
of cowards that disgraced me in the desert. I wish to see them
every one, and if any of them fail to appear, Muti shall answer
for the absentees at the peril of his neck.'

At the end of three days Mzilikazi was up at an early hour.
His *inkundla* was full of warriors. Six Bechuana who had
come in overnight, bringing tribute from the loyal Bakwena –
another Bechuana tribe which venerates the crocodile – were
introduced to the king by one of the indunas.

They found King Mzilikazi seated on his wooden throne,
which was covered with a tiger-skin. He was warming himself

near the blazing fire that subdued the biting cold of the sharp frosty morning. Facing the same fire in a semi-circle there sat to his right and to his left some of his indunas, awaiting the king's pleasure. The large open space was crowded by a mass of the tribe inside a ring of warriors, one end of the enclosure being filled by survivors from the misadventure of the desert, who now awaited the word that would seal their doom.

As was customary with most Native potentates of those days, the king seemed hardly interested in the things going on before him. When the six 'crocs' and their tribute were announced, he seemed as callously indifferent to their mission as though the tributes were intended for another; in fact, he proceeded to give orders and receive reports from the fops and flunkeys who shouted his praises and flitted to and fro, as though instinctively interpreting his silent and ruthless commands.

The six Bakwena gave various interpretations to this attitude. One thing they failed to read from the king's demeanour was any evidence of satisfaction at seeing them there. They shivered as they recollected the recent and ignominious defeat suffered by his warriors at the hands of another Bechuana tribe; how foolish they thought it was of their Chief Sechele to send them to the Matabele capital after such an event. One of the Bechuana trembled as he already anticipated visions of the six of them being eviscerated at the place of slaughter, while another imagined himself incapacitated by the simultaneous stabbing of one hundred Matabele spears. These fears were not allayed by the whispered murmurings they overheard among some of the tribesmen sitting round. These were to the effect that, that day was set apart for the killing of the survivors of the desert disaster – and possibly to be followed by the execution of thirty magicians unless their medicines proved strong enough to allay the king's displeasure.

All of a sudden, something fresh arrested the attention of the assemblage and likewise ruffled the meditations of the six Bakwena. This was the appearance of two young men who were ushered to the front by a dignified induna wearing a black ring on his head. They saluted 'The Lion' and fell before the feet of the king. Immediately there arose a volume of incantations by the large number of *mbongis* who sang the praises of the 'Great One'. Then one of the messengers reported:

'Yesterday, Oh King, while the flocks were grazing on the hillside and the Matabele boys were minding their cattle from the base, three red devils appeared as if from the skies and perched on the side of a hillock overlooking our cattle station. Each time a Matabele looked up to them there was a deafening crack, a cloud of smoke, and then a Matabele would reel over and die, bleeding from a mysterious hole in his body. One after the other they fell, for on the part of the strange devils on the hilltop, every pop projected a bullet, and every bullet had a billet, the billet in each case being the body of a helpless Matabele herd boy. There was no retaliation with these goblins for they are far – they do not come near to effect their mischief. They do it at a very safe distance. Fearing extermination the Matabele shepherds are now moving their outposts nearer home.'

A little while before this, Mzilikazi had sent one induna to ask Umnandi, his wife, for a striped squirrel-skin wallet which he had handed her the previous day for safekeeping. And just at this moment the man returned and reported to the king the disquieting news that Queen Umnandi had not been seen since the previous night. Several members of the household had been out on the search all morning but could find no trace of her. The consternation of the king upset the entire proceedings for this was the first news the king had had of Umnandi's flight.

Yet another group of men entered the ring and begged an

urgent interview with the now perplexed king. This being granted, Umzungu, the spokesman of the interviewers, expressed himself in the following terms:

'Silence, silence, warriors of the Matabele, guardians of the safety of the Great One, he who is Terror of the breadth of the world, and all that dwell within it. Silence! Listen. The world is in a state of turmoil and it sadly wants mending. We are surrounded by witches of a reckless type. Our ancestors have never known their kind. They will not scruple to exterminate our nation and obliterate all trace of us, if only their skins remain intact. If they could but retain their cattle, could plough, go hunting, eat meat, and marry the prettiest daughters of Matshobana to brew beer for them, they care naught what happens to the greatness of Mzilikazi or the rest of us. Hence we find our soldiers suffering disaster in the battlefield, our cattle vanishing and our young men dying by the smoke of spirits within full view of their helpless mothers and sisters. The country reeks with sorcery, people drop dead all round us and we know not how to help them. Poisons, sorcery, witchcraft! Have not the nostrils of the indunas smelt the sorcery with which the air is fouled? There is one such sorcerer I regret to say, Oh king, in my own family. Yesterday we were obliged to call in the aid of two magicians and, without a moment's hesitation, they smelt out my younger brother – Ngub'entsha (New Cloak) – as the cause of all the pestilence. The charm of the smellers-out is amply corroborated by our own observations, for I can assure the Great Hero, and you my chiefs, indunas and warriors, that since my father's death – I am certain he killed him – this upstart has entirely forgotten himself. He looks down upon his elders. I have heard him say with his own lips that he will not go to war to please anyone – no, not even the thing you call a king – (*sensation*) – he ignores his relatives (*cries of Where is he? Why have you not brought him here?*) – and as for me, his eldest brother, he regards me as nothing but the dirt beneath his feet.'

Now these reports both vexed and perplexed King Mzilikazi, who gave a sign for the speaker to cease his harangue. He called the thirty wizards into his presence, and in a thunderlike voice asked what they had done to counteract these dire fatalities. As the disconcerted wizards could offer no satisfactory explanation, orders were given for the immediate execution of them all.

'Remove these false sorcerers,' shouted Mzilikazi to one of the army leaders, 'along with the successful cowards who returned from the desert yesterday and brought a cowardly report of their defeat and flight. I will have neither cowards nor liars in my city,' he said, 'even if the liars pretended to live on smelling trouble. Take them far down to the ravine and leave them there.'

A scene of the wildest commotion followed this utterance and the populace at once prepared themselves to witness an orgy of killing. When the condemned wretches were driven to the shambles, Mzilikazi rose from his court to enquire personally into the mysterious disappearance of Umnandi. 'What had happened', he wondered, 'to his beautiful queen, the one woman in his harem, or out of it for that matter, whom he adored. What could be her reason for leaving her house; had the witches been at her?'

A little later, the tumult of the surging crowd with the frightened faces of the condemned army, were leaving the outskirts of the town. Some of the condemned men were absolutely listless, while others laughed at the faintheartedness of the witches (who by their machinations have so often brought down sentences of death upon others), now that they were about to be dosed with their own medicines. Two of the condemned soldiers thought it was a disgrace to be killed at the same time as such pigeon-hearted poltroons.

'Oh Fates!' exclaimed a third warrior, 'is this all the reward we get for serving Mzilikazi? After all the devotion we have shown this nation and its country, marching and fighting without water and without food, the king condemns our spirits to share the life beyond with such things as these! Yet no man knows better than our hero king that if we had had water, even without the food, we would have given an excellent account of ourselves and brought back a different tale from that bewitched desert enterprise.'

Yet said another, 'What cowards these witches are! Look, look, look how they quake! The ease with which they ordered the execution of pretty-faced girls made me think they were not afraid to die. What a pity they have only one life like other people; I would like to see witches die several times over in return for the many lives they have sent to the shambles.'

Just at this moment Gubuza appeared in view.

This is the doughty leader of the armies whose acquaintance we made at the great celebration early in the story; the marching throng stopped mechanically the moment he was recognised.

'What now?' enquired Gubuza. The awful judgment being explained to him, he gave vent to his consternation in the following terms:

'Mzilikazi knows not what he does. I am told that he has lost his pet; his favourite wife, Umnandi, vanished during the night, and he is not responsible for his actions.'

A thrill of terror and astonishment ran through the crowd of warriors as the whisper passed from mouth to mouth. 'Umnandi vanished during the night. Can her mystery have something to do with these death sentences on the doctors and ourselves?' queried one soldier.

But Gubuza went on: 'Go and slaughter the witches

according to the King's word, but spare me the soldiers, I need them, every one. Wild devils are infesting our country and I cannot afford the spilling of a single warrior's blood except in defence of the nation. Kill the witches and go back and repeat to the "Great One" that Gubuza took the soldiers alive to battle.'

Shouts of approbation followed this command, and hope sprang afresh in the soldiers' breasts. '*Inkos! Ndab'ezita!*' they cried. 'Take us to battle straightaway, and see how we shall fight with shields and spears and not with poisons as these hacks do.'

Now Gubuza was the general who commanded all the armies of Mzilikazi. He was as popular among the nation as his prowess was renowned among their enemies; so that even the king could not ignore his word. Mzilikazi therefore promptly countermanded the sentence of death upon the defeated warriors.

There was a sense of general relief all through the town and country when news of the terrible judgment was succeeded by the unexpected reprieve of the soldiers. Among anxious families who had made the welkin ring with their wails and lamentations, the fame of Gubuza went up by a hundred per cent and he was renamed Gubuza-Mkomozi (the Comforter).

There were but few to deplore the loss of the thirty witches. It was contended that members of that craft were having things too much their own way. It was also hoped that surviving magicians would henceforth bear in mind that they too were subject to the law and might not deal out death, as they pleased, to the innocent of the nation.

Chapter Fourteen

Light and Shade of Memorable Days

AT THE BAROLONG settlement of Thaba Nchu the day broke as if reluctantly, over a thick mist, which, mingling with the early morning smoke from thousands of hearths in the huts and courtyards, created a light fog. But this was soon dispersed when the African sun rose over the north-eastern horizon. The top of Thaba Nchu hill, visible for scores of miles in each direction, dwarfed every hillock and kopje round about as though standing sentinel over the surrounding landscape. It had been snowing the previous night, and the picturesque brow of the hill (skirted by a thick black forest round the sides) was enhanced by a clear white cap of snow that covered its peak. But, once the sun had risen, his rays were so powerful that one could scarcely realise the wintry weather or the recent fall of snow.

On this particular morning the Chiefs Moroka and Tauana had announced a big game drive, at which it was intended to count all the guns and other weapons of war in the place. This was a part of the plan for arming the tribe against the dreaded Matabele. The day's exercises, as previously arranged, were preceded by one of the favourite national sports, viz., a long foot-race by the men. The race was made a contest between the tribes of Ra-Tshidi, the subjects of Tauana, and of Seleka, the subjects of Moroka. Chieftains of both sections, mounted on swift Basuto ponies, went out as starters, the meeting point being a kopje, nine miles distant from Thaba Nchu town. Over two hundred young men took part in the race. The prize to be given by the chief of the losing clan was a huge bullock to be slaughtered at a subsequent feast in honour of the winners. In addition, a prize of one heifer was to be awarded to the young man who should carry off the emblem of victory, the switch end of a white ox-tail, and deliver it to one of the waiting chiefs at the goal. The competitors were up and off long before the first streak of dawn, so that they were already on the return journey when the sun rose. A long black train appeared in view and thousands of people, who lined the route to the goal, were waiting to cheer and encourage the leading runners in their final effort. At that distance it could not be seen who the leaders were, only a score of them having yet climbed the ridge. The rest of the train, following the graceful curve of the road towards the top of the incline, moved like a giant serpent nearly half a mile in length.

By the side of the string of runners the starters rode, Tshabadira and Motshegare, chieftains of the respective clans, each urging on his side.

Already the ears of the fleet-footed racers caught the shrill but clear notes of the *ooldoo-ooldoo-oo-oo* of the Barolong girls, and the runners did their very best. The silvery white switch could be seen fluttering in the morning breeze, held aloft by the leading runner who, coming nearer and nearer, was observed to be none other than Ra-Thaga. He was ten yards ahead of the next runner, and it seemed certain that he would carry the switch home; but as they came within four hundred yards of the goal, another man overhauled him and seized the white switch.

Ra-Thaga, still doing his best, was not reluctant to hand over the emblem of victory, for he found that his rival was Mapipi, his fellow clansman. He was running close behind the latter, when, after another hundred and fifty yards, Pheko of the Seleka clan ran level with him. Pheko sped along so fast that within a short time he took over the switch from Mapipi.

The imminent danger of losing the prize and the prospect of forcing his chief to pay incited Ra-Thaga to accelerate his speed and without knowing how he did it he was abreast of Mapipi, and past Pheko – who was still carrying the switch. With careful running and cool judgement he led the race, reached the goal, and received the coveted prize with the congratulations of both chiefs. Pheko, still bearing the emblem, tied for the second place with Mapipi.

The cheers of the spectators rent the air as more and still more of the runners arrived. By that time the winners had already taken up positions among the onlookers and were watching the advance of their own long trail.

In the meantime a faction fight broke out towards the rear between a number of young men of the rival teams. This arose through one of the Seleka tribe declaring that Ra-Thaga had not won the race for the Ra-Tshidi; for while reaching the winning-post at the head of the competitors, he had failed to take over the switch from Pheko and hand it to the chief as the winner ought to have done. Therefore, he argued, the race was between Pheko of the Seleka, the bell-bearer, and Mapipi of the Ra-Tshidi who carried no switch. But Pheko being abreast of him should be counted equally as a winner. In the speaker's opinion, no side had won and the race was a draw. This argument was resented by the winning side, who maintained that Ra-Thaga, their man, had outstripped the alleged winners by six paces.

'But,' shouted the other, 'the emblem was not in his hand.' 'Hang the emblem, hang the hand!' cried a chorus on the other side. 'They did not run on the emblem, nor on their hands; they ran on their feet.'

Arguments grew heated and changed into abuse, till one of the disputants getting infuriated, picked up a stone and struck an opponent in the face, causing it to bleed. The bleeding youth was led to the presence of the chiefs, who shook their heads with indignation.

The Chief Moroka in a serious voice asked, 'What son of a menial had perpetrated this outrage?' A headman pleaded that the wound was inflicted accidentally in the excitement of the moment by some rowdy youths after the race, and moreover, added the advocate, the wound was not very serious.

'Deliver the offender to me,' commanded the great Moroka; 'let me teach him, and others through him, that an assault is a crime according to Barolong law, even though the victim did not suffer any permanent injury. See how he bleeds. We abhor human blood. Assault not serious! Let it be known that we Barolong abominate human blood in any form. Do you people take my court for a den of beasts?'

'Mercy, Oh Chief!' shouted the crowd. '*A e ne modiga* (Mercy on him)!'

'Now', said the chief, 'listen to my mercy. Fetch me two bullocks from his father's herd and slaughter them for the entertainment of the youths who ran in the race this morning. In future, anyone spoiling for human blood may go and join the Matabele, and there slake his thirst for blood. They are the only nation I know who delight in bloody accidents. Assault not serious! Let me hear no more of such bloody sports.'

'Behold, here comes a stranger. A Boer; he looks tired and frightened. Make way for him, give him a stool. Be seated, stranger. Who are you?'

'I am Schalk von Merrel, Captain Marock', replied the newcomer, 'a messenger from Sarel Cilliers who trekked through here last year, but I am dying for a drink of water.'

'Bring him a gourd of cool water', said Chief Moroka. 'Well, Schalk, I and my councillors are pleased to see you. What is Sarel's pleasure?'

The seething crowd surged forward to listen to the startling story told by the young Boer after he had quenched his thirst. Not being fluent in the Barolong tongue, he was imperfectly understood; yet his news sent a shocking thrill through the heart of every listener.

After the Boer had spoken, Chief Moroka asked dejectedly, 'You say all your oxen are captured by the Matabele! In spite of all the guns you had?'

'Yes, Captain,' replied the young Boer.

'Did not Sarel and his Boers smoke at them with those wooden poles with the spit-fire noses?' asked the second chief. 'And they rushed on all the same through the fire and captured your stock? Had the Matabele firearms too? Then how did they manage it?'

'I hope', said the third chief, 'they captured none of your smoking sticks?'

'They did seize two or three rifles but they cannot very well use them, as I understand they have neither powder nor lead,' replied Schalk.

'His news is very disturbing,' said the fourth chief.

'King Moshoeshoe should be told of this,' said another. 'An overwhelming force must be organised and armed against the common foe. Death seems to have no effect upon this ferocious people. Truly, their warriors, like cats, have several lives.'

'Well said,' concluded Chief Moroka. 'Dismiss the crowd. Supply the Boer with some refreshments. I will take council with my headmen immediately. Let there be rain!' And shouts of '*Poolah!*' followed the remarks.

The people had scarcely begun to disperse when three men came forward through the throng.

Unlike the rest of the crowd massed in the *khotla* (assembly place), these three apparently had not come from their homes as they carried bundles on their shoulders like ordinary travellers. Chief Moroka recognised the leading man and returning his salute said, 'You are Rantsau, son of Thibedi, are you not? A much-travelled young man of considerable experience at home and abroad? You understand the language of the Basuto, and of the Koranna and the Hlubis, and the Boers down in Graaff-Reinet, don't you, Rantsau? Of course I know you. Have you not learnt to speak the language of the fish-eaters [English] yet? You must speak Setebele too? I would like to send you as a spy to Inzwinyani before we proceed to attack Mzilikazi. You will go? I know you will when I command you.

'Well, Rantsau, where have you been to this time? I have not seen you for a long while. Give us your news.'

Rantsau then addressed the chiefs. 'My lord and chiefs, I have no news, except that the Boers who passed through here several moons back, have suffered a catastrophe. They have been wiped out by the Matabele, and I am afraid that not one of them has survived to tell the story.'

'But,' said Chief Moroka, 'here is a Boer who says the others are still alive. He left them the day before yesterday.'

'Then,' said Rantsau amid sensation, 'he must have come from another party, not from Sarel Cilliers's army. No, my lord.' 'But he is from Sarel Cilliers's army,' said the chief. 'Sarel himself sent him here to me. Anyway, Rantsau, let us have your version.'

'The three of us were returning from Bapediland near the Vaal River,' proceeded Rantsau. 'When we reached the forest beyond the Namagadi River, we noticed two naked men emerging from the bush and looking in the opposite direction. They withdrew directly they saw us. I should explain, my lord and chiefs, that by this time we were not far from the place where on our forward journey, two moons back, we found Cilliers's army encamped. After passing this bush we saw another man spying at us from a treetop. He scrambled down from the tree directly upon observing that we were looking at him. We then hastened to put as much space as possible between us and that bush.

'Later we came across two Boers whom we warned that the Matabele were going to ambush them. Sometime after we heard the sound of many guns some distance off. The guns rattled and never ceased for a long, long time. As a matter of fact I have never heard such a din before. Judging by the incessant noise we came to the conclusion that the Matabele must have been massacred. Later three mounted Boers came into view hurrying forward a large flock of sheep. We climbed a ridge to give the alarm to the Boers, when we saw another mounted Boer galloping towards the three, shouting at the top of his voice "Mieklaas, Mieklaas! [Nicholas], come back, we are surrounded by the Kaffirs! Never mind the sheep, Mieklaas, return to the waggons." At this the Boers left the sheep and all rode away very fast. Late in the afternoon, a group of Matabele appeared. They rounded up the sheep and drove them off.

'Reaching the peak of the nearest hill, and looking about we saw huge clouds of dust and numbers of Matabele in the distance driving the herds and the flocks of the Boers and not a sign of the owners anywhere; no, not even the sound of a gun, so we came to the conclusion that the Boers had been surrounded and massacred, like our own people had been years ago at Kunana.'

No one listened more attentively to Rantsau's story than Ra-Thaga. He had always been nursing a bloody revenge in his heart, and the preparations for arming the tribe against the Matabele had been proceeding too slowly for his liking. He desired retribution before he died, and he was fearful lest some natural or unnatural cause should shorten his life before he greeted that glad day. But the news of this latest success of the Matabele against the well-armed Boers conveyed to his mind the staggering impression that this ferocious nation was superhuman, and that nothing in this world would ever punish them. Could it be a fact, he asked himself, that there is absolutely no power to exact judgment in return for all the wrongs and cruelties of the past, and for the loss of so many of his relatives who died guiltless deaths at the hands of the Matabele? The idea was revolting. Amid such thoughts Ra-Thaga scarcely heard the Chief Moroka thanking Rantsau for his news, unpleasant as it was.

At sunset the crowd began to collect at the chief's court to hear the council's decision on Sarel's message. It was on the night of the full moon, and the powerful rays of the big round aerial ball, mingling with the waning light of the passing day, seemed to dispel the settling dusk, and to prolong the twilight; and so it was not at all dark as old men and young men collected and sat down to hear the ominous decision. Many of the men had already taken up their places in the *khotla*.

The chiefs were a long time coming, and little knots of debaters automatically grouped themselves here and there. Soon there was a low but insistent hubbub in the centre of the open air court, for the discussions, carried on in low tones, were decidedly animated.

Some were for letting the Boers stew in their own juice, as the Barolongs had perforce to do years before; others were for combining with the Boers against the Matabele; some again were for letting the enemy well alone as long as he remained on the far side of the Vaal River – that river of many vicissitudes and grim histories – yet many believed that a scrap with the Matabele with the aid of the Boers would give each one an opportunity of avenging the blood of his relations before he himself joined his forefathers. Such were the conflicting views that found expression among the waiting throng. One grizzly old man with small jaws and very short teeth, touching his shins, said, 'Oh, that I could infuse some youth into these old bones and raise my shield! I would march against the vampires with spear in hand. Then Mzilikazi would know that among the Barolong there was a man named Nakedi just as the pack of lions at Mafika-Kgochoana knew me to their cost.'

One man raised a laugh among the serious groups. 'What a truthful thing is a proverb,' he said. 'According to an old saying "Lightning fire is quenched by other fire." It seems a good idea then to fight the Matabele with the help of the women, for they always kill women in their attacks. If Sarel Cilliers's women had not helped the Boers, they would not have defied Gubuza's army and Schalk would not be here to tell the tale.'

The chiefs arrived almost simultaneously and took their seats without giving any indication of what they had decided to do. There was some little delay after this. Every man bent forward expectant how the question, 'War, to be, or not to be', was to be decided. This delay severely taxed the patience of the waiting crowd, but it was unavoidable. One chief, representing a powerful clan, had not yet appeared and an announcement so momentous could not be made before his arrival.

Not until Chief Moroka had twice asked, 'Where is Morahti?' did he arrive and take his seat to the right of the presiding chief, Morahti (for that was the name of the latecomer) was not exactly of royal blood. He owed his eminent position to a rather liberal endowment of this world's goods, as the gods are partial in their bestowal of fortune; secondly, his position was due to his marriage to a princess of the first royal house.

Morahti sat down with an air of pomp as though proud of the fact that business did not proceed without him. One of his equals, in sarcastic allusion to the lateness of his appearance, indulged in a little banter at his expense. The object of the squib, turning round to his railer, said, 'How unbecoming to your dignity these frivolous remarks are on a serious occasion like this.'

'Quite so,' put in a third chief sitting just two chairs away. 'They are almost as frivolous as the flippancy of my cousin Morahti, who must needs keep the chiefs and people waiting while he stays indoors to watch how gracefully my cousin Neo – the latecomer's wife – puts on her anklets.'

'It must indeed be true,' retorted Chief Morahti, 'in the words of a Barolong proverb, that "kings sometimes beget dross" or else I could not account for a lineal descendant of the great Tau, attributing to me such weakness as that of regulating my actions by Neo's anklets.'

The chief was about to call the assembly to order when, in the waning light of the evening, through the twilight and the bright moonlight, a horseman was observed riding into the town. He was recognised as another Boer urging along his exhausted and hungry mare by repeatedly striking his heels against her flanks. One chief said, 'I hope that he is not coming to report that the Matabele returned to the attack and killed every Boer.'

'Nor that Gubuza is following hard on his heels,' remarked another.

They were soon set at rest, however, for the new arrival, a young Boer named De Villiers, came in the wake of Schalk to support his appeal for relief. The Boers, said De Villiers, were anxious to hear that the chief would come to their rescue before the enemy returned to surround them.

The meeting was then called to order.

Chief Moroka was not as great an orator as most of the Native chiefs but he excelled in philosophy. In that respect his witty expressions and dry humour were equal to those of Moshoeshoe, the Basuto king. He spoke in a staccato voice, with short sentences and a stop after each, as though composing the next sentence. His speeches abounded in allegories and proverbial sayings, some traditional and others original. His own maxims had about them the spice of originality which always provided his auditors with much food for thought.

He knew he had no right to join hostilities without the consent of the tribesmen, yet he delivered a speech which, while leaving no doubt as to his personal sympathies, left the main decision in the hands of the assembly. When he called for silence the stillness was like unto that of a deserted place. The crowd pressed forward and eagerly hung on to every word, but it is to be regretted that much of the charm is lost in translation.

'Men of the Barolong,' he said aloud, 'listen! Old people say that "the foolish dam suckles her young while lying down, but the wise dam suckles hers standing up and looking out for approaching hunters." This day has brought with it the most appalling news since we pitched our abode on the banks of the Sepane River. For the first time since we experienced their depredations, the marauders of Mzilikazi have forded the Lekwa (Vaal River). They are now prowling on our side of that deep stream.

'You all remember the visit of Sarel Cilliers, the Boer chief, who called on us last year and enquired the way. You saw his mounted followers and their flowing beards, you saw his women and children in their hooded waggons, like a moving city travelling northward, where they said they were proceeding in search of God. Well, they have found the Matabele instead.

'Crossing the Kikwe and the Kikwane, they forded the Namagadi River, and then camped at a place which we must now call Battlehill. Here they remained in their wheeled houses and peacefully fed their children on the meat of the springbok, the wildebeest and other antelopes of our plains. Then, while the Boers were quietly drying their venison in the sun, Mzilikazi, without a word of warning, sent his big man Gubuza with an army which cast a thousand spears into Sarel's city. A desperate fight must have taken place, for the Boer women left their boiling meat-pots on the fires and stood at the backs of their men to reload the guns as fast as the long beards could fire them.

'As the result of the fight, the attackers were driven off; but Gubuza, on retiring, looted every beast in the possession of our white friends. Now they are anxious to remove their families but have no draft animals left to pull their waggons. These young men have come to tell us that "the ox is found" (There is a state of war). Now I wish to know from you whether help shall be forthcoming and, if so, how quickly?

'Personally I think that, if we must perish, it were better to die fighting (for then our women could flee into Basutoland) than to wait until Gubuza's impis are in our very midst.

'Those of you whose mothers and grandmothers have perished at the point of the Matabele assegai must realise the danger to which Sarel's women are exposed if they remain any longer at Battlehill, for "no jackal-skin could possibly be sewn to a Matabele pelt."

'Gubuza, fortunately, has not yet seized my cattle and I have enough bullocks to pull Sarel's own waggon and bring his wife back. Will anyone else's oxen go up with mine, or must we leave the other wives stranded on the plains? What say the hammersmiths to the Boer appeal? What say the sons of Mokgopa-a-Mazeppa whose tribal totem is the iron? What answer is forthcoming from the descendants of Moroa-Phogole? Will these young Boers return to their parents smiling, or must they go back and say, "the Barolong are afraid; their chief alone will help us!" What say the sons of Kwena and the offspring of Mhurutshe who venerate the baboon?'

By this time the speech had stirred a feeling in the centre of the crowd. The commotion was made audible by the mention of the several sections of the tribe; and the various clansmen loudly responded, 'We are with thee, Oh Chief.' 'We will be there at thy command.'

A hurricane of enthusiasm arose from the throng as first one and then another of the men cried, 'My oxen will be ready at daybreak, Oh Chief.' 'I am going off to fetch mine from the cattle station.' 'Mine are available, they are pasturing just outside the city.' 'No woman brave enough to load a gun to kill the Matabele shall perish while I have a pack-ox.' 'The day will soon be breaking, let us wait no longer!'

The spontaneity of these offers showed that there would be more than enough oxen to go round. So the chief said: 'I knew the Barolong were no cowards. Our friends shall know that it is not wrought iron we venerate but that our tribal badge is a hammer made of tempered metal. Let the Boers come here and camp at the foot of the Black Mountain. Here Sarel and I will tarry.'

Chapter Fifteen

With the Boers at Moroka's Hoek

DURING THE BOERS' sojourn at Thaba Nchu, there sprang up a lively friendship between De Villiers, the young Boer, and Ra-Thaga. The two were constantly together, at the Boer settlement, at Moroka's Hoek, and at the Barolong town of Thaba Nchu proper. They made up their minds to learn each other's language, so De Villiers taught Ra-Thaga how to speak the *taal* and Ra-Thaga taught the Boer the Barolong speech. They were both very diligent and persevering and, having ample opportunities for practice, they both made very good progress. There was one special bond of fellow-feeling between them, namely, their mutual aversion to the Matabele.

Ra-Thaga could never forgive the sacking of Kunana, nor De Villiers the loss of his cattle and those of his relatives. His Boer pride was repeatedly hurt when he recollected how badly they had been worsted by the wild folk whom his people called 'nude kaffirs'. He thought likewise of his particular cow,

Driekol, which yielded abundant supplies of milk. When he remembered that enemy children were being fed on the milk of his cows, while his own brothers and sisters lived partly on Barolong charity, the soothing words of his mother could scarcely allay his wrath. Sometimes he would burst out in her presence saying, 'Oh that our cattle were captured by friendly Hottentots, or reasonable Natives such as the Barolong, instead of those wild savages!'

Whenever he confided his grief to Ra-Thaga the effect was only to fan the glowing embers of revenge that were burning in his breast.

Then Ra-Thaga would exclaim: 'Whenever I visit the homes of other men and see the beautiful dishes that their mothers-in-law prepare and send over to them, and find no one near my dwelling to mind the babies when Mhudi goes a-faggoting, I think of her and say, "This faithful child of my mother, so lonely and forlorn, is without help, because without a mother's advice! Shall I ever forgive the Matabele! But for them, my mother-in-law would be alive and active." And when I see a sheepmaster select the fattest wether in his sheep kraal and proudly send it to his mother-in-law, I grieve and wish that she were alive, for then my cattle-fold would hold no kine, my sheep-pen no fat-tailed mutton and my hunting snares would catch no venison too good for her. The plains would feed no game, the silver jackals grow no furs and no eland falling to my musket would have forequarters so fat and tasty but would be all hers.

'Yesterday again I was looking at my poor wife at work, and there was that everlasting gap which only a mother-inlaw can fill; and it was poignantly brought home to me that I have married an orphan, and am thereby orphaned also.'

At times they fell into a discussion and schemed and plotted for means of avenging these wrongs. If their secret maledictions did not affect the Matabele far away, they always seemed to increase their liking for each other.

By this time Ra-Thaga's admiration for the Boers embraced not only De Villiers's family, but other members of the Boer settlement. Almost every time he went up to the Hoek he returned to his house with tales of fresh virtues he had discovered among the Boers. Their unerring shooting, their splendid horsemanship, the dexterity of Boer women with the needle; the beautiful aroma of the food they cooked (possibly due to the fact that their iron pots were always systematically scrubbed and cleaned), and the lustre of their eating utensils.

Ra-Thaga's intense love of the Boers, however, was not shared by his wife, for Mhudi could not understand why they were so hairy, and why they were so pale. But her husband always said, 'Wait until you taste the beautiful food they cook, and you will fall head over heels in love with them all.' She wished she could believe her husband, but somehow she could not master an inexplicable dread that lingered in her mind.

One day Ra-Thaga induced her to accompany him to the Boer settlement and the Hoek. He succeeded in getting De Villiers to speak to his wife the few Rolong words he had taught him in exchange for his own Boer vocabulary. This had a reassuring effect on Mhudi who met at least one Boer who could talk her language. De Villiers and her husband visited other parts of the Boer camp and left her with De Villiers's mother, but they could not understand each other's language. The Boer lady gave her some cookies which were exceedingly tasty, and she made a parcel of them to take to her children; she began to reflect that after all her husband had not exaggerated the virtues of the Boers. It was fortunate for these feelings that she could not understand their language, for some of the Boers who eyed her curiously, exchanged among themselves several remarks about her that were not too complimentary.

De Villiers and Ra-Thaga were away rather long, and Mhudi, as her husband had predicted, really began to 'fall in love with every Boer'. How wrong she had been in her first dislike of her husband's friends! She already began to reproach herself for having doubted the wisdom of her resourceful husband, when something occurred that shook to its foundations her newly found faith in the character of the Boers.

Outside one of the huts close by she observed a grizzly old Boer who started to give a Hottentot maid some thunder and lightning with his tongue. Of course Mhudi could not understand a word; but the harangue sounded positively terrible and its effect upon the maid was unmistakable. She felt that the Hottentot's position was unenviable, but more was to come. An old lady sitting near a fire behind the waggon took sides against the maid. The episode which began rather humorously developed quickly into a tragedy. The old lady pulled a poker out of the fire and beat the half-naked girl with the hot iron. The unfortunate maid screamed, jumped away and writhed with the pain as she tried to escape. A stalwart young Boer caught hold of the screaming girl and brought her back to the old dame, who had now left the fireplace and stood beside a vice near the waggon. The young man pressed the head of the Hottentot girl against the vice; the old lady pulled her left ear between the two irons, then screwed the jaws of the vice tightly upon the poor girl's ear. Mhudi looked at De Villiers's mother but, so far from showing any concern on behalf of the sufferer, she went about her own domestic business as though nothing at all unusual was taking place. The screams of the girl attracted several Dutch men and women who looked as though they enjoyed the sickly sight.

Mhudi's first impulse was to rush to the rescue but, suddenly remembering that every Boer had a gun, she feared that such cruel people might as easily riddle her with a score of bullets, for she was revolted by their callous indifference to the anguish of the unfortunate girl.

At last Ra-Thaga and De Villiers came back and Mhudi appealed to her husband to help the girl. Ra-Thaga explained to De Villiers, and the latter immediately went up to unscrew the vice and the grateful maid, still screaming very loudly, fell at his feet and thanked him.

Mhudi, whose love for the Boers was thus shattered as quickly as it had been formed, retained a strong confidence in the sagacity of her husband who apparently had the sense to make friends with the one humane Boer that there was among the wild men of his tribe. And when they left, she shook the dust of Moroka's Hoek off her feet and vowed never to go there again.

That night Ra-Thaga could scarcely go to sleep. Mhudi pestered him with questions about the Boers and her interrogations continued almost to the small hours of the morning. 'What sort of people are these friends of yours?' she would ask, 'Have not the Boers got a saying like ours, *a e ne modiga?*'

All next day callers were told of the cruel episode of the previous afternoon. Every now and then she would exclaim, '*My husband's friends!* They looked at the girl squirming with pain, with her ear between two irons and they peacefully smoked their pipes like a crowd of people watching a dance. Give me a Matabele rather. He, at any rate, will spear you to death and put an end to your pains. *My husband's friends!*'

After this the Boers occasionally heard themselves referred to as 'Ra-Thaga's friends'. The Barolong women using Mhudi's own words called them 'My husband's friends'. Not knowing the origin of the phrase, the Boers thought that they had made a fresh impression of friendliness among their hospitable black benefactors, and so took it as a compliment.

Now Ra-Thaga, during his numerous visits to the Hoek, had seen several instances of severe flogging of Hottentots, but his mind being always occupied with the subject of his visit, he minded his own business and overlooked these instances. But since his wife had made her caustic observations, he could not help remarking that, compared with the larger population in the Barolong town, the rate of flogging among the small population at the Hoek was disproportionately high. Besides this he remarked that the Boers inflicted corporal punishment by using the birch upon their own children very much like the Barolong; and that, like them, when a Boer child was chastised, someone always shouted pardon, though not as readily as the Barolong did. He noticed further that no Boer ever interceded when a Hottentot was flogged. That in punishing Hottentots the Boers used dangerous weapons, the most familiar being the sjambok made of sea-cow hide; or the buckled end of a belt. Further, he noticed that the number of lashes they applied to their servants was excessive and sometimes appalling. In these cases, the Boer onlookers would gather round and even assist the castigator. So he was obliged to admit the justice of his wife's allegations.

One day Ra-Thaga returned from a long journey far out on the Thaba-Tilodi plains in the direction of Basutoland. The day being hot he felt tired, and as he was to pass near the Boer settlement, he thought he would call on his friend for a piece of ash-cake which he was sure he would get on mentioning his hunger. Outside the camp he observed a number of Hottentots drawing water; among them there were a few Boer children playing round about the spring. Tired and thirsty as he was, he saw a vessel full of cold water and at once proceeded to help himself. He had hardly stopped drinking when the loud cries of a Dutch boy interrupted him. The boy, howling at the top of his voice, was yelling 'the Kaffir, the Kaffir!' Soon a number of Boers were scrambling towards the pool gesticulating so rapidly and loudly that his Boer vocabulary proved useless to him. With the exception of a few abusive terms he could not distinguish much of what they said, but it soon became clear that the loud profanity was meant for him. For a while things looked very ugly, for he had never seen the Boers so angry. As they approached he collected his little bundle, and adjusting his attire was on the point of running when an elderly Boer from the top of a waggon shouted to his infuriated brethren to return and leave the Barolong alone. They did not return, however, before making use of a few more expletives and shaking their threatening fists at the same time.

As Ra-Thaga was a long time revisiting the Hoek, De Villiers called for him a few days later, and assured him that no Morolong could be hurt by the Boers while they enjoyed Barolong hospitality. The cause of the rumpus, he said, was that Boers at their own homes never allow black people to drink out of their vessels. The Boers cannot understand why black people when visited by white men show no scruples. De Villiers added that whenever Ra-Thaga had been served at the Hoek it was always from vessels reserved for the use of Hottentots, and were he not a Morolong he would have paid for his presumptuous action with a lacerated back. After this information, Ra-Thaga's visits to the Hoek became less frequent. Ra-Thaga and De Villiers both agreed not to let Mhudi hear of the latest escapade of 'her husband's friends'.

For some time the chiefs had been planning to send a spying expedition into Matabele territory and Rantsau was selected for the job. As a companion the council suggested Ra-Thaga-a-Notto-a-Motila-a-Dira-a-Sehuba. So the two attended at the awe-inspiring hut of a magician to be thoroughly charmed for the success of their mission. The ceremony being through they started out for the distant north. They were accompanied on the trip by De Villiers and another young Boer, Viljoen by name. Carefully eluding any Matabele scouts that might be wandering about, they travelled by night and hid by day till, after crossing the Vaal River, they eventually reached Mogaliesberg.

Mogale's people are an eastern section of the Bakwena tribe, who instead of the crocodile – the tribal totem of Sechele's Bakwena – venerate the elephant. But they spoke the Rolong tongue with a peculiar accent so beautifully that the spies were not very sure that the quaint accent did not improve the sound of the language. Mogale's people also paid taxes to the Matabele but lived comfortably among their cornfields and cattle-posts, as Mzilikazi only required from them a nominal tribute in recognition of his supremacy.

The Natives hereabout had never seen a white man before, and the hut in which De Villiers and Viljoen lay concealed by day was daily besieged by curious Bakwena. The spies began to fear that the surprise and searching questions of the crowds would eventually reveal their presence to informers who would carry the news to the Matabele and frustrate the object of their mission. Tlou, the headman, was obliged to restrict the callers and permit only those who could be relied on not to say a word about it afterwards. At last Tlou entirely prohibited the visits of the curious; only such men as came on business sometimes managed to catch a glimpse of the Boers.

Still that did not deter the people from coming. Women found all sorts of pretexts for visiting Tlou's village; and in order to be admitted to De Villiers's retreat they came loaded with presents of meat and milk and vegetables; others brought wild fruit and honey, and the hostesses and attendants had a royal time. The women invented ingenious excuses for bringing their children with them. A spry old lady said she had heard that the strangers were fond of sweet-cane, and had brought with her her daughter who carried a bundle of sugar cane; and as she herself was 'half-lame and short-sighted' she had to be led by her grandchild; a son, she said, would be coming later on with a goat and possibly his smaller brother would help him to lead the animal as an offering to the strangers.

Such donors being privileged visitors used to crowd into the enclosure at the back of the hut where the strangers sat and asked them all sorts of curious questions. They were at first very timid, scampering away whenever a Boer would move himself, but growing bolder and bolder they addressed to them first a few simple queries, and were highly amused at De Villiers's peculiar pronunciation of the Native language. They distressed him very much by telling one another that the broken Sechuana he spoke was probably the Boer language. When their shyness wore off, their persistent attentions became to him so disagreeable that De Villiers pleaded to be spared the gentle solicitude of the Bakwena women; but his host and hostesses would not hear of checking them lest they should restrict the almsgiving, so the fair visitors laden with presents continued to pour into the place and to torment De Villiers and Viljoen beyond endurance. They stroked their hair, they asked them to pull off their shoes and they counted their toes. They remarked on the buttons on De Villiers's jacket, and sometimes asked him to unbutton his shirt. Saving him the trouble at other times they personally did the unbuttoning and, baring his chest, they would ask De Villiers to account for the contrast between his pallid chest and ruddy face. This exhibition went on for days while Rantsau and Ra-Thaga, in pursuit of their mission, made long excursions into the territories occupied by Mzilikazi's people before returning to rest with their Boer friends. It used to be a relief to De Villiers when his Native friends returned with news, for then these visits by relays of inquisitive women would mechanically cease.

A month had elapsed since the spies left Thaba Nchu so a Boer party was despatched from Moroka's Hoek to find them. They were strictly enjoined to avoid contact with Matabele outposts, and to turn back the moment they found themselves in their proximity. The search party returned after ten days and reported having actually fired a few shots at some Matabele scouts, but failed to obtain any news of De Villiers and his friends. At home they were told, however, that some travellers who had seen Rantsau had reached Thaba Nchu with news that they were in high spirits and continuing their work. Rantsau, so the intelligence went, regarded the two Boers as valuable assets to the expedition, as the donations given them by Tlou's people might have fed a small army.

The search party looked foolish as they brought no news, but the climax of their incompetence came a few days later when a Basuto chief sent an ultimatum to the effect that the Boer party had killed two of his men and maimed two more who were peacefully hunting on the Vaal River. For this damage Chief Moseme claimed heavy compensation, failing which he would descend on the Boer settlement with an armed force to compensate himself. But thanks to the intercession of Chief Moroka, a satisfactory compromise was effected.

The stay of the Boers at Moroka's Hoek largely influenced the Barolong mode of living. Sarel Cilliers and some of the chiefs were often together quietly discussing the impending reprisals against the common foe; and the following was not the only instance on which he took part in the national trials.

One day the sabbath calm of Thaba Nchu was rudely disturbed by a tremendous scandal between two great families in the town, and unlike other scandals of the kind, there was not one woman only, but there were two concerned in the case.

On the southern end of the town there lived a prominent Ra-Pulana named Noko (Porcupine) and north of the town there was a Mokwena headman named Poe (Bull). Now, if these were common people, the proportions of the scandal might have been limited. But since each of the men had extensive connections in Barolong society, the gossip disclosed wide and distressing ramifications. Noko had stolen the affections of Mrs Poe, a litigious female of a cantankerous disposition, and the farmer's wife, so the gossipers said, had, by way of reprisal, successfully made love to Poe, who was also said to be enamoured of Mrs Noko. The relatives grumbled and bad feeling became pronounced; old men and young people of the respective clans joined in the strife and exchanged harsh words. High expletives from the 'Bull-ring' were let off for the delectation of the inmates of the 'Porcupine-den', and the latter never failed to return the compliments with compound interest. Abuses and imprecations were periodically hurled forward and reciprocated with alacrity. The time came when the children also took a hand in the battle-royal but it was an unequal contest: a dozen of the Poe boys met seven of the Ra-Pulana children and belaboured them mercilessly. Their elders found on the bodies of some of their children enough bruises and other evidence of violent treatment to support in the chief's court a case of 'unwarranted assault'. A huge crowd attended the trial either as witnesses or to take part in the adjudication. And, of course, all the parents attended followed by numbers of their several households. The mother of one big-bellied piccanin, whose face wore distinct evidence of his lion's share of the blows, insisted that she was not going to be satisfied with empty apologies. 'Apologies', she said, 'cannot mend the bruised body of my child. I want the fattest animal out of Poe's flock – a sheep with a very fat tail – as I require the dripping to anoint the wounds of my injured son.'

The whole of Thaba Nchu was agog with excitement, and when the chiefs lined up in all their courtly dignity to arbitrate in the case, they took a grave view of the proceedings. They knew that a Solomonic decision had to be delivered that day; evenhanded justice was expected of them and evenhanded justice they must dispense or there would be donnybrook (uproar) in Thaba Nchu. Each parental party was out for Barolong justice and either side clamoured for it in large quantities.

Naturally the evidence followed the wide ramifications and intricate connections underlying the original scandal until the complexities were laid bare to the very roots. The aggrieved relatives on both sides attributed the whole mischief to the machinations of Mrs Poe, and eventually the drift of the forensic eloquence almost lost sight of the children's fight and centred round the marriage tangle until the case resembled a double action for restitution of conjugal rights. Mrs Noko first appeared to demand the lost love of her spouse, and it seemed that Poe wanted his wife back. In tendering their evidence neither of the supporters of the four persons held back anything that might prove damaging to the other side; each of the parties finished up by renouncing his or her original spouse, with whom they said future family peace was entirely out of the question. There was bad blood between the two men, but as for the two women, they made no effort to conceal their utter contempt for each other.

In such long cases there are no adjournments for refreshments. This case too had lasted from early morning, without intermission, and it was still in progress late in the afternoon, when Sarel Cilliers turned up, accompanied by six other Boers. The Boers dismounted at the assembly place, and were invited to take part in the discussion. Cilliers and his friends had previously attended Barolong trials but were amazed to find so many women taking part in this one. Having outlined the case for their information, Chief Moroka said, 'Now, friend Sarel, the dispute was really between these little children, but the trial has given birth to a much greater case. We have heard all there is to be said on either side. It would save time if we tried the double marriage question straight away, as I do not wish to be troubled by it again. These men have stolen each other's wives; each of the two wives exonerates both men and accuses the other wife of stealing her husband. Our minds are made up about the children's case, and we would now like to hear your views as a stranger on the larger issue.'

'Well, Moroka,' replied Cilliers, 'this is a complicated matter.' 'I should have told you,' interrupted the chief, 'that Poe says (and the woman corroborates) that he has loved Mrs Noko ever since they were children and meant to marry her. He went out elephant hunting fifteen years ago and avers that on his return, he found that Noko had stolen and married his girl with the connivance of her parents, but against her will. And so when he speaks of his rightful wife he means the other man's wife, for he never really conquered his infatuation for her.'

'In that case,' proceeded the Boer, 'we would ask the woman to cling to the husband she is married to, and forget all about her childhood's love. The parties should remain with the spouses they were wedded to before these disputes arose. That would be my award if I were the judge.'

Chief Moroka giving judgment said, 'Now you have all heard diverse views on the marriage tangle before us. You have heard the views of old men; you have heard the views of younger men and the views of women too; you have heard the views of white men. And neither side can complain of having been ignored. As a child I remember being told of a case among the Bangwaketse almost like the present one. It was regarded as an abomination for a case of that sort had never previously presented itself for arbitration. It was heard by the late King Chosa and this was his judgment: he fined the two men five head of cattle each and sentenced the women to be birched with berry-wood twig for their share in the intrigue. He then ordered the wives to return to their original husbands and threatened them with death if they repeated their offence.

'Unfortunately we do not live in Chosa's days,' continued the chief. 'The Barolong of today are more refractory than the Barolong of my grandfather's days. I can see by the faces of these women, especially that little woman over there, with eyes like a yellow snake's, that it would be a crime to sentence her to spend the rest of her days with a man she has ceased to love. Both these women might well poison the two men if we compelled them to go back, and I have no desire to turn potential mothers into witches. Each man loves his stolen wife better than his own, and in my opinion theirs was not a bad exchange. My judgment is: From today, Noko shall take Mrs Poe to wife; and Poe shall have Noko's wife, the woman he says he loves. Each of the two men must pay a fat bullock to satisfy the children in their little case. The women shall go to their new men straight from here, and never trouble each other again. The past must be forgotten and I shall deal severely with anyone who reminds them of its unsavoury details.'

The two women could scarcely hide their satisfaction with what appeared to them the only wise decision. All tongues stopped wagging and they went to their new homes rejoicing. Each shook the dust of the old home from the soles of her feet, and spurned in disgust every relic of her first marriage. The general satisfaction restored the sabbath calm of Thaba Nchu for the two husbands also shared their views. As for the children, whose fight precipitated matters to such a head, they ate so much beef when the fines were paid, that they wished there could be a children's fight every now and again.

Chapter Sixteen

Queen Umnandi's Flight

SAD WAS THE GLOOM over Inzwinyani when the news spread that Umnandi, the brightest star in the social circles of the Matabele and pride of their king, had disappeared without leaving a trace. Only two women and a man (Nomenti, Nomsindo and Umpitimpiti) could throw some light on the mystery; but they did not dare open their lips for fear of being accused of her death. At least the two women knew that she had fled, but they also thought that the king was secretly aware of the cause of her flight. But Umpitimpiti, who had been sent to accuse her before the king, was not acquainted with the manner of her disappearance; and when he saw how genuine was the king's distress he felt it was only natural after he had taken the life of one so dear to him. But the strange thing was that no one seemed to have any evidence of the actual facts. Had any execution taken place, surely, thought he, there should have been some final incident or some last message from Umnandi to her people which could scarcely have been suppressed. Someone must surely have witnessed what happened at the

SOL T. PLAATJE

execution of so popular a queen, unless indeed she had been assassinated in her sleep, but by whom? Yes, by whom? He vainly sought for an answer to these questions, and although burning with curiosity, he could not venture to express his anxiety.

One day, the performance of his various duties took him to Nomenti's hut. He lingered about looking for a favourable opportunity, until, finding himself alone with her, he cautiously asked, 'Mother, did you ever learn what became of Umnandi since the night you told me of her evil deeds?'

'Oh,' said Nomenti snappishly, 'she was not the only sorceress put away that day. Did not the king order the execution of a whole company of witches – her companions in evil – so why should you single her out for special enquiry?'

'In that respect, mother, I am in good company,' ventured Umpitimpiti timorously. 'No children ever sang a dirge over the slain sorcerers, as they did when the news of Umnandi's disappearance got about. None shouted a wail over them as they did over Umnandi; and the king is consulting nearly every diviner in the country to detect her whereabouts. Indeed no search parties ever issued out of Inzwinyani in such numbers as those sent out to scour the woods and hills for his lost wife. Warriors have been threatened with death should they fail to return with her alive. Why should he grieve if he is acquainted with the circumstances of her disappearance?'

'Oh Umpitimpiti,' said Nomenti, 'are you going to ask me to probe the secrets of my lord, whose intentions are hidden as much as the acts of the gods? Cannot you reason for yourself? Would all these diviners and these search parties fail to locate her if my lord desired her return?'

Umpitimpiti remained unconvinced. He said, 'I have heard of miracles like those of the mysterious devils who kill our boys on the pasturage; no one can tell how, but I doubt if they are half so startling as the circumstances surrounding Umnandi's death. It was strange enough that one so highly placed as she should become unfaithful.'

'Away with you, you madman,' ejaculated Nomenti in disgust. 'What was noble in the actions of that witch?'

'Perhaps it was natural,' Umpitimpiti proceeded, 'in view of the accusation, that she would be executed – not that I think the imputation was justified – but it is the subsequent behaviour of those connected with this case that baffles a man's imagination.'

Nomenti suddenly chipped in with the question, 'By the way, Umpitimpiti, what did the king say to you that night when you brought him your report of her evil work?'

To this unexpected question Umpitimpiti knew not how to reply. He kept quiet for a time till Nomenti asked again, 'What said my lord, Umpitimpiti?' Again there was silence and the lady, losing her temper, cried, 'Speak, fool! Don't you hear me?'

Umpitimpiti then hazarded this evasive remark, 'I have always been wondering, mother, why you have never asked me that question before. I am surprised', he continued gingerly, 'that it should only come today - ten nights after the event. Your silence, too, adds to the mystery of the whole thing.'

'What did Mzilikazi say to you, Umpitimpiti?' repeated the lady impatiently. Her reference to the King by name – usually forbidden to Zulu wives – so startled Umpitimpiti that he almost lost his reasoning powers, but after further hesitation he stammered, 'I thought perhaps he might have told you himself before now.'

Nomenti, with an effort just managing to control her fury, asked again, 'Umpitimpiti, do you hear my question or have you forgotten your tongue? Tell me, was the king angry, when you told him, or was he not?'

'Really, mother,' he said, 'so many things have happened since then that I am trying to recollect what the king did say that night.

But what may his word have been to you, mother?' Nomenti burst out, 'Idiot, am I asking you or are you asking me?'

Umptitimpiti could not explain that he had been too frightened to deliver the dreadful message, and that he had left the king to find out things for himself; but, much as he dreaded a charge of dereliction of duty, he also shuddered at the idea that, if the king were really sincere in his grief, it would go ill with him once it were known that for ten days he had held a clue to the mystery and never disclosed it. While Nomenti was boiling with indignation, visions of exaggerated possibilities passed swiftly through Umpitimpiti's mind. He imagined himself a grovelling figure in the presence of his infuriated king, convicted for his long and culpable silence. He tried hard to suppress these fancies, but they shook his mind and body from head to foot. Nomenti on her part, feeling insulted by his obstinacy, grew beside herself with rage; Umpitimpiti, on his part, had almost ceased to be conscious of her presence. He wished himself a hundred miles away. Not only were his knees shaking at the awful possibilities before him, but the frown on Nomenti's face did not ease his nerves in any way.

Suddenly Nomenti forgot her rage and Umpitimpiti suppressed his horrible fancies. The atmosphere was quickly changed, for their ears caught the voices of two men speaking outside the hut, who had stopped almost in front of the door. This is what they heard: 'Did the old people ever relate an occurrence of this kind where a wife vanished like the wind, leaving no trace behind her? The queen could not have been carried away by a four-footed beast, for there is neither paw-mark nor blood trail to indicate the event. It cannot be a human being that ran off with her; or he too would have left some clues. Someone would have noticed a struggle or heard a scream. The only reasonable supposition, therefore, is that Queen Umnandi was caught by some flying creature that snatched her up without giving her time to cry for help.' 'And what might that be?' asked the second voice. 'Impundulu (thunder and lightning-bird) or some aerial monster.'

'Did you ever hear of the lightning-bird doing anything of the kind in the early days?'

'In the early days they never related a case where a cloud of smoke caused someone to bleed to death almost a mile away.'

'I feel certain your surmise is correct. These goblins that have been killing our herd boys must have descended from the skies; and they must have had something to do with the abduction of Umnandi. After all, those spirits are sensible; they know a good woman when they see one, for they abducted the best wife in the kingdom.'

If Nomenti was convulsed with jealousy on hearing this complimentary reference to her missing rival, both listeners were soon to receive a thrill of terror as one of the speakers went on.

'I wish that whoever kidnapped this wife, be he man or beast, would bring her back before Mzilikazi lops off the heads of every one of us. The king wants his wife back, and, not knowing where she is, he demands her from whoever has the misfortune to come across him. Now just think of poor Dlhadlhu.'

'What's the matter with Dlhadlhu?'

'It has leaked out that the poor man's Barolong maid disappeared mysteriously about the same time as the vanished queen; and she too has not been heard of. Now the king is fuming with new rage. He wants to know why Dlhadlhu kept that information to himself until it was forced out of him too late. I would be very much surprised if Dlhadlhu is still alive by sunset,' concluded the speaker.

'Impossible!' ejaculated the other man. 'Behold, here comes Umpitimpiti, the one man in this city who has the freedom of the royal harem. *Sakubona*, Mpitimpiti.'

Umpitimpiti, who had just left Nomenti in the hut, returned the salute, making a supreme effort to appear calm.

'I hope', continued the first speaker, 'that there are no other wives missing, Umpitimpiti, for it seems that the disappearance of one only is going to set this kingdom on fire. How about Queen Umnandi? If she stays away much longer we had better all prepare to die.'

Umpitimpiti laughed aloud, rather with his teeth than with his feelings. At that moment he cared not what became of Nomenti, who stood petrified with fear as she overheard the conversation. He was only anxious to get away from the place before his alarm was noticed; so he left the two men to continue their conversation. Hardly knowing where he was going, Umpitimpiti walked through the courtyard into the open space where the assemblies are held and cases were tried. There he found himself in the midst of a large crowd of men. Two of them cowering in front of the king were closely guarded by four stalwart young soldiers. Umpitimpiti pressed his way into the thick of the crowd until he could hear what was being said. He understood that one was a doctor, who on being commanded to divine the whereabouts of Umnandi, had prophesied something which proved hopelessly inaccurate. The second man was Dlhadlhu who had failed to report the disappearance of his missing Rolong maid; he was shaking with fear like a reed at the mercy of the wind. Umpitimpiti also trembled when he remembered how hopelessly implicated he himself was in the same case; presently he heard the angry king raise an imperious voice, saying, 'Their ears have heard my anxious inquiries but paid no heed to them. Cut off their ears!' This order was promptly obeyed by the four warders in charge of the unfortunate men.

'Their feet walked out of my way so that useful information

might not reach me until too late,' proceeded King Mzilikazi. 'Chop off their feet!'

'Their tongues lied to me in my distress. Cut out their tongues!'

'Their eyes have seen the cause of my anguish. Pluck out their eyes!'

All these drastic commands were obeyed as soon as they were uttered, for any hesitation on the part of an unwilling attendant might have increased by one the number of victims. If Umpitimpiti had been standing alone and not wedged in between a group of other men where the crowd was densest, he would have fallen down through fear, as the mutilated bodies of the former owner of a Rolong slave girl and of a noted soothsayer were carried away; and if there had been some doubt in his mind, he now felt certain that, whatever Nomenti did or said, Mzilikazi knew nothing of the cause and circumstances of Umnandi's disappearance.

How he wished himself equally ignorant! On the contrary, he was far from innocent, for Nomenti had entrusted him with a message which he was afraid to deliver. Perhaps, had he done so, the whole tragedy might have had a different climax. Now he had seen and heard the plot that preceded Umnandi's disappearance; further, he had participated in it and failed to apprise the king. Did he deserve to retain his own ears, eyes, and tongue which had failed to testify to the facts? He knew further that his feet carried the secret from the King instead of carrying it to him. And if Mzilikazi came to find out how much he knew about Umnandi's flight, he would surely sentence him also to forfeit his eyes, ears and feet as well as his tongue.

Umpitimpiti spent a very bad night. Repeatedly he resolved to go up and make a clean breast of it before he should be found out, but as promptly changed his mind when he recalled the agony of the victims of Mzilikazi's wrath. Finally he decided to rise and escape from his home under cover of the darkness. This he regarded as by far the safest course, for if he were met by any of the tribe he could always say he was in search of the vanished queen; and if on the other hand he were fortunate enough to come across her (which was at best but a remote possibility) the honour of restoring Umnandi would make him a hero of the first rank. Then there was Nomenti; she could explain her complicity much better in his absence.

But wait, what about the doctor from Zululand, whom Nomenti had accused of seducing Umnandi? Why had she never mentioned him? Surely he could throw some light upon the subject. And why had not the king charged him with the heinous, not to say treasonable crime? The mystery thickened. For even if unconnected with her disappearance, he, as a clever magician, ought surely to have been asked to divine her whereabouts. Why had he not been consulted? Of all magicians the Zulu doctor should be able to offer a solution of the unexplained killing of the shepherds, the queen's disappearance and Nomenti's accusation. I will find him out, treacherous wretch, and bring him to judgment. I will go right out.

In a short while the midnight silence of a small hut on the outskirts was disturbed by a nocturnal visitor who announced himself as 'Umpitimpiti, come to consult the Zulu wizard, privately, on a very urgent case.'

He was admitted. The owner of the hut got up and, by the light of a wood fire which he rekindled on the fireplace, he scanned the countenance of his visitor and, after inhaling a pinch of snuff from a ramhorn that was suspended by a string round his neck, the old man said 'The doctor is not here, and I am afraid we shall not see him again.'

'What has happened?' asked Umpitimpiti, with a fresh shock of disappointment.

'Well,' replied the old man, rubbing his nose again,

'he seemed very much concerned about the judgment on Dlhadlhu this afternoon, and when the other doctor came up for trial beside Dlhadlhu, I could see him shaking like a leaf. I am surprised that other people did not notice his terror, for when the sentence on the other two men was pronounced and executed, his eyes were turning red with terror like one who was a party to the crime. All evening I have been waiting but have not seen him again. His most important medicine bag is missing and so is his best cloak, and no doubt he has left this town and neighbourhood, and will never return until the queen is found.'

This information decided Umpitimpiti, and a day later it was noised abroad that two more persons – Umpitimpiti and the Zulu doctor – had vanished like Umnandi.

Chapter Seventeen

The Spies – Their Adventures

DE VILLIERS, LIKE MANY other young Boers, could not write; so that during his absence his friends heard from him only twice when travellers who had met the spies reached Thaba Nchu. These verbal messages, however, not proving satisfactory as to the safety of their sons, the Boers engaged two Natives to accompany to Mogaliesberg another young Boer, Van Zyl by name, to recall De Villiers and Viljoen or bring back authentic news concerning them.

Meanwhile a traveller, named Lepane, was journeying from the land of the Bapedi in the east accompanied by a young man, going to the land of the Bahurutshe in the west. They passed through Mogale's country and heard some whispers about Barolong spies and white men.

The travellers after leaving Tlou's village, where De Villiers and his friends were hiding, took a rest under a shady tree at the foot of a hill where they fell asleep. On awaking they beheld half a dozen Matabele emerging from a thicket in the depression below their hiding place. Naturally the sight struck terror into them. For a moment they knew not what to do. But the younger man, more resourceful than Lepane, suggested to the elder that they were less likely to be seen if they hid in separate places. So advising Lepane to press close up to the tree trunk, he crawled through the grass and the bushes to find another hiding place.

This plan might have worked very well had not Lepane's nerves unfortunately given way at the near approach of the foe. Terror-stricken, Lepane, before being descried, shrieked aloud. 'Oh, spare me!' he cried. 'I will tell you of some undesirable persons in King Mzilikazi's country. Just let me live, I tell you, I am not alone.'

'He's a liar!' shouted his astonished companion from the bush hard by: 'Kill him, he's alone.'

The humour of the situation appealed strongly to the Matabele. They burst out in contemptuous laughter at the timidity of the two men who thus revealed their own presence. Proceeding to bring the two together, the Matabele forced them to make a full confession.

The younger man, of course, had nothing to confess, since he was a harmless wayfarer to Sebogodi's land. Lepane, on the other hand, was eloquent. If the honourable the indunas would spare his life, he pleaded, he would guide them to a place where white men and black men were spying the land, using the foreign spells and medicines, vowing to capture King Mzilikazi alive, overthrow his government, butcher his people and compass a lot of other mischief.

The Matabele first did not know what to make of him. 'Kill the vagabonds!' said one. 'No, wait,' said another, 'let them show us the witches who have the impudence to talk of catching the King.' The Matabele, finally deciding to investigate the matter, proceeded to Tlou's village, with Lepane as their guide.

It was the dreariest march that Lepane had ever undertaken. He knew that his freedom depended on his finding the spies. He had not personally seen them but rumours of them were confirmed when he passed through Mogale's country and heard the two Boers were actually at Tlou's village.

'But, what if the spies have left?' he thought, 'and if the villagers should deny that they were ever there!' Grim fears possessed his mind. 'Supposing we find the white men, and Tlou, the village headman, hands them over, what about me? My people would surely kill me as a traitor. Why did I shriek and reveal my hiding place to these Matabele?' These and similar thoughts haunted Lepane all the way up to the end of the journey.

There was consternation among Mogale's people when the party arrived and enquired about the Boers. These had been hidden in a cave for safety while Ra-Thaga and Rantsau had been disguised as members of Tlou's tribe. No one would give the spies away. Threats and intimidations only elicited evasive answers from men and women. Finally the enraged Matabele demanded the spies from the village headman.

Tlou's explanation was that Lepane's story was but a hallucination caused by an exaggerated fear of death. And when the Matabele threatened to spear Lepane, the headman retorted that no harm would result if society were rid of such a coward. 'He must die someday,' said Tlou, 'so why not take on the job of killing him now while you have the chance. Here's my village, search every hut, you will not find a white man here.'

His captors, having satisfied themselves that no white men were hiding in the village, asked Lepane if he had anything to say before they beheaded him. This turn of events of course did not diminish Lepane's ordeal. He had been standing with his small bundle behind his back, resting his chest over his hands on the nob of his walking cane; he quaked from head to foot and could scarcely keep his knees from knocking against each other; scarcely able to keep his limbs straight, he seemed in danger of tumbling over with fright when the question was put to him. 'Stay your hand,' gasped the terrified man. 'Let us to the spruit where the children are watering the stock and ask them. Perhaps they are not such accomplished liars as their elders have proved to be.'

'Give him that chance,' said Umbebe, the Matabele induna. 'Take him to the fountain as he suggests. He must be thirsty after his long march, and he will die better with his belly full of water.'

A large party proceeded to the brook, where boys were watering their stock and women filling their cans. All were alarmed as the party approached, but as the Matabele descended on them, the would-be runners had to scamper back to the pools and await their fate. Some of the bigger boys were questioned. Lepane, the slender thread of whose life hung on the answer, heard with great relief the answer of the first boy. 'I'll take you to where the white man is,' said the young one readily. 'We passed him down the valley as we came up this way with our cattle.'

'Lead us to the place,' cried Umbebe, and very soon the boys were running in front of the party which followed with Lepane as captive. They reached the tree under which lay the young Boer and his Barolong guides. The three were promptly arrested and taken to the Matabele capital.

There was weeping and wailing at Thaba Nchu when news came of the arrest of 'all the spies'. Rantsau's family and Ra-Thaga's friends, not to speak of Mhudi – that mother of sorrows – were in deep grief. The Matabele who had murdered their nearest and dearest relatives at Kunana, had now slain her one succourer. He too, she thought, had met the same fate as his white friend, De Villiers, the one humane Boer she had ever found at the Hoek. Friends came and offered her their condolence, for, as the rumours had it, the men were dragged before Mzilikazi, who ordered their massacre along with thirty witchdoctors.

'Why are the Gods so cruel?' Mhudi asked herself. 'Now I have only my sons to live for, how can I support them without a husband and without any brothers.'

At the Hoek, grey-haired Boers stroked their flowing beards and thought long and seriously. Women wearing kappies looked up to the skies and asked why heaven was so merciless. 'How long must it last, Oh God?' they demanded, as though expecting an answer by return post.

The mourning for the 'butchered men' had been in progress for three weeks, when one day the sound of shrill voices of Barolong women was wafted on the breeze from Thaba Nchu town and echoed round the surrounding hills. The Boers knew that such noises were only heard when Barolong warriors returned victorious from a battle, or from a successful chase with pack-oxen laden with carcasses of royal game. Presently a mounted messenger rode into camp and delivered to Sarel Cilliers a message from Chief Moroka. It was, 'Rejoice with me, Sarel friend, for our boys have come back with good news. The youths De Villiers and Viljoen are also back and look much the better for their long experience.'

When the once lamented young men reached the Boer camp at Moroka's Hoek, they were welcomed like men returning from the dead. Joyful Boers shook their hands, the women congratulated them and children welcomed them home. Scenes similarly cordial were taking place at Thaba Nchu with Rantsau and Ra-Thaga as their centre. 'How agreeably unreliable was news from a far country,' was the comment of men.

The wanderers brought the first authentic news of the

arrest of a white youth, and two Natives, one afternoon of tense anxiety during the trip of the espionage, all through the timorous loquacity of one Lepane. They heard for the first time who the prisoners were; but of their subsequent fate they knew nothing.

All this did not diminish the bellicosity of the Thaba Nchu young men of both races. They became more impatient and eager to get at grips with Mzilikazi before his impis had time to import and acquire the use of firearms.

Chapter Eighteen

Halley's Comet – Its Influence on the Native Mind

NOW A PROUD RACE like the Matabele had no idea of the systematic espionage that was carried on among them on behalf of their enemies, even by the very messengers who came to their capital laden with tributes from friendly Bechuana chiefs. Any valuable pieces of news about the movements or the intentions of the Matabele impis were carefully listened to, and just as carefully and promptly conveyed to Thaba Nchu. The Matabele, on the other hand, did no spying; they relied mainly on their spears and felt secure in the frightful terror they would instil in the hearts of their neighbours. They did their usual hunting and cattle-herding and never troubled about a possible danger directed against them.

Since Gubuza's success against Cilliers, they had not again been troubled by mysterious spirits. The strange people who sniped at their herd boys at a safe distance from the tops of a hillock, never revisited the country.

Once during the intervening years a small Matabele army under a smaller induna labouring under an excess of zeal, travelled far afield and carried a raiding expedition to the cattle-posts of the Basutos. Having seized some unprotected cattle they followed up their temporary success into Basuto land until they came in contact with a wing of King Moshoeshoe's regular army.

The Basutos inflicted upon the raiding Matabele such a severe punishment that they ran down the mountains and retired across the plains in scattered formation, leaving behind them on the mountain slopes several dead and wounded; and when after a very long run they halted for a rest, they were overtaken by a number of Basuto driving a herd of bullocks. The leader of the party – a Mosuto named Tshephe – approached the leader of the raiders and delivered to him a friendly message from King Moshoeshoe. 'The Basuto king', so the message sounded, 'had heard that some boys belonging to the nation of the great King Umzilwegazi, had been about Basutoland and felt so hungry that they actually helped themselves to Basuto cattle. He was sorry that the impis of so great a king were famishing in his land, and he sent them the herd of bullocks as provision on their way back to Inzwinyani.'

The magnanimity of the Basuto king amazed the Matabele soldiers. The tone of the message was so unusual that the defeated raiders could scarcely believe their ears and eyes. They wondered if this was not a new and unheard of form of sorcery, for they had never heard that after being put to flight, a beaten enemy was ever supplied with provisions.

'All these bullocks', Tshephe went on to say, 'are yours with the exception of the white ox. King Moshoeshoe knows that Matabele soldiers, when defeated, are usually punished with death. The King therefore desires you to take the white bullock as your ransom to the great Mzilikazi with Moshoeshoe's greetings; by this ransom he pleads that your lives should be spared by your King. And it is his desire that you depart in peace and convey the news to his brother Umzilwegazi.'

The raiders were not quite certain that all this was not a dream. But they received the cattle and went forth. The news of the generosity of the Basuto king caused a peculiar sensation among the Matabele. It proved too much for the credulity of the whole nation for such magnanimity had no parallel in the history of Native warfare. For a generation thereafter it was a byword among the Matabele that Moshoeshoe, the Basuto king, was an enigma, and nobody would dare think of doing harm to any of his people. The Matabele always referred to him as 'Moshoeshoe, the wonderful'. And of course, Moshoeshoe's ransom was accepted by Mzilikazi, and the lives of the soldiers were spared.

A few months later, Mzilikazi called his magicians together and asked the principal national wizard to throw bones, and communicate any omens he could divine. The execution of thirty doctors, a few years before, was still fresh in the people's minds, and they wondered if the next slaughter would be confined to magicians only.

The magician duly attended at court, and found the king seated and surrounded by his principal chiefs and a large crowd of men. The wizard prophesied that Umnandi, the favourite wife of the King, now lost for seven years, was alive and well among strange people to the East. That the elements were not propitious for a search party to be sent after her, but if the Great One – the King – would exercise a little patience, Umnandi, the beautiful, would voluntarily turn up one day and appear in all her regal beauty, and she would be the source of much comfort to His Majesty.

Picking up his bones once more, he cast them down in different positions, and repeating the operation a few times, he critically examined the lay of every piece and, having praised his bones again, he said, 'Away in the distance I can see a mighty star in the skies with a long white tail stretching almost across the heavens. Wise men have always said that such a star is the harbinger of diseases of men and beasts, wars and the overthrow of governments as well as the death of princes. Within the rays of the tail of this star, I can clearly see streams of tears and rivers of blood.' Having praised his bones once more, the wizard proceeded. 'I can see the mighty throne of Mzilikazi floating across the crimson stream, and reaching a safe landing on the opposite bank. I also perceive clear indications of death and destruction among rulers and commoners but no death seems marked out for Mzilikazi, ruler of the ground and of the clouds.'

At this there were loud applauses and several mbongis began to vie with one another in singing the praises of the king. But he motioned them to stop and the wizard continued: 'On the other side of this river of blood, I can see large tracts of forest lands teeming with giraffe, elephant, buffalo, eland, koodoo, rhinoceros, sable antelope, zebra and other game, too numerous to mention; further, away in the distance, I can see a deep crystal stream of sweet drinking waters alive with all kinds of fish and water snakes, as well as ferocious crocodiles and the portly hippopotami. I can see the Matabele first wading through this stream of blood, many men and women and children falling in the stream, yet many of them survive and cross the wilderness until they reach the crystal stream beyond. There they cleanse their blood-stained limbs and, refreshed and invigorated, they leave the second stream and go forth to the north; penetrating the forest they spread panic and terror among the bushmen. They return to a new royal kraal with much booty of livestock, ostrich feathers, ivory and precious skins. Here they establish for their lord, Mzilikazi, a great kingdom whose greatness stretches right up to the dome of the skies. They go out again and capture food and serfs and many new wives for the rising generation of warriors.

'The bones tell me that there will be much of death and tribulations before the new haven is reached. Instant emigration, therefore, and arrival at the new place before the appearance of the star is the only sure way of escaping these troubles.'

One old grey beard asked: 'You say you saw a star with a tail?' Here the wizard invited the questioner to pick up the charmed emblems. The bones being picked up and thrown down once more and praised again, the wizard chanted: 'A star . . . a big giant star . . . the biggest that ever appeared in the skies. Its tail will spread from the eastern to the western clouds, remaining visible for many a night. Cattle will die, cattle will be captured, chieftains will sicken and die, and so will their wives and daughters and sons. There will be wars in Zululand, fighting in Basutoland, a stream of blood across the world. It will soak and drown many people in Inzwinyani. Yes, and we may escape it if we move to the north before the appearance of the star and the flooding of the red river.'

'Stop this child's play!' cried Mzilikazi. 'I remember hearing similar nonsense about the star with the tail when mad devils killed our herd boys and stole our goods. What was the result? I killed the chatterers and ordered Gubuza to go and hunt down the spirits who infested our pastures and whose depredations oiled the tongues of seers and witches. Where is that star now, and where is the tail? Has anybody seen either? If so, why has he not told me? Gubuza, in whose veins ran the pure blood of our fathers, squelched the offending sprites and we have not moved the city to the north, as the witches suggested we should do. As for this present announcement, I repeat now what I said three years ago. A Zulu never stepped back for any man. If death threatens me I shall stand my ground, face it and receive the fatal stab on my broad chest – not on my back. If any man considers himself a foeman worthy of my spear, let him come. I shall spit him out of here – (*spitting*) – like the saliva from my mouth. I am astounded at the disloyalty and audacity of these bonethrowers who fain would frighten me with visions of imaginary stars and jackal tails across the sky. Shall I drop my shield and fly from a tail and go to northern forests and northern rivers? Have I fallen so low in your estimation! You shall know from today that I have a shield and a driving power in my right arm. Let an enemy try conclusions with me and the vultures shall gorge themselves with his flesh and the ants shall fatten on his blood. An enemy! A long-tailed star! Bloody rivers and what not! Am I afraid? Go and sharpen your spears and keep them ready for the predicted trouble. Up everybody.' And the assembly dispersed.

As the vast crowd left the king's court there were comments on the happenings of the morning. Men importunately asked one another about this dangerous star with a long tail. They dreaded the idea of waiting at home for trouble, especially after the very clear warning from the head doctor, corroborated by other magicians.

'It is all very well for a king to stay at home and say he is not afraid, I tell you, Zungu,' said one old jet-black Matabele. 'I am going to find a way out of this place before the star appears and before the rivers turn red.'

Presently they noticed some excitement outside the enclosure to the king's court. Children ran and women shouted, and a garrulous crowd was collecting around a group that was coming towards the enclosure. The excitement increased as the din grew louder and some of the men who had heard the prophecy of the morning began to look up to the skies to see if the long-tailed star was already there. At this time the oncoming crowd had reached the enclosure, and was proceeding to the centre where the king and the chiefs sat, but the concord was so vast that those outside could not see the cause of the commotion in the centre. All they could hear were remarks that came from within the crowd. 'These are the spirits who killed our herd boys the year before last; truly, these are they. What are we waiting for? Let us to the ravine and lose them there.'

The cause of all this commotion was Van Zyl and his guides, who were arrested by Umbebe's impi near Tlou's water pool on the occasion when Lepane lost his nerve, and brought to Inzwinyani. Whilst the majority were for the immediate execution of the men, there were some who advocated milder measures, but mercy found very little favour with the dominant section. One old warrior, who had clearly passed his dancing days, cried, 'What! spare his life? Where will he stay? In Inzwinyani? Go out into the valley early one morning and find a frozen cobra, or some other snake; catch it while it is shivering with the cold; put it inside your cloak till it gets warm and then see what would happen. Save this ruddy witch! Save him and you will die before you had time to regret it. Where are our herd boys? Ask him; ask him before you suggest that his life should be spared.'

Very little could be seen of the captives in the midst of the throng, much less could be heard of what the chiefs said. But there was no mistaking their decision for at once Van Zyl and his guides, with their hands manacled, were led out in the direction of the place of slaughter, where the Matabele witches were slain three years before. Their belongings were taken from them, and so was Van Zyl's rifle which was still loaded. As they were being led away, one of the Barolong guides pulled the trigger of Van Zyl's gun then in the hand of a Matabele. The leaden bullet pierced the air with a hiss that seemed to penetrate the very clouds in the highest space; then there was a loud explosion which scattered and terrified the Matabele. Hundreds of men, including those in charge of the prisoners, fell down and hid their faces, as they saw the very smoke which was said to cause people to bleed to death. A good many recognised the sound with which they had become familiar when, under Gubuza, they attacked Cilliers's camp south of the Vaal River. But the majority of the frightened Matabele had never heard that sound before – they called it a man-made lightning.

The confusion caused by the report of the gun influenced public opinion in several directions, the consensus of opinion now being that the strange witches should be allowed to live.

'These must be the people who took away the king's beautiful wife,' said one Matabele excitedly, many others concurring, 'and yet he says he is not afraid. Why does he not go to their den and bring his wife back?'

'No,' commented an old man, 'I must leave this place. Spirits were never good neighbours; not even the spirits of one's ancestors. But this is wild and unknown sorcery! I am going to leave this place while the leaving is good.'

Hopelessly surrounded as they were by armed men in the centre of the city, the captives could not think of running away, so they stood by while the astonished Matabele discussed them. 'Why kill the sprites?' some of them asked aloud. 'Of what use will their dead bodies be to us? Have you all forgotten the action of Moshoeshoe, the wise king of the east? He fed his tormentors and ransomed his enemies. Don't you think that that is the secret of Moshoeshoe's strength?'

'No,' rang the drum-like voices of dozens of excited Matabele, as the discussion continued long and lively. 'Spare the life of the sprite and he will show our doctors the secret of the magic of his explosive witchcraft. Let him live and show us how to create explosions and clouds of smoke.'

Yes, keep and feed the sprite,
Especially the hairy sprite;
Yebo, yebo!
He'll show us how to crack magic out of poles
So that we'll scatter and slay our enemies,
Then nobody will do us harm
While we use this wonderful charm;
Yebo, yebo!
Let the hairy spirit live
Let him live, let him live.
Yebo, yebo!
Yebo, yebo!

Chapter Nineteen

War against the Matabele

POTGIETER HELD HIS last council of war at Thaba Nchu. He told the Barolongs that the Boers had their forces and munitions all complete, and, if the Natives would join them, they were ready to march against the Matabele. He sincerely hoped that the Barolong would keep their word and help him to rid the country of the Matabele impis. Further he gave them his word of honour that after killing off the Matabele and looting their property, they would make a just division of the spoils by keeping all the land for the Boers and handing over the captured cattle to the Barolong.

'What an absurd bargain!' exclaimed Chief Tauana of the Ra-Tshidi, 'what could one do with a number of cattle if he possessed no land on which to feed them? Will his cattle run on the clouds, and their grass grow in the air? No, my lords: I would rather leave the Matabele where they are and remain a sojourner with my people in the land of the Selekas under my cousin, Moroka.'

'What would you have then?' asked Potgieter.

'I will go on one condition only,' replied Tauana. 'If we succeed to dislodge Mzilikazi, I want the land of my fathers back. The Boers could keep all the land to the east, but I want the whole of the Molopo River and its tributaries. I have asked the Griqua king to send an army to help us in the expedition and he was generous enough to agree to come and help me in the recovery of my lands.'

'On Tauana's terms,' said Chief Moroka, 'I, too, am prepared to help with the further condition that, while you all share the lands at present occupied by the Matabele, I remain at Thaba Nchu and continue in possession of my present territories.'

After much wrangling and arguing the Barolong terms were accepted by the Boers and communicated to the Griqua king who sent two hundred horsemen equipped with firearms; and in due course the expedition, armed to the teeth, set out against the Matabele. Sarel Cilliers led the Boers, Motshegare (Chief Tauana's son) led the Barolong, and a brave horseman named Dout led the Griquas, the whole army being under the supreme command of Hendrik Potgieter. As they proceeded north from day to day, the allies were joined en route by large numbers of Bakwena, Bakgatla and Bahurutshe who lived in the neighbourhood through which they marched.

A month after leaving Thaba Nchu, the expedition swooped down upon the outlying Matabele outposts and captured many cattle with their shepherds and cowherds. Some of the young herds were taken captive and permanently retained by the Boers as slaves. Those who resisted or tried to run away were shot.

Potgieter encountered his first serious opposition on the plains between the Matloang and the Matloasane Rivers. This was a stand by a hastily collected army of about a thousand Matabele determined to hold the invaders in check until

Mzilikazi's main forces should arrive. The Matabele, however, soon found out that against mounted men armed with firearms their assegais were of no avail. Helplessly outranged, terrified by the deafening noise of the guns and outmanoeuvred by the mobility of their enemy's horses, they rapidly turned and fled, leaving the field strewn with their dead and wounded. In the rout and confusion many of their cattle were scattered and lost.

Meanwhile a large army of Matabele were gathering near the source of the Marico in answer to Gubuza's call. They had been massing there during the day, and sunset was given as the time they should start so as to reach and attack the invaders. Swift runners had been arriving with news of the first day's encounter and these acted as guides to lead the army back to where the enemy was supposed to be.

When Gubuza, the brave commander, marshalled his huge army the warriors hailed him as the hope of the nation. As the serried ranks marched out under their several indunas, they constituted a formidable mass of black humanity. Going through their initial exercises, thousands of limbs would straddle after a thousand different patterns; innumerable spears described circles in the air as if slaying as many visionary enemies; myriads of shields waved to and fro or vertically up and down as if to parry a host of imaginary thrusts; and they chanted a war song to the rhythmical tramping of countless feet. 'Death before dishonour!' they cried, and swore to vindicate their king and the glory of Matabele arms. The guides on the other hand were not so sanguine. They had participated in the initial skirmishes and knew that in the face of firearms, their assegais, however well aimed, could make no impression on the invaders.

The army marched all night. Towards dawn their attention was drawn to the eastern skies where they saw the tail of a comet transfixed above the horizon. The repeated prophecies of Matabele seers at once came back to mind and many of the soldiers began to murmur. They complained that they were driven to fight against the forces of aerial sorcery which were far above the powers of their own witchcraft.

'I know', said one sable warrior, 'that our doctors can perform miracles on earth; but I am also sure that I have never heard of any Matabele whose wizardry planted a lodestar in the skies to confound his enemy and lead his warriors to victory as our present enemy is apparently doing. Don't you see! Look, look at the tail of that star,' and many heads were turned upward 'Why, the tail is pointing straight in the direction of Inzwinyani! What could we, poor mortals, do to a heavenly rod which, predicted years ago by our own wizards, is now visible to the eye of the uninitiated?'

Gubuza too remembered the prophecies. He knew how the apparition would affect the minds of the men of his army, but he did his best to cheer them on.

Behind a distant ridge, the invaders waited with beating hearts, their fingers on the triggers, and prayed that the Matabele arrival should be delayed till after daybreak, when the good light would aid them to shoot more effectively. Gubuza's great army continued to advance and gathered fresh courage as the sun rose above the treetops; but with dramatic suddenness there emerged from the top of the swell four hundred horsemen of the allies who galloped up to meet them and Gubuza ordered his men to the attack. The horsemen stopped, dismounted and fired. The crash of the volley was as frightful as the effect of the fire. The Matabele had never seen horses before; and, to them, each horse with a man on its back resembled one hideous monster. Hence the mounted men advancing in mass presented a spectacle so grotesque as to form a horrible apparition. When the riders dismounted to shoot, the Matabele were further bewildered by the strange action of creatures dividing themselves into two parts and still continuing to act.

Gubuza, a warrior by profession and a genius by intuition, had arranged the march of his army in semi-circles – one within the other – so as to surround the invaders. Each such circle marched inside a larger circle; a mile beyond that there came another, and yet another semi-circle with its flanks stretching for miles to the east and west behind the others. Thus, when the inner circle was broken up by the first volley, Gubuza's indunas would marshal the next circle, and so on. But the bulk of these mobile crescents were soon reduced to carrion for the vultures of the air.

The first volley threw the inner circle back into the next one, the riflemen of the allies finding enough time during the resulting confusion to reload their muskets. The next circle coming up to reinforce the confused ranks of its predecessors suffered the same fate. The battle was a one-sided affair; only Matabele could keep on rushing to such certain death, and even they discovered that they were engaged in a struggle hitherto unknown in human warfare.

The devastating machines of war had spread a pall of death and desolation over the plains. The forests shook with the awful thunder of the guns, which stirred a wild agitation among the denizens of the day. Terrified game of every description scattered in all directions and fled for dear life; oxen bellowed in surprise and wild hounds yelped, wolves and jackals ran as though possessed by a legion of devils.

Wild birds rushed out of their nests and protested loudly against this unholy disturbance of the peace of their haunts. The very bees hived in hollow tree-stems swarmed forth as if to enquire what the matter was. Meeting the charges and counter-charges of the two armies, they probably demanded a reason for the upheaval. Of course, neither the Matabele nor the invaders understood the language of the bees, who, failing to get a satisfactory explanation, proceeded to attack the intruders in mass formation. Myriads of them distributed their stings impartially among the ranks of the allies and of their foes. The Matabele being undressed of course suffered the worst from the bee-stings. At this they were convinced that they were now fighting the evil influences of the comet which had illumined the skies the night before.

The riflemen continuing to drive home this traditional advantage in their favour still further decimated the now demoralised armies of Gubuza.

The sombre shades of evening fell upon a field bestrewn with dead and wounded Matabele. A general retreat was ordered; but, as the order failed to reach all ranks, the scattered groups continued to attack and suffered severely.

Gubuza was a dignified personage of powerful build who carried himself with a lordly gait. He had certainly been marked out for nothing if not for the role of an army leader but that day's fight had proved too much even for his wonderful resources. The demoralisation of his army was humiliating. Only one consideration deterred his men from deserting him. It was the belief that they would be executed, according to custom, if they returned home defeated. Their general on the other hand was glad that such a false fear kept his men together. He knew that the flower of the Matabele army had been severely mauled; that it needed a superior force to put a defeated army to death. Such a force no longer existed, and the execution of his army therefore was out of the question.

None of his warriors had been able to sleep. In the night he was obliged to interview each messenger before sending him off with a message. He could neither shout his order nor call anyone aloud for fear of helping his uncanny adversaries to locate his whereabouts. This meant that he had been running incessantly throughout the night; and, cool as the night wind was, just before dawn Gubuza found himself drenched with perspiration as the sweat oozed from every pore of his ample physique.

Bechuana villagers, near the Marico, who had been for years paying tribute to the Matabele king, now saw the sorry plight of their tormentors, and hurried to the allies' camp to offer their congratulations. Many dead logs, remnants of majestic mimosa and camelthorn trees that waxed for years and withered with age, were burning to cinders, and chunks of beef were roasting on the live coals. Such a magnificent slaughter of kine had never before been witnessed in that part of the country. The effect of this display was that everyone who visited the camp of the allies was given enough beef to eat and a portion to carry to his home and celebrate with his family the victory of the allies.

The atmosphere reeked with the smell of roast meat, and prolific beef eaters like the Bechuana thought that war was a blessing indeed if one's sympathies were on the winning side. The Bechuana had themselves fought battles and knew that winners always got cheap meat, but not in such superabundance. It seemed to them that white men in warfare first slaughter the owners by the hundreds, then help themselves to the dead men's cattle without any opposition. Having enjoyed the roast beef, the villagers proceeded to discuss the wonderful effect of white men's firearms.

No people need be poor, who are allied to these Boers, they said. In fruitful years folk could revel in plenty; and when supplies ran short they could always raid their neighbours, kill off the people with little opposition, round up their stock and distribute the raided cattle among the needy.

'How will Mzilikazi claim further taxes from us after this?' asked one enthusiastic admirer of the Boers.

'He won't be left alive to claim any,' said a bystander, 'for if he be alive at this moment his body will be food for the jackals before many suns have set.'

Villages in the vicinity resounded with a thrilling song of joy. The inhabitants told one another that the hour of deliverance from Matabele domination had already struck. On many a hill could be seen puffs of smoke burnt by friendly wizards whose incantations breathed malediction upon Mzilikazi's impis and invoked further victories for the allies; and many were the praises sung in honour of the Boers.

In other villages where there were converted Natives, they gathered in their grass-thatched chapels and sang other songs to the God of Moses, of Joshua and of Gideon. Their supplications were for new priests to blow the ramshorn and the trumpet, bring down the walls of the modern Jericho on the banks of the Marico, and thus hasten the emancipation of all the Bechuana tribes.

At home at Inzwinyani some old men gathered round their king and supported a large number of wizards who were employed in dispensing other charms to propitiate the fates in favour of Gubuza's army. Stragglers from the first day's attack had already arrived with gloomy accounts, depicting the deadly fire of the foe, but with the hopeful assurance that Gubuza's main army might yet turn the oncoming tide in favour of the distressed nation. They little knew that Gubuza and his lieutenants were at that time in serious trouble, with their broken armies fleeing in wild disorder.

While the ceremony of the propitiation was in progress the courtiers whiled away the time in conversation on other topics in anticipation of better news from the front.

In the course of this conversation one greybeard asked, 'Do you men know what? When I got up this morning I noticed in the sky a star with a long tail?'

'Yes,' replied another, 'I saw it there yesterday morning and wondered what it portended. I was told by Ntongolwane that it was there two mornings previously, and that its tail is growing longer and longer every morning.'

'H'm,' grunted Umbiko, 'it must be the star prophesied by Doctor Maji some time back. He said it would cause us terror and destruction unless indeed we move the nation from here.' 'Most extraordinary!' said another. 'What was it like?

'Wiseacres say that such comets never appeared unless they portended the downfall of kings and destruction of nations by wars or sickness. Have you heard the latest news? I overheard today the Great One telling Somebebe that Dingana, king of all the Zulus, was no more; and if great trees like those crumble down over their own roots, what must become of shallow sprouts like the Matabele strangers in a strange land?'

'What did he die of?' asked a number of men.

'I don't know. Some say he was sick, others believe that he was bewitched by his brother Mpanda, while others assert that he was killed by the very witches who are attacking us today.'

'Impossible!' exclaimed several voices.' 'Are they then flying across the world and slaying everything in their way? What about Moshoeshoe! What about the Barolong and these Bechuana lapdogs?'

'I don't know about the Barolong,' said another, 'but a wise man like Moshoeshoe would surely send them a white ox and pacify them before they reach his country.'

'Oh, woe to us!' exclaimed one portly Matabele. 'Our fathers were idiots to advise us to leave Zululand and follow a madman like Mzilikazi. In Zululand at any rate we would have perished in our own country, but who will recognise our bones in this unfriendly part of the world? If Mzilikazi had only listened to the wise words of the doctors and moved us away, all might have been well, but he is as obstinate as a gnu.'

Groups of Matabele were soon discussing the comet and

Dingana's death, almost forgetting that the court was at that time expecting important news about the luck of their armies. The discussion grew more animated and several 'ringed-heads' raised their voices on purpose that their words should reach the ears of the King. These grumblers wished him to understand, though indirectly, that if the star were there next morning the nation should forthwith evacuate the city according to the wise words of the magicians. But if, on the other hand, the star was not visible next morning, the people were to know that doctor Maji and other oracles had misread the destinies of fate, and stay where they were.

During the night, King Mzilikazi received two swift runners with a message from Gubuza, the supreme commander of his armies. 'Come forth, my sons!' he said, 'and let me hear your message.'

'Hail, Great King, Animal of the Wind and Storm! Gubuza salutes thee and says: Tell Mzilikazi my king that I have previously fought witchcraft but not after this fashion. This day we have been fighting not human beings but thunder. Lightning flashes are dangerous enough when they explode in the air whence they have not been known to strike the same place twice. Today we had thunder in the hands of witches who scattered it over the battlefield with a series of detonations that wrought havoc among our ranks. For all the Matabele that fell this day, and all the cattle captured by the enemy – and no man can count them – we have not inflicted any appreciable injury on the foe. My advice, therefore, is that the Great One should evacuate the city and move the nation to the north. The forces arrayed against us are supernatural and no human effort can stay their advance.

'I have seen my men mown down as if they were so many ears of corn. I have not seen any spears or darts cast at them yet unseen missiles issued from the clouds of smoke that screened the enemy gashed, on the bodies of our helpless warriors, wounds from which they bled to death; and the miracle is how I managed to escape. The runners will explain to the Great One the valour of the armies and the valiant princes and gallant warriors who fell to the thunder of these witches. Had they fallen on one spot and not over a wide field their blood must certainly have cut a big red river, and I cannot but believe that today's events were the harbinger of the disasters foretold by the magicians. If the invincible foe would permit our retreat, two days' forced march should land our remnants at Inzwinyani. This is hardly time enough to evacuate the capital, but it must be done if the complete destruction of the Matabele is to be avoided. This is a discouraging message to send to a king as great as Mzilikazi, but believe me, Great Ruler, we have done our best.'

This message being accurately delivered word by word, by a Matabele endowed with a strong memory, the news of the humiliation of the flower of the Matabele army caused the nation to shudder. Everyone made up his mind that, orders or no orders, comet or no comet, Inzwinyani was a good place to get away from. After receipt of the alarming news men and women spent a restless night arranging their portable belongings so as to start with the first streak of dawn. Indeed, some of them actually started before daylight, but the bulk of the nation waited for the word of command. In the early morning a shout went out to the outskirts of Inzwinyani, by calls from hut to hut, and the exodus had begun.

Whether the command to start was due to the appearance of the comet, or to the entry of the enemy, no one knew. Everyone was aware, however, that Gubuza, the hope of the Matabele, supported by the crack regiments of the nation, had been completely defeated by the invaders. And when at length the comet became visible in the sky, several voices moaned lugubriously. The predictions of the magicians having proved so accurate in regard to the long-tailed star, there could no longer be any doubt that the further prophecies, regarding the rivers of blood and other calamities, would likewise be fulfilled. Few of the people knew where they were going, and fewer still could estimate the length of the journey before them, and what they would encounter on the road; everybody had but one impulse, namely, to hurry forward, as fast as their burdens of babies and other impedimenta would allow, to safety in the unknown north.

Some days after the allies struck camp, and having moved their waggons two days' march into the interior, they bivouacked at a place on the edge of the forest along the trail of the army. Here the drivers disposed themselves among the waggons. Several of them lay in the shade and smoked, some prepared the food and the camp-followers went to water the cattle.

Chapter Twenty

Mhudi's Leap in the Dark

MHUDI WAS SUFFERING from an attack of malarial fever when the armies of the allies left Thaba Nchu. Although she was growing worse, she assured Ra-Thaga that she dared not prevent him from carrying out his long-nurtured revenge against Mzilikazi.

Two days after the departure of her husband, her condition was causing her friends some anxiety. Old women came to massage her, and herbalists cast bones and consulted them on her illness, but all with unsatisfactory results. As her condition became more serious, her friends fetched away her two younger children, and left only the eldest boy to run her messages.

One night, a week later, while Baile was watching by Mhudi's bedside, the patient fell into a deep sleep. She dreamt that she was gazing upon the battlefield and saw the clash of the two armies. The Matabele hosts advanced with spears aloft as they did on the night of the sacking of Kunana. She beheld a Matabele giant leading the impis and coming to grips with her husband. They were next wrestling in a hand-to-hand struggle, and, as Ra-Thaga measured strength with the giant, another Matabele drove his spear into her husband's body. At the sight of this the dreamer screamed aloud. Her scream woke her drowsy cousin with a shudder.

'What is the matter?' asked Baile, quickly. 'Are you delirious?'

'Oh!' replied the patient, 'I am so glad it was only a dream! I hope it is not true.'

Then Mhudi rose, and Baile noticed a wonderful change in her condition, for she no longer appeared ill. But before she had had time to congratulate her cousin on her improved health, the patient made an unexpected proposal that almost took her cousin's breath away.

'Baile,' she said, 'I would be pleased if you will do me a real cousinly favour. That is, take care of my hut for me while I go away for a few days, or, say, for a month. The children could stay with Matsitselele while you mind the hut. Now, don't ask me any questions, cousin mine, for I must depart. I had a call in my dream which I must obey. I feel strong and healthy now – I will not wait until morning in case I have a relapse. Don't disappoint me, coz.'

Before her astonished cousin could think of an effective remonstrance, Mhudi had tied up a bundle with some boiled maize and some parched corn and, throwing her arms round Baile in a farewell embrace, went out into the darkness. 'Of course,' thought Mhudi, as she went along, 'I may not locate my husband, and yet again I may. He is with the biggest army that ever went to war. It would be impossible to miss the trail of a force of such dimensions.'

She had been gone some time before Baile recovered from her astonishment, and wondered how in the morning she would explain her cousin's absence.

By that time Mhudi had cleared the outskirts of the town and was already traversing the plains of Thaba Nchu, and proceeding in the direction of Moroto. She had not gone very far when she observed a dense cloudbank swelling in the southwestern horizon growing longer, higher and thicker as it rolled onward. It was accompanied by a deep rumble that grew louder and louder, while a dense, dark shroud covered the sky and intensified the blackness of the night. Successive peals of the thunder shook the earth as the clouds ascended higher and higher, while flashes of forked lightning played all round the dark heavens. Speedily there followed a cloudburst which deluged the earth, and covered it with a lake-like sheet of water; still the rain kept falling, the flashes continued to blind her eyes, and the thunderclaps kept up their awful detonations. But in spite of the fury and rage of the storm the brave woman struggled along her chosen route. There being neither trees nor shelter of any description, she had to endure in full the heavy onslaughts of these angry elements. It was as though the legions of nature were in conflict, and she – poor little human wreck – a mere plaything at their mercy.

Before daybreak the winds subsided and the storm ceased, and the clouds were swiftly passing away; and Mhudi, still pressing forward, waded through the water in wild hope of rescuing her husband. The unprecedented severity of the storm, far from depressing her spirit, only served to inspire her with hope. According to the belief of her people, Jupiter Pluvius is the god of good fortune, hence she regarded the downpour as his special benediction on her journey. At sunrise she stood near the side of a kopje, and saw the plains spread out before her in one great prospect, still covered by the moving sheet of water.

Oppressed by the vastness of the country stretching before her and the uncertainty of ever finding Ra-Thaga, she wondered how long her journey would last. The peltry she wore was ruined by the rain. But, drenched as she was, her determination remained unshaken and, having wrung out her garments, she proceeded on her perilous journey.

She travelled all day across a trackless and unpeopled country, and by the next evening she was passing over some ridges, the names of which – if they had any – she would probably never know. Fortunate for her it was that the rain had ceased the previous night, for, refreshed in the soft balmy air of the cool atmosphere after the thunderstorm, Mhudi travelled quite thirty miles that day. Late at night she wrapped her little lambskin kaross around her, and lay down to rest upon the slope of a hillock. In her exhausted condition she slept – as the Natives would put it – like a wolf that could be skinned when asleep without waking.

During the next day Mhudi ate nothing but boiled maize and cold water. She saw more than one drowned spring-hare floating on the floods but, without a fire, they were of no use to her. As she picked her way along the hillsides, she frightened several coveys of meercats which, scampering away from her, never stopped until well out of her sight. Their burrows being flooded out, the little creatures were compelled to seek shelter in the open.

The watercourses having ceased to roar, there was a dead silence over the immense plains, broken occasionally by the music of the birds as they chirped their songs on the hilltops. But Mhudi missed the forests and the cooing of the wood-pigeons of Bechuanaland. She missed the compact *mokgalo* and *mogonono* trees, the leaves of which had provided her with excellent awning when it rained, by day or by night; and longed for the leafy undergrowth which, during her early wanderings, had shielded her from the cold winds.

Travellers in Bechuanaland, when accosted by a lion or a buffalo, have saved their lives by scrambling up a tree. 'What', thought she, 'could a lonely woman do in this desolate and treeless land should the king of beasts appear over that ridge and attack her?'

She remembered how, when moving from Maamuse to Thaba Nchu, she and her family traversed those windswept plains and spent their nights in the open, exposed to every blast; throughout that journey of many days they had never seen a shadow except the passing flitter of a vulture's wing.

She recalled the number of travellers through this unshaded country who stopped at her home in Thaba Nchu, and related stories of dreary journeys under the sun. She recalled the adventures of another wayfarer through the same unsheltered territory who was badly wounded and almost pelted to death by hailstones, the size of a hen's egg; there being not a tree and not a cave under which he could take cover. 'How barren is this level country! All grass and kopjes, nothing useful. Truly,' she sighed, 'this is the most inhospitable land my wanderings have shown to me.'

Still, all this did not damp her ardour; on the contrary, she put her best foot forward and eagerly pursued her way. As she proceeded, Mhudi roused myriads of multi-coloured ladybirds and butterflies which flittered hither and thither in variegated liveries that challenged the colours of the rainbow; the damp ground was quick with the unceasing activities of red ants and centipedes while full-throated bullfrogs announced that they too were among the denizens of the wilds.

Passing a miniature lake – called a pan in South Africa – filled with the waters of the recent flood, Mhudi paused to admire a flock of wild ducks swimming gracefully on the still water and inviting a number of wild muscovies to join their cruise; but the latter seemed unsociable.

Climbing to the top of the next ridge, another expanse of level country was exposed to view. Here the country was overrun with antelopes, and as far as her eye could reach, the barren plains swarmed with springbuck and blesbuck. 'Some luscious bulb must be sprouting here,' she thought, 'to have attracted so much game, for buck from all points of the compass seem to have congregated here.'

Now in the distance there emerged a drove of gnu with a speed as great as if they were fleeing before a hunter's pack. Near the edge of the horizon, the mirage floated like a succession of moving lakes. Into this shimmering gleam, the running wildebeest plunged and glimmered in the rays of the noonday sun. They had to cross the mirage before she could make out what they were. As they approached her, galloping furiously through the herd of buck, she could see the switches of their white tails fluttering in the air. Mhudi soon discovered that they were running away from their bull, which vainly attempted to round them off into the opposite direction. Before they disappeared behind the horizon, the wildebeest outpaced their angry sire, which indignantly lagged astern.

Late that night she sought another unsheltered rest, and, stretching her tired limbs, she lay exposed to the heavy fall of dew.

Before sunrise, she was up and wading through the dewy grass. It was not until the morning of her fourth day of travel that Mhudi saw a man driving a flock of sheep and goats. She knew that this was not enemy stock, as the armies of the allies would long since have accounted for them, so she confidently walked up to the man, who proved to be a Hottentot in the service of a Boer caravan going north in the trail of Potgieter's army. Joining the Hottentot, she helped him drive his sheep along until they overtook the Boer waggons beyond the ridge.

The demands of the war had necessitated the bulk of the Native servants of the Boers being at the front with the armies. In consequence, the Boers who remained behind were suffering from a shortage of Native servants, therefore Mhudi's presence as an additional help at the waggons was very welcome to them.

Chapter Twenty-One

Mhudi and Umnandi

THE FRIENDSHIP BETWEEN De Villiers and Ra-Thaga had not suffered in the least from the events of the past few days; so leaving the waggons among the trees near the dell, they went to sit under a shady wild syringa, a little distance apart from the camp.

De Villiers examined and permanganated his wound once again; and having readjusted the sling round his arm, he proceeded to use his ramrod on his own rifle and that of his wounded black friend. By the side of the kloof, not far from where they sat, was a trickling fountain. The tiny perennial streamlets that oozed from it had furrowed the escarpment, leading first through a patch of bulrushes; then, widening and deepening its course, the water wound its way underneath two rows of *modubu* trees down to the dell below. Near the foot of the scarp the stream spouted and widened into a creek whose banks were rich with the verdant grass and other luxurious undergrowth. These provided food and shelter for the numerous herds of game that quickened the surrounding woods. Lilies and daisies along the glen had long since succumbed to the cold breath of autumn and left their tender stubbles to mark the spots where once they bloomed. Fallen petals of withering wild poppies littered the earth beneath the mopane trees, but the hardy marigolds survived the blast and garnished both sides of the rivulet which, unmindful of the seasons, wended its way beneath the water-lilies and rendered a perennial tribute to the great Marico River some miles to the west.

Leafy trees with creepers round their stout stems stood on the fertile banks of the rustling creek, where their branches furnished many an aerial tryst for birds of every plume. Nature had spread a peaceful calm around the oasis, and it were gross sacrilege for man to rupture this sublimity of the wilderness with his everlasting squabbles.

'I do wish the Matabele would come,' said De Villiers, still pushing and tugging at the ramrod, cleaning the guns.

'And what would you do with them?' asked his sable companion.

De Villiers: 'I will catch Mzilikazi alive, and tie him to the waggon wheel; then Potgieter will make me his captain, and you will be my right-hand man.'

Ra-Thaga: 'That will not do, for your people will not tolerate me. If they get enraged by nothing more than a drink of water out of their water-pail, they are not likely to allow me a place near their captain.'

De Villiers: 'But to tell the truth, I get on much better with you than with many of my own people. I owe you more than I could ever repay. But for you, Mogale's people would have killed me, or handed me to the Matabele as they did with Sarel van Zyl. And since his disappearance, I realise all the more forcibly how much I am in your debt. If ever I become a commander, you must come and stay near me.'

Ra-Thaga: 'Oh no! I am not going to abide with a boy. You should get a wife first and take your place among men before thinking of that. What would my children think of me if I were to be the right-hand man of a wifeless youth?'

De Villiers: 'Are those your terms?'

Ra-Thaga: 'Without joking, it is time you did. Look at the advantages. Besides, marriage will give you two mothers – your own and the wife's; the latter the greatest of the two.'

De Villiers: 'Is that the reason why your people call them the plain mother and the fine mother respectively?'

Ra-Thaga: 'Yes, and let me tell you why I am so glad Mzilikazi is getting a beating. When he is killed, I shall return to Kunana, walk around the old place and venerate the ground where lived and worked my mother-in-law whom I never saw. I shall go down to the field of carnage, bestride the old battlefield, and say: Here fell the noble Rolong woman who gave life to my faithful Mhudi. Somewhere here lie the remains of the woman who mothered my wife and nourished every fibre of her beautiful form. Then I will call to her spirit and say: Come down from the heights and approve of the feeble cares I am trying to bestow on the noble treasure thou hast bequeathed to me. My mother, Oh cradle of my wife! That after all thy pains and nursing, thou shouldst have been hounded out of this life without receiving a pin from the worthless fellow who wived thy noble offspring!' (After a long pause). 'Now, seriously, why don't you marry, De Villiers?'

De Villiers: 'Well, you see, the girls are – er – er . . .'

Ra-Thaga: 'Are what? I have been to Moroka's Hoek and seen the Boer girls. They are all crazy about you. I heard several of them say so.'

De Villiers: 'Which one?'

Ra-Thaga: 'Every one.'

De Villiers: 'But you know that I cannot marry them all.'

Ra-Thaga: 'Why, don't you fancy anyone?'

Again there was no answer, and Ra-Thaga continued:

'A man was not made to live alone. Had it not been for Mhudi, I don't think you would have known me at all. She made me what I am. I feel certain that your manhood will never be recognised as long as you remain wifeless. Marry a wife, De Villiers, and you will soon understand the Barolong, and – listen! After taking to yourself a wife, you will realise that you knew nothing at all about your own people, the Boers, for you will begin to understand them properly when your young wife has unbosomed herself to you. Now, De Villiers, why don't you marry Van Zyl's daughter?'

'Which one? Annetje? And why?' De Villiers's impatience was noticeable as he put the questions in rapid succession.

'I will tell you why,' said Ra-Thaga. 'I don't go about Moroka's Hoek with my eyes and ears shut. She has got a pair of bewitching eyes, and the moment you appear I have noticed that she always slips away like a mouse at the sight of a cat. She will either go to play at the far end of the camp or disappear into the interior of her mother's hut. Most of the time she spends working with elderly women, mending clothes, cooking food or boiling soap, and her ways are so admirable I have often said to myself that this daughter of Van Zyl is fit to marry the future king of the Boers.

'Do you remember when we returned from the spying trip? I noticed that many of the girls were openly shaking your hand and hugging you, glad to see you back. I was wondering where she was until I saw her in the interior of the hut, shyly devouring you with her dreamy eyes, but not daring to give vent to her raptures in public. De Villiers, that's the nonnie for you! I tasted her roast meat only once since I have known you, and I think her cooking beats your mother's by far. And, oh! how beautifully she talks!'

De Villiers, who had been listening to these rhapsodies, remained quiet for some little time. The silence of the moment and the girl's absence, hundreds of miles away, were to him symbolical of her retiring disposition. He felt a strange sensation all over him as thoughts of Annetje flitted across his mind. He could not account for these unaccustomed thrills. He mopped his brow, but that did not stop the flow of his perspiration. Modest and retiring as Annetje van Zyl had always been, he could not forget the occasions on which he discovered her peeping coyly at him through the folds of her rappie; and how quickly she would get out of his way and feel embarrassed if he surprised her anywhere by herself. He saw again in imagination the pure white face, the tender blue eyes and gentle smile. He thought he heard her mellifluous voice, and there was a kind of glow all about him, for Ra-Thaga's praises of her stimulated all these feelings. Finally he exclaimed: 'Man, Ra-Thaga, I always told you that you had a brown skin over a white heart, but you wouldn't believe me. Do you know I have been thinking of her too; I was too shy to ask anyone's opinion and now you have given me yours without asking. There are times I seem to lose my head over her. The night before last I was dreaming of her in the camp. Now you have made me crazy and I will never get the frenzy out of my head.'

Suddenly the confabulation between De Villiers and his solicitous matchmaker was disturbed by a rush of men from the camp. They ran forward to meet a party just arriving. Everybody wanted to be the first to meet the newcomers, and hear from them the very latest news from the front.

'Is Mzilikazi shot yet?' several voices asked.

De Villiers and Ra-Thaga jumped up and looked in the same direction. The piercing eyes of Ra-Thaga having at that distance established the identity of some of the new arrivals, he too raised his voice and shouted, 'Praise, De Villiers, praise the god of the Boers.'

'What is the matter?' asked De Villiers in surprise, still looking intently.

'The girl's brother!' replied Ra-Thaga.

'What girl?' queried De Villiers, impatiently.

'Van Zyl, the spy we thought was killed; and there is Taolo who was with him.'

For a moment De Villiers did not know how to act; he seemed dazed with joy. He was not sure if in such circumstances his best course was to move forward or sit down again. He thought of Annetje far away at Moroka's Hoek. He remembered how she had wept over the supposed death of her lost brother, and he wondered if she would survive the reaction that must be caused by his reappearance. How he wished he could be the first bearer of the glad news and break it to her very gently. He knew not how to meet the returned friend, and so Ra-Thaga again rose to the occasion.

'You don't seem to believe that this is the brother of the Nonnie we have been speaking about,' said he.

'Now, what would you have me do?' enquired De Villiers, rather sheepishly.

'Go and offer him your good wishes,' replied Ra-Thaga. 'Tell him how sorry we are that we missed him when he came in search of us. Offer him some food, and, while he eats, relate to him the experiences of our mission of espionage. I will be there to supplement your remarks wherever necessary.'

De Villiers at once darted forward, and was soon struggling in the crowd that hurried to reach Van Zyl, whom he succeeded in monopolising. They strolled about together a little among the waggons, being the while immersed in discussing their adventures. After refreshments which De Villiers procured for his friend, they listened to his story of the sudden condemnation to death and dramatic reprieve of the spies after their captors had heard a rifle shot; how they were retained in order to teach the Matabele the use of the gun; and how they wasted their ammunition and asked to be allowed to go for a fresh supply. How after repeated refusals Moremi was sent, Van Zyl and Taolo being detained at the Matabele capital.

'He was a long time coming back but we postponed the fatal day,' said Van Zyl, 'by constantly reminding our captors that Colesberg, where the powder comes from, takes months and months to reach. If the allies' attack had been delayed much longer, we must certainly have been put to death for the Matabele patience was well-nigh exhausted. However, when the alarm was raised, and panicky reports arrived about the defeat of the Matabele armies, pandemonium reigned in the city and with the aid of some Bahurutshe cattlemen we took advantage of the confusion and effected our escape.'

The conversation was interrupted by a sensational movement in the camp. '*Basadi, basadi!*' (women, women!) shouted the crowd.

Everybody looked round and saw a small party arriving near one of the waggons with three women among them. Ra-Thaga and De Villiers were dumbfounded to recognise Mhudi among the new arrivals.

Glad as Ra-Thaga was to see his wife, he found himself repressing a feeling of anger. He inwardly resented her appearance, because he feared that he would in future be chaffed by other men and called the poltroon who took his wife to war.

Ra-Thaga, still carrying his arm in a sling, came up to the waggon and, hiding these feelings, affectionately greeted his wife. 'Have you come to show us how to kill the Matabele, Mhudi? Could you not have trusted us men to do the work?

Now, sit down and let us hear how you are going to do it.' They carried on a dialogue.

She laughed and replied. 'I am not after Matabele, I am after you. What's the matter with your arm?'

'Where are the children?' he asked, without answering her question.

'At home with their aunts.'

'How did you manage to get here?' he asked again.

'Have I not the use of my legs and both arms? What's the matter with your arm?'

'Come over here, sit down and have some meat, then tell us all the news.'

Mhudi and her friends having had refreshments, she said in answer to Ra-Thaga's questions that she had been very restless since he left. She became indisposed and as the doctors failed to cure her she thought she would go and find her husband. So leaving the children with her relatives she departed, and the sickness left her the day she set out on her journey.

'Alone?' exclaimed Ra-Thaga in amazement.

'Yes, alone,' she replied.

'Silly woman! And did they allow you to do it? Where did they expect you would land?'

'Exactly where I am now,' replied Mhudi triumphantly. 'I did not ask anybody's permission. Besides, the wake of the army is unmistakable unless one deliberately intended to get lost. After a weary tramp of four days through a dreary country, I overtook some Dutch waggons and travelled with them till after we crossed the Great River. Parties returning from the front with cattle were often met with and their good reports about the fight excited everybody. But some of them told us you had been killed. Thereafter the waggons travelled too slow for me and I left the Boers behind. I am thankful to them, however, for I could hardly have crossed the Great River alone. Besides, they provisioned me for several days.'

'I thought you always found the Boers such awful people?' said her husband with a smile.

'Wait until I tell you what happened at the river,' she retorted.

'And what was that?' asked Ra-Thaga.

'As we were crossing the Lekwa, I sat in the rear of one of the waggons. Behind us, the Hottentot leader of the next waggon's team swam so near that he often touched the brake of our waggon. I could easily speak to him from where I sat. Suddenly something went wrong with his team. Two of the middle oxen got entangled with their yoke and chain and the waggon stopped amid stream. His name was angrily shouted and abuses were hurled at him by nearly every Boer, each trying to outdo the others in their expletives. It was Dancer this, Dancer that and Dancer again and again, in a chorus of profanity that conveyed to me much meaning but very little intelligence. The Boers in our waggon also shouted their imprecations at Dancer – they frightened me terribly, for I feared they were going to fling me into the water. Perhaps they might have done so if the trouble had been among our oxen. Fortunately we got through and they unhooked our team and extricated the next waggon with the two teams of oxen.

'As soon as the convoy got through, Dancer was tied to the waggon wheel and flogged till he was half dead. For the life of me I cannot understand why a leader, any more than the other people in the waggon, should be flogged for a tangle among the bullocks. But that was not all. After Dancer was beaten, there were loud calls for another little Hottentot. I never found out what was his crime, but the Boers called out, "Jan, Jan!" Poor little Jan, who was minding some sheep hard by, was dragged along, tied up and mercilessly punished.

'A pretty Boer girl in the waggon in which I came

remonstrated with her mother for keeping quiet while Jan was being beaten for no cause whatever. The Boers are cruel but they sometimes breed angels,' concluded Mhudi, 'and Annetje is one of them.'

'What is her name?' asked Ra-Thaga quickly.

'Annetje,' replied Mhudi, 'the girl whose brother was killed by the Matabele while out spying with Taolo and Moremi.'

'And where did you leave their waggon?' he asked impatiently.

'I believe the name of the river is Matloasane, two days' drive this side of the great Lekwa.'

'And who are your friends?' enquired her husband, looking at the two women with whom Mhudi shared her food.

'This beautiful lady,' she said, 'is queen of the Matabele –'

Ra-Thaga started. 'What! Mzilikazi's wife? Where did you find her, and what does she want among us?'

'Sh-sh, not so loud or you might frighten her. This good lady was turned out of their city through the evil influences of her rivals three summers ago, and she has been hiding among Mogale's people; but hearing of her people's plight she felt she must at all hazards return to them. She is on her way to find her husband, take her place by his side and share in all his troubles.'

'What a noble woman!' exclaimed Ra-Thaga in admiration. 'She is as well-bred as she is fair of countenance. But how will she get through? Mzilikazi is probably killed by now. Still death has become so tame that I am yet alive after having been twice accounted dead. Mzilikazi too might be just as fortunate, notwithstanding that report has killed him about six times during this campaign. Where did you meet her?'

'I met her two days ago, and being on the same quest we quickly fell in love with each other. The other one is a Rolong girl who has been captive among the Matabele since her childhood when Kunana was sacked. She wept for very joy on seeing me and talking once again to one of her own folk in her mother tongue after so many moons; but so attached has she become to this noble queen, that she realises the inhumanity of deserting her now in this war-devastated wilderness. After my own alarming experiences I cannot but encourage the girl in her sympathy for the lonely queen, for indeed it is a shame that one so dear and so good-hearted should be a Matabele.'

Ra-Thaga abruptly broke the interview with his wife and ran after a young Boer.

Umnandi, the Matabele queen, shuddered on seeing him start off. She thought he was going to betray her to the Boers. Mhudi, however, assured her that her husband, unlike many men, did not have a heart of stone.

'What is your wife after?' enquired De Villiers, who stopped in answer to Ra-Thaga's call.

'She has come to tell us that Annetje is not hundreds of miles away as you said a while ago, but only a day or two's ride from here.'

This was greater news to De Villiers than the expected information from the front. He was at once overwhelmed with ideas. His head was reeling with excitement and he wished to fly and meet Annetje. He could not desert the commando without disgracing himself, and possibly losing Annetje in the bargain – the natural punishment for such unmanly behaviour. He could not hope to disappear for two days and return to camp before he was wanted. What then was to be done? Oh! If he could only persuade the Field Cornet to send him back with the next field-post, he might be the first to break to Annetje the news of the dramatic return of her brother who was supposed to be dead. How could he manage this?

In due course the scouts reported that the woods were clear of the Matabele impis. The news of their rout being established,

Potgieter gathered his burgers to his laager outside the ruins of Inzwinyani, where they held a service of thanksgiving to the God of the Boers.

'You know,' Ra-Thaga used to say, 'the Boers can do many things in this world but singing is not one of them. On that day, however, the Boers sang as they never did before or since. I have been to Grahamstown and heard English congregations sing with a huge pipe organ that shook the building with its sound, like the pipes and brass horns of English soldiers on the march; I have been to Morija and heard Pastor Mabille, the best singer that ever held a church service, and the Basuto congregations render their beautiful hymns in answer to the signal he gave; I have been to Bethany and heard the most perfect singing by Native choristers under German leadership; but touched as I was by the rhythm of their drumlike voices, they always left something to be desired, when I thought of the manner in which those Boers sang that morning in the level valley bottom near Inzwinyani ruins, their old hymn "Juich aarde, juich alom den Heer"' (The old hundredth in Dutch).

Even those who knew not their language felt that they were listening to a stirring song of deliverance expressed by the souls of a people who, for the time being at any rate, felt profoundly grateful to their God.

By daybreak next day a detachment of Barolong were ordered to return with some cattle, and De Villiers was placed in charge of the company and ordered to relate to the Boers all the news about the war. Ra-Thaga, who was one of the company, returned home with his wife – she had been deftly attending to his wound, which had now healed. Before their departure, Mhudi took an affecting farewell from Umnandi and wished her a safe journey and reunion with her consort.

'Good-bye, my sister,' she said. 'I am returning to Thaba

Nchu for I have found my husband: mayest thou be as fortunate in the search for thine own.'

'Umnandi salutes thee also and thanks thee for the brief but happy time we have spent together. Thou hast a welcome destination in Thaba Nchu while I (supposing I meet my husband) know not what the future may have in store for me.'

'Nay, not so, my Matabele sister, for the gods who protected thee from the wrath of Mzilikazi will surely accompany thee in the search; seek him and when thou hast recovered the lost favour of thy royal lord, urge him to give up wars and adopt a more happy form of manly sport. In that he could surely do much more than my husband who is no king.'

'Nay,' retorted Umnandi ruefully. 'Thine is a royal husband, the king of the morrow, with a home and a country to go to. What is my lord without his throne, for what is a defeated king with his city burnt? It is no bright destiny I look forward to, but a blank gloom. I shared the glory of Mzilikazi when his subjects came and prostrated themselves before him, for then they always called at my dwelling to do me homage. The jealous machinations of my rivals drove me from out the city and forced me abroad to seek for shelter; but now that I hear Mzilikazi's glory is overthrown, I regard it my duty to seek him and share his doom if he will but permit me.'

'How wretched', cried Mhudi, sorrowfully, 'that with so many wild animals in the woods, men in whose counsels we have no share, should constantly wage war, drain women's eyes of tears and saturate the earth with God's best creation – the blood of the sons of women. What will convince them of the worthlessness of this game, I wonder?'

'Nothing, my sister,' moaned Umnandi with a sigh, 'so long as there are two men left on earth I am afraid there will be war.'

'Already the dustclouds of the waggons are receding in the distance; the darkness will overtake us ere I reach them and make it difficult for me to trail my people; so we must part. Good-bye, my sister,' continued Mhudi as the two women clasped each other. 'Farewell, thou first Matabele with a human heart that ever crossed my way. Mayest thou be as successful in thy quest as I have been in mine. May the gods be forgiving to thy lord and make him deserve thy nobility, and may the god of rain shower blessings upon thy reunion. Good-bye, my Matabele sister; may there be no more war but plenty of rain instead.'

'Oh, that I could share thy hopes', rejoined Umnandi plaintively. 'Good-bye, my beloved friend. Peace be to thee and thy husband. I am going into the wilderness and will not rest till I have found Mzilikazi. *Sala kahle* (Fare thee well), my Mlolweni sister.'

'That thou wouldst find him, is the ardent wish of Mhudi. Urge him, even as I would urge all men of my race, to gather more sense and cease warring against their kind. Depart in peace, my sister. *Tsamaea sentle* (Farewell).'

Chapter Twenty-Two

The Exodus

MZILIKAZI WAS THE LAST to leave with his bodyguard. Trembling under the weight of the sad news from the front, he quailed at the sight of the deserted huts of his great city. In the middle of the morning he overtook the bulk of his people resting in the woods. He at once sent word to collect the veterans and returned soldiers with the object of making a final stand against the invaders of his land. This army he himself would lead, while the women and children with the cattle should push further north.

These orders, which were executed with remarkable promptitude, revived the hopes of the jaded nation. Magicians immediately set to work making sacrifices, muttering incantations and burning all kinds of charms. Praises of the king were profusely and vociferously sung, while the men tested their shields and spears and chanted the ancient Zulu war songs. These martial exercises and the death-defying enthusiasm of the warriors restored public confidence, and the hope was expressed that the king's own impi would turn the scales where Gubuza had failed, and shortly after midday the army was on its way.

The vanguards of Mzilikazi's veterans, having reached the summit of a high hill, saw in the direction of Inzwinyani what looked like a rising cloud-bank growing more and more dense. It was the smoke ascending from the hundreds of deserted huts of Inzwinyani which lay scattered across two valleys.

For a time the sight damped the ardour of the *majahas*, for they had not until then realised the near proximity of the foe. Someone suggested, and it was hoped, that perhaps the burning was done by Gubuza with the laudable intention that no valuable loot should fall into his pursuers' hands. But Gubuza at that time was resting his tired army about twelve miles to the west of the burning city. In passing through it, early that morning, some of his men had actually entered the capital for a hurried examination of the ruins of what used to be their home, and to see if they could conveniently carry away anything left behind. Many valuable articles, flung away by the people in their haste to get away, lay strewn about the huts. Indeed, while thus occupied among the huts, the soldiers heard a few shots on the outskirts and flames began to shoot up, thus forcing them to cut short their inspection and hurry out of the place.

In order to elude his pursuers, Gubuza ordered his flight along a well-wooded depression where his retreating forces could less easily be seen. It was because of this strategy that the advance of the King's impi escaped his notice. Mzilikazi's army soon came in contact with the invaders' scouts. The latter, having now acquired a supreme contempt for the feeble resistance of the Matabele, were recklessly riding over the country. The impi promptly surrounding them, killed four Boers, four Griquas and twenty Barolong, captured their horses and arms and put the remainder to flight.

This enterprise, led by the king himself, was the first success of the Matabele in a running fight that lasted nearly a month. The whole army came back in an orgy of rejoicing and trampled upon the dead bodies of their uncanny foes to make sure that they should not rise again. Some headmen suggested, and the suggestion was adopted, that the hearts of such brave warriors should be cut out to prepare charms to inoculate the impi with their valour. One Matabele who could ride – Qanda by name – mounted one of the captured horses and proceeded to scatter the good news among the fugitive tribesmen and women in the bush.

On arrival at the temporary refuge, Qanda, who at first was mistaken for one of the invaders, created consternation among the fugitives. Women at the sight of the horse screamed, believing that the enemy was already in their midst. Till then all war news from the front was to the effect that the mere sight of the invaders was sufficient to cause death; so having seen the horse, these women covered their faces, laid themselves down and prepared to die in the rays of the flaming tail of the notorious star of ill-omen; in this way a number of babies were injured.

But when his identity was established by the panic-stricken people, Qanda's message sent a thrill of joy through the encampment and there was a sensational demonstration of relief. It was supposed that the dead scouts comprised the whole of the army of mischief-makers and loud were the praises sung in honour of Mzilikazi, the redoubtable ruler of earth and skies, who had definitely destroyed the agents of the fatalities of a bewitching comet.

The glad news reached Gubuza that night, and he at once led his retreating forces back to rejoin the king. It was a depressed army, however, that returned. The impi had witnessed a succession of disasters with nothing to cheer them;

they had been fighting and marching for days and nights with very little sleep and hardly any food; yet they were hopeful that the king had by a miracle freed the country from the implacable devils, whose thunder they had been subjected to since the invasion commenced.

By daybreak King Mzilikazi effected a junction with his disappointed commander. To them the golden dawn broke drear and hopeless, for, before Gubuza had time to render a full report of his generalship and the losses of the preceding days, their pickets ran in to say that a yet more imposing body of the allied forces was marching upon them and at once the impis scrambled to meet their fire.

'Oh Gubuza, my brother,' was the lament of the despondent King, his melancholy voice sounding like a dead weight upon the disconsolate spirit of his general. 'Would that I were with you on the day of the big fight; to share in the terror of your brave men! What sorcery are we faced with, my brother? Your experience has indeed been greater than the most thrilling battles of another age. Truly your indunas were more daring than the bravest Zulu warrior who ever cast a spear. What would you advise under this heavy cloud of death? Speak, for you alone bear the amulet that could shield us from the edicts of fate. Even now do I hear the thunder of their murderous weapons.'

They advanced to a more elevated position, and looking down toward his warriors and the one-sided battle raging before him, Mzilikazi beheld with an all too vivid realisation the actual cause of the rout of his people.

There they were, marching spear in hand and shields aloft according to their ancient formation; but alas! only to fall in masses before the fire of the musketeers.

'*Bona! Bona!* (Look! Look!)' said the broken-hearted Gubuza to his despondent King, pointing a solemn finger at the frightful scene of massacre, 'it is thunder, lightning! None but the superhuman can resist it. My advice to the Great One is, take the bodyguard, return at once to the people and remove them to a place of safety while I remain behind to delay the enemy's advance.'

King Mzilikazi, adopting the advice of his commander-in-chief, turned and retraced his steps. He had for years been cherishing a beautiful ideal. He had made preparations for overpowering and annexing adjacent tribes and augmenting his armies with the fighting forces of the conquered peoples; and, having trained and inspired them with Matabele courage, he had dreamt of possessing the most invincible army that ever faced an enemy; then, with his power thus magnified, he had looked forward to a march upon Zululand and the establishment of an idyllic empire, stretching from the sandy woods of Bechuanaland to the coast of Monomotapa, and along the Indian Ocean, through Tonga- and Swaziland, as far south as the coast of Pondoland; and then he should hem in and subdue the wily Moshoeshoe of Basutoland! So much for human ambition.

Marching back to his waiting people, the king heard the lament of his guard, mourning the loss of Prince Langa, 'the bravest son of the Great One.' This was an unparalleled blow. 'My son, my son, my gallant son and glory of my eyes,' he groaned. 'He fell beside his brave uncles Dingiswayo, Motambo, S'tonga, Tabata . . . and Dambuza, the warrior orator, is also among the slain.'

Mzilikazi quavered under the lash of these reminders. He recalled with a pang the patriotic speeches of Dambuza and the others, now killed, and the poignancy of the new situation in which Gubuza, who, in the heyday of their rejoicings, was accused of being a coward, now remained his sole pillar of strength. 'Where is that bombastic spirit now?' he asked himself. 'The wind, which at one time seemed to be under my sway and that of my invincibles, continues to blow as if nothing has happened; the leaves of the great modubu and mopani trees are waving in the breeze as if gladdened by the flight and melody of birds of every plume. The mountain mist like a giant pall still connects the peaceful earth with a dull sky and the clouds roll heedlessly by in the same manner as they did during the height of my glory; everything retains its natural serenity, the fatal comet has not blighted their existence. Only one giant is uprooted and overthrown. Low lies the city of Inzwinyani. *Mayebab'o!* (Alas!) Shall not my greatness survive? Could not the storm have been averted? Yes, then why was it not avoided? Forsooth, the cataclysm was not unexpected.'

He wished that he could meet the authors of his extreme misfortune and smash their skulls for them. He felt that he could not entrust their execution to a deputy but would lop off their heads with his own hands. 'Who was responsible for this calamity?' he asked himself once again.

Looking about him he regarded the sympathetic faces of his bodyguard, then remembered with a tremor that none but Mzilikazi was the culprit and muttered: 'I alone am to blame; notwithstanding that my magicians warned me of the looming terrors, I heeded them not. Had I only listened and moved the nation to the north, I could have transplanted my kingdom there with all my impis still intact but – Mayebab'o! – now I have lost all!'

Following this reverie, the king vividly recalled the death of his wife, Nomenti, who succumbed to a mysterious disease the day after they evacuated the capital. The flight of his nation kept him preoccupied, so that he had been unable to give her a queenly burial. He further thought of the still more mysterious disappearance of Umnandi, the jewel of bygone days, once so dear to his heart. 'That daughter of Mzinyati', he said to himself, 'was the mainstay of my throne. My greatness grew with the renown of her beauty, her wisdom and her stately reception of my guests. She vanished and, with her, the magic talisman of my court. She must have possessed the wand round which the pomp of Inzwinyani was twined for the rise of my misfortune synchronised with her disappearance. Yet she was not the only wife in my harem. How came it about that all was centred in her? What was the secret of her strength? It is clear that calamities will continue to dog my footsteps until that wife is found. The combined efforts of my people have failed to bring her back to me. How could she be found? Yet she must be found. I shall have her found.'

These thoughts tormented Mzilikazi all the way, until he reached the crest of the last slope, from which elevated position he could see his people resting among the woods. He heard the bitter wail of the children who hungrily shrieked aloud for food. He saw anxious mothers pressing their empty breasts into the mouths of crying babies, but the teats of starving mothers failed to still the gnawing pangs of hunger and the little ones kept up their weak, discordant wail.

All this seemed to affect Mzilikazi tremendously. He alarmed his guards by muttering to himself aloud: 'Of what use are these things to me? The bones of my sons and nephews and those of my great fighters lie still and lifeless on the battlefields. Their arms are powerless and never again shall wield the assegai. Give me neither spear nor shield,' he thundered. 'Find then some other weapon if I am to live in this world. Give me the lethal weapon that will frustrate the wiles of my pursuers; bring me the sword of fire to pierce their craven hides,' he exclaimed like one in delirium.

Surveying the ruins of all his hopes and remembering the rich, red Matabele blood sacrificed so lavishly, in hopes that the end would justify the means, and contemplating the inevitable gloom with which he stood face to face, Mzilikazi heaved a deep sigh and wished that he held the keys to open the gateways of the elements of thunder and lightning, so as to command these forces to hurry down and annihilate and blot out forever the armies of his tormentors.

Then, passing his hands before his eyes, as if to wipe out the calamities of which he was the victim, he drew himself up to his full height – a noble and kingly figure, despite adversity – raised his voice and with something of his old dignity he addressed the gathering crowd: 'Amandebele, Oh people of Matshobana, listen to me! We escaped from one tyrant in the land of the rising sun and fought our way through Basuto, Mantatise and Bechuana, until we found a resting place in this country, surrounded though it be by vile treachery. You are my witnesses. Have I not been kind to these Bechuana traitors? It was my desire to incorporate them with ourselves so that together we could form one great nation; they pretended to be willing, yet they have always played me false. When they failed to bring tribute I slew them not; yet at the first opportunity they did not hesitate to abuse my kindness. Those Barolong dogs assassinated my indunas; the Bangwaketse beasts led into a desert trap one of my regiments; the Koranna dissemblers helped my enemy; the Bahurutshe and Bafokeng, while professing to be my friends, constantly sowed thorns in my path; the deceitful Griquas also laid snares for me. Sechele is the one friend I found in this country; yet when I appealed to him for an army to support me in my present plight he promised one next moon, when he knew it would be too late. Nevertheless, I do not wish to quarrel with the doubtful friendship of his Bakwena. As for those other Bechuana robbers, the infernal spirits they have invoked upon me will recoil on them. Tradition tells of no instance where a man has ever found a neighbour in spirits of that kind. Spirits are not of this world and the witch who associates with them does so at his peril.

'Those bearded Boers who killed my herdboys and stole my cattle are today helping them to destroy me.

'The Bechuana know not the story of Zungu of old. Remember him, my people; he caught a lion's whelp and thought that, if he fed it with the milk of his cows, he would in due course possess a useful mastiff to help him in hunting valuable specimens of wild beasts. The cub grew up, apparently tame and meek just like an ordinary domestic puppy; but one day Zungu came home and found, what? It had eaten his children, chewed up two of his wives, and in destroying it, he himself narrowly escaped being mauled. So, if Tauana and his gang of brigands imagine that they shall have rain and plenty under the protection of these marauding wizards from the sea, they will gather some sense before long.

'Shaka served us just as treacherously. Where is Shaka's dynasty now? Extinguished, by the very Boers who poisoned my wives and are pursuing us today. The Bechuana are fools to think that these unnatural *kiwas* (white men) will return their so-called friendship with honest friendship. Together they are laughing at my misery. Let them rejoice; they need all the laughter they can have today for when their deliverers begin to dose them with the same bitter medicine they prepared for me; when the kiwas rob them of their cattle, their children and their lands, they will weep their eyes out of their sockets and get left with only their empty throats to squeal in vain for mercy.

'They will despoil them of the very lands they have rendered unsafe for us; they will entice the Bechuana youths to war and the chase, only to use them as pack-oxen; yea, they will refuse to share with them the spoils of victory.

'They will turn Bechuana women into beasts of burden to drag their loaded waggons to their granaries, while their own bullocks are fattening on the hillside and pining for exercise. They will use the whiplash on the bare skins of women to accelerate their paces and quicken their activities: they shall take Bechuana women to wife and, with them, breed a race of half-man and half-goblin, and they will deny them their legitimate lobola. With their cries unheeded these Bechuana will waste away in helpless fury till the gnome offspring of such miscegenation rise up against their cruel sires; by that time their mucus will blend with their tears past their chins down to their heels, then shall come our turn to laugh.

'Rally now to your burdens, Amandebele mothers; strap your babies to your waists; let us direct our toes to the north for there is a refuge there. The Mandebele assegai has served us well in the past. It shall be the indicator of our road to the land of plenty, in a far country that is good for raising corn and the grazing of cattle. We shall ford the Udi and cross the Mocloutse; we shall traverse the territories round Nchwapong, where Sekgoma holds sway, then we shall enter the land of ivory, far, far beyond the reach of killing spirits, where the stars have no tails and the woods are free from mischievous Barolong. Our hunters up in the north have discovered some fertile territories whose rivers abound with endless schools of sea-cow; whose forests are alive with long-horned families of rhinoceros; whose jungles are marked by the tracks of elephant and giraffe; where the buffalo roam and the eland browse, where the oryx and the zebra invite us to the chase.

'Arise, Ama-Ndebele! Let us from hence. *Pambili lonke* (Forward, everybody)!'

Chapter Twenty-Three

A Happy Reunion

IT WAS A HOPEFUL nation that moved forward, and for months afterwards the Bechuanaland forests were alive with swarms of Matabele travelling persistently towards the land of promise to found a new Matabeleland.

Before finally settling at Bulawayo, far, far up north, the trek bivouacked for several moons on the banks of the Shashe River. There the Matabele erected a wide stockade in the centre of which they built temporary dwellings for their sorrowing king. Within this enclosure, King Mzilikazi resumed his indabas and issued commands from an improvised throne placed at a corner shaded by a row of mopani trees. During the trek northward he had lost much of his surplus flesh and other outward signs of dignity and was the object of much sympathy. The gap created by Umnandi's disappearance, so painfully evident in the domestic life of the nation, seemed to overshadow all other troubles. His warrior sons had fallen on the battlefield. The principal wife had died under mysterious circumstances, and the hopeless inefficiency of his surviving consorts left him gloomy. The dances and ululations of the fair maidens of the nation were a dismal affair and their forced gaiety proved ineffective, even for the usually responsive heart of Mzilikazi.

He continued to hold his councils and arbitration courts. Swift runners went south and east and returned to assure the King that there were no enemies in the wake of his trek. His young men, who conducted periodical hunting and raiding expeditions into the unknown jungles of the interior, also carried instructions to inspect the land for a suitable location for a permanent settlement. From many of these forays they returned with ivory, the choicest ostrich plumes and furs of every colour. One party went to far-away Zimbabwe and returned with pack-oxen loaded with ivory, rhinoceros hides, lion skins and hog tusks. They reported finding a people whose women dug the mountain sides for nuggets and brittle stones, which they brought home to boil and produce a beautiful metal from which to mould bangles and ornaments of rare beauty. That was the Matabele's first experience of gold smelting.

One morning an induna came to the king's place and announced the approach of Thipa, a Kwena courier from Chief Sechele. The king received the visitor without delay, and welcomed Thipa by handing him the gourd of corn beer which he held in his hand.

'Drink and slake your thirst, messenger of the sons of Kwena,' said Mzilikazi, handing him the gourd, 'and acquaint me with the wishes of Sechele. I knew I had a sterling friend in him, but I hardly thought that your chief would remember me in these days of my bitter adversity. What tidings do you bring? Tell me and quench my thirst for news.'

'Hail, Great Lion!' began Thipa, 'monarch of the woods and glades and ruler of the hills and vales! Sechele greets you and says: "Tell my brother, Mzilikazi, that since his trek to the far north, Sechele's courtyards have been greatly honoured by the unexpected, yet nonetheless welcome, presence of a courtly visitor in the person of Queen Umnandi, the fairest among royal wives. She was eager to follow up the trek of her lord and mine, but I detained her until I could have sufficient provision and ample escort to ensure her safe arrival by the side of Mzilikazi our king! She asks me to intercede on her behalf for the king's pardon, since the displeasure and pain occasioned by her disappearance was the work of others. Thus, remembering her bounty and the charm she lent to the king's court at Inzwinyani, where so many of us worshipped her person, I was glad to do this by my trusted messenger, Thipa, who will assure the king on my behalf that Umnandi would gladly be a faggoter and water-carrier for the king's meat pots, without the status of a wife, if that will insure her pardon; for this cause I entreat the great Mzilikazi in the hope that domestic reconciliation will bring contentment to my gallant lord and his brave tribesmen!'"

'What woman speak you of, Thipa? Has Sechele sent you here to mock me in my misery?'

At that moment the crowd surged asunder and allowed a passage to a group of travellers . . . 'Umnandi! my long-lost wife!' cried the King. 'Not dead – not dead!'

His voice was drowned in bursts of rejoicing, as the vast concourse recognised Umnandi and her faithful Barolong maid. The welkin rang with the ponderous shouts of the men and the joyous shrieks of the women. This glorious welcome amazed the returning wanderer. Her fern-draped feet shook with excitement and exultation, for instead of being a suppliant for the king's pardon, she found herself a national heroine, acclaimed as such by a people that had been profoundly grieved and perplexed by her disappearance.

Clapping Umnandi's hands to make sure she had returned in reality, Mzilikazi said: 'Is it you? Oh Umnandi, is it you? Or is all this a fleeting dream from which I shall awake to find myself a lonely and disappointed man?'

Crowds hurried from the utmost ends of the scattered encampments and rushed to the scene of excitement in answer to ejaculations such as 'a great magician has arrived! He makes the dead to walk . . . He resurrected Queen Umnandi! She is walking and talking like one who never died! All our slain soldiers have arisen and are on their way here! . . .'

Many could not get near for the press and had to be content with these rumours and fables.

Young men were dispatched to the cattle-posts to bring sheep and bullocks to the slaughter poles to prepare a magnificent feast and celebrate the return of Umnandi from the mysterious unknown.

But the king ordered that none should partake of the feast. He, too, was not going to touch meat until Umnandi should prepare a meal for him by her own hand; likewise none might taste of beer until the deft hands of his beloved Umnandi had ground malted grain and prepared for him her familiar and delectable brew. Accordingly, the welcome was postponed for three days during which all the men and women of the tribe were fasting.

Early in the morning of the fourth day chunks of beef and portions of mutton and venison were spread on the hot glowing embers where stacks of dead wood had been burnt to cinders through the night. And as the food sizzled over the fire, King Mzilikazi, surrounded by the heads of a joyful nation, entered the court and proclaimed the homecoming of his queen. For the first time, the Matabele learnt how she had been cajoled into leaving her home. The clever magician from Zululand, who disappeared as mysteriously as Umnandi herself, had been vainly urged by threats and promises of rewards to poison her. This he would not be persuaded to do; instead he handed her an amulet to give to her husband as a result of which she would bear a son and heir to the Matabele kingdom. And so the faithful daughter of Umzinyati had treasured that charm through the years of her enforced exile, and on the day of her homecoming handed it to the king.

When the populace had finished cheering, Queen Umnandi, headed by a procession of fifty young girls, and followed by the same number of singing women, emerged from the royal quarters and entered the enclosure. She was easily recognised by the prominence of her bejewelled costume, rich with beads and ornaments. Her kirtle of foxes and young leopard skins exposed amazing bangles of ivory and wristlets of solid gold while necklaces of rare value added to her barbaric splendour. There was continuous cheering as she stepped gracefully in the procession to the tinkling of the cymbals and ululations of the dancing girls, reinforced by the ponderous cadences of the drum-like voices of the male section of the gay crowd.

King Mzilikazi joining in the contagious merriment cried: 'Sechele, my brother Sechele! What friendship is so strong as yours to dig up the very grave and restore my dead love to me! Have you not brought back the central pillar of the life of Mzilikazi and the Matabele nation? Hawu Thipa, your mission is greater than the return of successful hunters and more welcome than the soaking rains that fertilise the sun-scorched fields!

'Thipa shall drive home to his chief, Sechele, a herd of ten snow-white cows to symbolise the pleasing satisfaction in my heart, so that the Bakwena may also rejoice with us.

'Now,' concluded the king, 'let us feast for three days and nights; let us sing and dance and be merry, and invoke the spirits to propitiate the magic of the sullen spirits of our dead ancestors.'

The voice of Mzilikazi starting a brand new tune, and leading the singers by tapping the time with the handle of his spear against his shield, rang out clear and strong above the others:

> Sing on, sing on! Mzilikazi's a youth today,
> For since we left the bewitched valley –
> I never did feel so great before,
>   Sing on, sing on!
> I never did feel so young before;
> The pillar of my house is here,
> I never did feel so glad before,
>   Cheer on, cheer on!
> Not since we left the vale bewitched
> Inzwinyani, the place of sorcery,
> I never did feel so strong before,
>   Dance, on dance on!

And as the crowd of leather-lunged men reiterated the refrain, the ground reverberated with the stamping of many feet to the rhythmical sound of tom-toms. The siren-like voice of one *umfazi* rang out in thrilling repetition after each verse. 'Sing on, women, sing on!' she shouted. 'We have suffered only tribulation since Umnandi's flight, now let her bring back to us the joys of bygone days. Dance on, women, dance on!'

In due course the Matabele having struck the Shashe camp, established a new capital, named Gu-Bulawayo, in the very far north. There a magnificent feast was repeated a year later, for Umnandi had presented the king and nation with her son, the newborn prince! In the course of a prosperous life during which the Matabele grew in power and affluence, Umnandi's son extended the awe-inspiring sway of his government to distant territories of the hinterland; and when at length he succeeded his father as Matabele king, he wielded a yet greater power than that of his renowned father.

Chapter Twenty-Four

A Contented Homecoming

DE VILLIERS ON receiving the order to go back, was overcome with joy. He saw before him the image of Annetje and looked forward to a happy reunion with her. On the road he often left his party and the slow moving oxwaggons, spurred his mount and galloped to the endless hills lying to the east and west of the beaten trail, thus reconnoitring the country from the peaks of the hillocks, lest in the trackless wilderness he should miss the girl of his heart, by going south whilst she and her parents came north.

When the bird trilled its lay, to his ears it sounded for all the world as if its chirrup was a repetition of her name. To him the clattering of the hoofs of his mare sounded like the same articulation, 'Annetje, Annetje', all the while. Visions of Annetje van Zyl formed and re-formed themselves before his mind every hour of the day, and in his dreams during his sleep. This enchantment continued until one day his party came upon Van Zyl's waggons bivouacked on the banks of the Khing Spruit.

De Villiers received a rousing welcome from Annetje's

parents and the other Boers encamped beside the rivulet, all of them eager for authentic information from the front. All the war news he related consisted of the unexpected successes of the allies, which, of course, was very agreeable to the Boers. Some of it caused the women folk to weep in gratitude; this was concerning the return of Sarel van Zyl, whose parents and friends up to that moment had counted him among the slain. De Villiers related that Sarel, too, would have come, but the commander-in-chief wished to offer him a stretch of land in the conquered territory in reward for his own adventures in the interest of the cause. Sarel himself had in view a cosy estate of which he wished to claim the freehold before another claimant could forestall him. For all this news the Van Zyl family knelt down around the fire and returned thanks to the Higher Power.

As for Annetje, she had been overjoyed by the arrival of De Villiers from the war. The sight of him surrounded by a company of elderly men who were voraciously devouring every word that fell from his lips, as if he were an oracle, was glorious and all-engrossing. All the time that De Villiers was the centre of attraction she behaved like one treading on enchanted ground; but the climax of her bliss was reached when she heard, late that evening, that De Villiers had asked for, and received, the consent of her parents to 'sit-up' with (court) her. This was in accord with her most fervent desires and expectations. That evening, when drowsy people disposed themselves as travellers usually did, two ecstatic young persons clasped hands gingerly under the wide canopy of heaven, with the evident belief that they were already part of each other. That night, the two young souls, with hearts beating in unison, formally pledged their troth, in the light of the full moon, to live and die the one for the other. Next to the young couple, no man was better pleased than Ra-Thaga at this development.

During their stay at Khing he relieved De Villiers of all cares regarding the waggons and livestock, while De Villiers devoted more time to his love affair.

Mhudi fully shared the pleasure which her husband felt in the betrothal of the young people. The succession of coincidences startled her. She had pronounced De Villiers 'the only humane Boer at Moroka's Hoek'. In her last journey to the north she incidentally crossed the Vaal River in the waggon of Annetje's father. During the few days she travelled with them, she had been charmed by Annetje's disposition which seemed to her a shining contrast to the general attitude of the other Boers; 'but who could have guessed', she exclaimed in wonder, 'that my two favourites would finish up by one day becoming man and wife.'

Old Van Zyl, with the concurrence of the other Boers, considered it useless of De Villiers to continue his journey south with his convoy, as all the Boers had left Moroka's Hoek and were on their train north.

The Van Zyls were also anxious to find Sarel, but were resting their animals at Khing and would remain there pending the arrival of an itinerant pastor to unite De Villiers and Annetje in the bonds of holy matrimony.

De Villiers vainly tried to persuade Ra-Thaga to break with his people and remain with him. Annetje too had fallen in love with Mhudi. She said if she lived to have little ones of her own, surely they would be proud to have for an ayah, such a noble *mosadi* as Mhudi. But, unlike the two men, they knew not each other's language, consequently she made a less favourable impression on Mhudi than De Villiers did on her husband. Nevertheless their parting was mutually sincere and friendly. Besides Ra-Thaga's own loot, consisting of several head of Matabele cattle and valuable skins he gathered, when the allies rifled the huts of Inzwinyani, De Villiers suggested that in token of their friendship, his Mhudi, the only Rolong woman who had been to the front, was entitled to some permanent and useful souvenir of her own adventure. He therefore presented her with an old waggon and its gear. In making the presentation De Villiers said: 'It is in rather a poor state of repair; but two bullocks paid to a blacksmith will turn it into the best waggon in Thaba Nchu.' Accordingly he gave her from his convoy two oxen for the purpose. The Van Zyls, especially, and the other Boers at Khing, feeling outraged at De Villiers's treatment of the Kaffir and his wife, regarded these acts of generosity as being grossly extravagant. Indeed they began to doubt the sanity of the young man. The Boers were God's chosen people, so they argued, and had never seen a heathen treated with so much consideration; they remonstrated with De Villiers and held that it was unnatural to reward a Kaffir for anything he did as liberally as if he were a baptised Christian.

The young man's pithy retort stung them at their most vulnerable point. 'What did Paul mean,' he asked, 'when he said to the Galatians, "There is neither Greek nor Jew, bond nor free, male nor female, White nor Black, but all are one in Christ Jesus."'

To the Boers, a race of proverbial Bible readers, who profess Christianity to the point of bigotry, the retort was unanswerable for, amongst them, it would be gross heresy to dispute a single word in that sacred book – God's Holy Word. And when they flinched and recoiled under the force of De Villiers's scriptural rejoinder, Annetje exclaimed proudly: 'I knew that he was right, for I felt certain that De Villiers would do nothing except in obedience to the Lord's commandments.'

A few days later Ra-Thaga and his party left for the south. The young Boer couple accompanied their Native friends a little distance on the road. They saw the trek safely across the spruit with Mhudi on top of her own waggon. Ra-Thaga remained in conversation with De Villiers and Annetje as the waggon went across.

'Who would have thought', said De Villiers to him, 'when you and I plotted and schemed against Mzilikazi, that he would be routed within a year?'

'Who would have thought,' retorted Ra-Thaga, 'that when I urged you to play the man and woo Sarel's sister, you would have her within the same month?'

Annetje guessed that the reference in the Native tongue concerned herself, and pressing her closely to his bosom, De Villiers said to Ra-Thaga: 'Yes, I always told you that this world was round and you refused to believe me; but now that you see that it has spun round like a waggon wheel at Mzilikazi's expense, you must believe that it is indeed round.'

'Yes', said Ra-Thaga 'whether this be a round world or a flat world, you and I have had our revenge, Mzilikazi will not burn any more cities, nor will he capture any more women and cows. Not in Bechuanaland anyway.'

De Villiers's hands reached out once more and embracing Annetje he called her all kinds of dainty little names. Upon this Ra-Thaga remarked: 'Well, if you call Nonnie "the point of your heart", then Mhudi must be "the whole of my pluck".'

'I wish you two would speak Dutch', said Annetje softly, 'and give me the benefit of your talk.' The above conversation being repeated in the *taal* for her information she said: 'Your boys should be proud of their parents, Ra-Thaga. You bear the scars of a tiger's claws on your face; a tiger's fangs on your arm and Mzilikazi's spear on your shoulder; and, although the wounds were inflicted far out in the wilderness, their mother turned up each time and nursed you back to health. I am glad to call you my husband's friends, but it will take me very long to forgive your refusal to remain with us.'

'Oh Nonnie,' replied Ra-Thaga, 'wait till you have little

ones of your own, and you will forgive me soon enough, for then you will understand why Mhudi was so anxious to return to Thaba Nchu.'

'But can't I persuade you to come back after a good long rest and bring your boys with you?'

'Oh no, Nonnie,' protested Ra-Thaga emphatically, 'you white people have a way of writing down conditional promises and treating them as debts.'

'Well, well', said De Villiers, 'it wouldn't be Ra-Thaga if he missed a joke. But this is not time for humour, for I tell you I shall feel this wrench.'

'Make him forget it, Nonnie,' said Ra-Thaga to Annetje; 'the proverb says, "there's always a return to the ruins, only to the womb there is no return."' One more good-bye, *tot wederzien* and the young couple returned to camp enraptured with visions of a future happiness after the pastor should have come and done his work.

De Villiers grievously offended his people's susceptibilities by openly fraternising with the black couple, and when the Boers had seen the backs of Mhudi and Ra-Thaga for the last time, they were glad to draw the curtain on what they regarded as a most disgraceful spectacle.

De Villiers and Annetje returned to the camp by the longest way round. They came arm-in-arm as if heedless alike of the temper of their stern-visaged elders as of the divine melody of the cackling of the heath-grouse, and the glory of the sunset. They had been stepping quietly over the dreary veld, with their spirits lost in a newfound bliss, more like a pair of dreamers careering through space on a seraph's wings.

'Oh, when will the predikant reach this god-forsaken place?' exclaimed De Villiers as they neared the encampment. 'It will be our happiest hour on earth when he shall have merged our two souls into one. Oh, when will he come, dear little heart?'

'Do be patient, De Villiers,' muttered Annetje softly, depressing the immature swell of her bosom in order the better to hide the intensity of her own impatience. 'The proverb says, "a hasty dog always burns his mouth". Is it not enough to know that while my heart yearned for yours, feeling that it alone could quench the fire of my intense desire, your soul, too, was yearning to mingle itself with mine? I know now what I have to live for; so, come soon, come late, I am satisfied.'

In the centre of the waggon away on the low road sat Mhudi, the happy proprietress of a valuable 'house on wheels'. Her husband having boarded the vehicle from the rear came to sit beside her. Side by side they watched the team of tired oxen lumbering along slowly in the direction of Thaba Nchu, where a warm welcome was awaiting them. The vast plains were dotted by conical kopjes now donning their purple mantle in the waning light. Already the stars began to twinkle overhead as together they viewed the surrounding landscape. He recalled with delight the charm that attracted and held him to her since first they met. He mused over the hallowed glories of being transported from place to place like white people, in their own waggon.

Gone were the days of their primitive tramping over long distances, with loads on their heads. For them the days of the pack-ox had passed, never to return again. The carcase of a koodoo or any number of blesbuck, falling to his musket by the roadside, could be carried home with ease, leaving plenty of room in the vehicle for their luggage. Was it real, or was it just an evanescent dream?

These pleasant thoughts occupied their minds in the gathering darkness while the old waggon meandered along and the racket of the waggon wheels on the hard road made a fierce yet not very disagreeable assault upon their ears.

'Tell me,' said Mhudi, raising her voice as the waggon

rattled along, 'why were you so angry with me when I found you at the front? Promise me,' she went on, 'you will not again go away and leave me, will you?'

'Never again', replied Ra-Thaga, raising his voice above the creak-crack, creak-crack of the old waggon wheels. 'I have had my revenge and ought to be satisfied; from henceforth, I shall have no ears for the call of war or the chase; my ears shall be open to one call only besides the call of the chief, namely the call of your voice – Mhudi.'